To Tia
Enjoy H
Jou

EMBRACE
OF THE
SHADE

Part One of The Berylian Key
Book One in the Pantracia Chronicles

Written by Amanda Muratoff & Kayla Hansen

www.Pantracia.com

Cover design by Andrei Bat.

ISBN: 978-1-7337011-0-5

Fourth Edition: February 2022

Co-writing a long series has been a time-consuming labor of love, accomplished despite hundreds of miles between us.

Instead of testing the bond we've had for more than half our lives, this endeavor has strengthened our friendship and brought us closer. Our mutual passion for writing and story telling made Pantracia possible. This fantasy world wouldn't exist with only one of us, as our partnership is the keystone from which these characters breathe.

The Pantracia Chronicles:

Visit www.Pantracia.com for our pronunciation guide
and to discover more.

Prologue

Winter, 2609 R.T. (recorded time)

Bellamy fought the Shade's grasp, kicking against the crumbling marble.

The temple doors shuddered shut, swallowing any remnants of dying daylight.

As the darkness of the chamber enveloped him, Bellamy couldn't avoid the coming consequences. It all began when he willingly walked the same path he was now being dragged down, deep into the vine-choked ruins.

An iron tight grip yanked at his collar, and Bellamy's breath escaped in a betraying sob. Fear squeezed his chest, raking his insides like a rabid wildcat. The acrid scent of a fire, crackling on the broken altar, burned his eyes as tears blurred his vision. His bruised ribs ached with each breath.

Defeated, Bellamy ceased his struggle and hung limply in the Shade's grip.

His captor huffed at the sudden shift of dead weight, but spun Bellamy, forcing him to face the dancing bonfire.

Bellamy avoided looking at the monstrous shadow of his master. The man he'd betrayed.

"Bellamy." Disappointment oozed from the master's sickly sweet voice. His shadow swelled to envelop the distant exit.

Dread erupted in his gut, fueling a final attempt to free himself. Bellamy kicked at his captor's ankles, clawing at the arm holding him. His nails dug into the Shade's branded arm, eliciting a hiss of pain. The geometric tattoo given by the master hosted a far more

I

prolific array of shapes than Bellamy ever managed to achieve. He counted the number of tasks his captor had completed to distract from the roiling fear.

Twelve.

The distinct shapes composed the tattoo on the Shade's arm.

Twelve completed tasks.

Bellamy had only stomached two.

He cried out as the Shade jerked his head back by his hair. His hands instinctively moved to break his fall as his aggravated captor threw him to the stone steps. The jagged edges of the broken granite scraped his palms, making him grunt as red smears tainted the floor.

Bellamy caught another glimpse of the Shade behind him.

Ghost-like, his pale eyes reflected the fire. The Shade tore at the rolled-up sleeve, pulling it over the tattoo on his right forearm, now dotted with blood. Thick, dark hair fell over his brow and stubbled his chin in a thick beard. One of the few indications that the Shade had lived, and served, almost a decade longer than him.

I'll never even see my twentieth birthday.

The hem of the Shade's onyx cloak swayed at his ankles as he sidestepped the shifting shadow of their master. Ripples spread among the darkness, convulsing like a pit of writhing snakes.

Like a mother scolding her child, the master clicked his tongue. The black abyss of his shadow fell over Bellamy in a suffocating blanket.

Breath became difficult to draw. His skin prickled at every pore, as if he plunged into an icy lake in the dead of winter.

He distracted himself by thinking of the last time he felt warmth, when his cell-mate in Lazuli held him before her release from the prison he'd confined himself to. The Art-blocking cuff Helgath had used hid him from his master temporarily, and he found solace in a friend.

I hope you're safe. I'll keep my promise and never take up the power again, no matter what he does to me.

Burns scalded over his right arm, delving deeper than his skin and into the bone. He struggled to rip off the bandage that covered the cuts he'd carved across the pair of inverted triangles tattooed on his forearm. Disgusted by them, he'd tried to remove the infection by mutilating his flesh. He should have known the attempt would be futile.

"I didn't know." Bellamy sucked in a despairing breath as he sought pity from the Shade who'd brought him to his death. The haunting fire-colored eyes of the man, who must have once been someone like Bellamy, held no empathy.

How does he just stand there and watch after I spared his life?

"Of course you did." The master, who lured the naïve to give up a piece of their soul, spoke calmly. His shadow lashed with power, a serpentine tendril rising from the ground. It reached for Bellamy, ravaging the exposed skin on his arms and neck. Another slithering shape joined it, dragging searing pain up the length of his leg.

Relentless shrieks erupted from his mouth as the tendrils consumed his flesh. Bellamy's body convulsed as he fell to all fours.

"I consider my price minimal for what I have given you!" The master's voice reverberated as the shadows engulfing Bellamy forced his chin up, ceasing their assault.

Bellamy dared a look at the beast who ended his life with the gift of power he thought he needed and saw merely a man.

The master's formal beard, carefully trimmed on his wide and angular jaw, suggested nobility. The kaleidoscope of gold and black marred the stormy blue-green of his eyes. Within them, Bellamy saw no soul.

"You know the punishment for one who betrays my gift?"

With a gut-clenching sob, Bellamy nodded. His lips couldn't form words, his tongue swollen, tainted with the coppery taste of blood.

"Master." The Shade's interruption sent a twitch through Bellamy, but it prolonged his moment of reprieve, allowing Bellamy to take another breath.

He'd known his captor once as an ally, but couldn't recall his name.

A quiver rippled through the tentacles, tightening to twist Bellamy's arm. His vision flashed, accompanied by the sickening crack of bone, an abrupt numbness seeping over it.

Ears ringing, the rest of the conversation eluded Bellamy. Their voices murmured as the coils of darkness wriggled around him.

"Do you understand the task before you?"

Bellamy expected the reverential bow given as the Shade revealed the tattoo on his arm once more. A new shape blessed the mark and man with greater power.

"I do, Master." The Shade's baritone echoed over the stone. "I will see it done."

"Good." The master roughly patted the shoulder of his servitor as if the gesture would assuage his guilt before turning and climbing the granite steps. "Go."

Bellamy locked eyes with his master, to plead with whatever shred of humanity might still lie within those soulless eyes. But his vision blurred, washed out by tears.

"I have further lessons to teach." The master smiled, a skeletal flash of white teeth against his lips as he drew on the Art.

Shrill cries erupted from Bellamy's lips, sounding distant as fresh torment coursed through him before everything collapsed into shadow.

 Chapter 1

Spring, 2610 R.T.

Kin huffed to catch his breath after trekking the precarious climb to the top of Capul's greatest hill. He didn't bother slowing the door behind him, and it sent a thunderous echo through the library's foyer as it slammed shut.

The stale air reeked of ancient knowledge. Kin preferred the salty eastern breeze outside, ushering in spring and banishing the goddess Nymaera's winter.

Even though he was in good shape, the venture to the Great Library of Capul left him winded. Its purposeful location would deter would-be thieves of historical treasures. The towering structure, which Kin thought a palace at first glance, stood as a zealous guardian to the secrets hidden within.

The garish mosaic of a sun dominated the floor in front of him as Kin eased his breath to slow his heartbeat. Beyond the foyer, the narrow tower widened to the expanse of the library, where shelves brimmed with texts. The warm glow of artificial orbs hung from solid wooden beams. They provided just enough illumination to see by, crafted by practitioners of the Art who could manipulate the energy coating the lands of Pantracia.

Little other light existed between the crowded shelves. The library didn't have many windows, protecting its contents from the rays of the sun. It created a dim but comfortable environment which reminded Kin of a late night in front of a tavern's hearth.

With a lingering glare, the librarian evaluated Kin over the wire rim of his misshapen glasses.

Well, that's not the face of a helpful public servant.

He tossed the edge of his worn black cloak over his shoulder, the library air too stifling for the thick linen he wore. Tugging, he loosened the laces of his padded maroon tunic to allow air to reach his chest. His boots tapped as he approached the balding old man.

The librarian's eyes returned to the book resting on the desktop in front of him.

As he approached, Kin reached into his pocket, and the librarian shifted. He presented a slip of parchment torn at the edges. Scrawled on it was a book title he'd hastily written before he could forget.

Slim, ink-stained fingers accepted the paper. The librarian lifted it towards his spectacles and into the light. "Pre-Sundering Aueric Ley Lines and Myth, Volume..." He squinted.

"Three."

The librarian's eyes moved to take in Kin again. A quizzical, bushy eyebrow rose as his eyes narrowed.

Please, don't make this harder than it has to be...

The ledger within a rare tome belonging to the Great Library would aid his task. A negligible amount of research had informed him what to expect when he arrived, but he hoped to avoid spending several days in the city finding the right book.

Kin forced his charming smile wider. He refrained from touching the hilt of his sword and waited for the librarian's response.

The librarian delayed before he heaved a sigh and placed the paper on the tabletop face down, sliding it towards Kin. "Sorry, son." The librarian returned the fake smile with one of his own. "That text isn't available to the public."

"Excuse me?" Frustration colored Kin's tone before he could control it.

This is what I get for asking permission.

He glared down at the balding head which had gone back to ignoring him. Kin hoped his somewhat noble appearance would aid him in being taken seriously. Lethargy made him less tolerant of the complication to his plan.

"Not available." The librarian's voice brought forth a hidden strength which Kin hadn't guessed possible from his slight frame. "I'm certain you can understand and respect, young man, not all knowledge is equally accessible."

Kin eyed him and silence settled between them, each stubbornly waiting for the other to bend.

A door opened deeper within the library.

Kin frowned at the thought of having someone outside his field of vision. Giving in, he shook his head and tucked away his slip of paper.

"If you'd like..." The librarian smirked. "You may peruse the volumes behind me and find something else of interest. Perhaps a nice tome about Zionan battle procedures." His voice dripped with sarcasm.

Women and fighting. How little he expects of me...

Ziona boasted an impressive military force composed of primarily female fighters, unlike any other country in Pantracia.

Kin glared at the old scholar before stepping around the desk towards the shelves the librarian suggested. They provided cover as he slid between the first two aisles. Once he figured out where the restricted section was, he could decide whether force or deception would be required.

"Caisus. This is the fifth edition. I need to see the first."

Kin peered through the gaps in the shelf towards the origin of the feminine voice. Long, dark-auburn hair framed the face of a youthful woman who stood at the librarian's desk. Dim light reflected off her shimmering hair and the fair skin of her delicate facial features.

"Samitha, that's the best I can do for you." An evidently common response. "You know the first edition is one of a kind and not available to the public." His voice strained at the words, but he seemed less intent on insulting her than he'd been with Kin.

Curiosity overtook Kin as he looked at the woman while he pretended to skim a text on Feyorian beast training.

A thud echoed through the foyer as Samitha dropped a book onto the librarian's desk. "You don't understand, Caisus." She sighed. "Mister Gretter needs to know what the original text says on a matter. They have eliminated the section from all later editions of the book. If you could just do me this one little favor..." Her charming voice trailed off, leaving her fate in the librarian's hands.

Caisus paused, considering her for a moment before he solemnly shook his head. "I'm sorry. I can't grant your request. We don't allow open access to the east tower. Our most cherished and protected volumes reside there. Gaining permission requires paperwork and diplomatic approvals from the universities, which will take some time. I can get you the forms, if you'd like?"

Kin hadn't received the same offer and regretted his lack of feminine curves.

"Shall I return this to the shelves for you?" Caisus motioned to the book she'd placed on his desk.

She nodded and thanked him, conceding to a verdict she'd likely encountered more than once before. "I'll try to find the answers he seeks within a different text in the meantime." Her eyes fluttered over the aisle which led to the east tower before she gazed at the main area of the library. "I'd very much like to complete the forms to gain access, if you don't mind."

"Of course, my dear." Caisus smiled and grabbed the cloak draped over the back of his chair. "If you'd like to check the sixth edition, just in case, you can find it in the fifth aisle down. I'll fetch the forms while you look."

She gave a grateful nod as he stood to leave his desk.

He pulled his cloak over his shoulders and opened the enormous oak door, exiting outside. It closed with a quieter thud than Kin's callous entrance.

Samitha exhaled, a soft sound Kin couldn't help but enjoy with a half-smile. With the librarian gone, his vision moved east. He closed the book in his hands, glancing at the woman to evaluate if she'd create a problem for him.

The charming smile had left her face, replaced by a furrowed brow. "East tower." A certain stubborn quality laced her voice. She set off, black boots clicking on the hard-tiled floors. Tucked inside her riding boots, black leather breeches clung to her legs. Her movement held Kin's attention, and he leaned forward to savor the sight.

Her dark-blue cloak fell loose around her, leaving the short sword at her left side exposed, along with the dagger strapped to her right thigh. Peeking over the top of her breeches was a white, long-sleeved tunic, covered by a fitted black leather vest with ties on the sides, and black bracers at her wrists to keep her sleeves in place.

Kin didn't stop his eyes from falling to the curves of her body, swaying as she strode in the very direction he needed to go. He shoved the book back onto the shelf and stepped after her, careful to minimize the thunk of his boots to keep his presence unknown. Pulling his cloak off his shoulder, he let it fall around himself again.

Samitha wound her way through the aisles, familiar with where she was going. Halfway to the east tower, she halted. Standing still one aisle over from where Kin crept, her voice reached him as a whisper. "Why are you following me?" Her voice contained none of the abundant charm from before, only the distinct edge of someone who didn't want extra eyes on her.

Kin froze mid-step and gazed through a small opening between books to see the profile of her face.

His heart hitched as it responded to the adrenaline of being caught in the act of something unbecoming. But the breath passed, and he grinned. No longer hiding the sound of his steps, he came up beside Samitha, pushing aside the volumes in front of his face to look at her through the open-back shelves. As her eyes met his, he took in the rich hue, like the deepest waters.

I bet they hold just as many secrets.

"I apologize. I overheard we were heading the same direction. Caisus was less than helpful to both of us." He mimicked Samitha's tone when he said the librarian's name.

She turned to face him with an unimpressed expression, an eyebrow rising at his words.

Kin returned the look. He hoped she would consider a temporary partnership, one of convenience. While he preferred to work on his own, an opportunity such as this couldn't be passed up. On top of the potential benefits of having a beautiful partner, it also occurred to Kin that once she tried to break into the east tower, the library's security would stiffen.

Allow yourself the company. It's the preferable complication.

Chapter 2

Standing there, looking through stacked books at a man she didn't know, Amarie debated her options.

This opportunity, with Caisus absent to fetch paperwork, was one she'd been working to create for hours. It'd taken every ounce of charm she could muster. The idea of someone interfering now infuriated her.

He's just seeking an advantage. To use me for his own means.

She had little time, and her mind raced to reach a decision.

While Amarie had been in the library, under the alias Samitha, she'd spent most of her time watching the archway that led to the east tower.

Only two people passed through while she was there. They each left after a short while, with nothing in hand. They walked under the unguarded east tower's carved keystone archway with no resistance, escort, or visible key.

A dull hum tickled at the back of her mind, confirming it wasn't as simple as they made it look.

The Art-manipulated energy centered within the doorway. How the Art-crafted barrier knew who to let through wasn't clear at first, but didn't take her long to discover.

The first person to enter was a woman, who Amarie merely watched. The second person was a man, older than herself but apparently not wiser. He hardly saw past the low neckline of her shirt as she bumped into him on his way out, dropping several books she needlessly carried and apologizing profusely.

The blunder allowed her to slip her hand into the outside pocket of his robes, where he'd stashed his east tower access charm. Her fingers found the cold surface of the spherical stone with ease. The dull, pulsating buzz of the Art hummed on her fingertips.

She inspected the item after he walked away, oblivious. No bigger than an inch, the charm had intricately sculpted imagery on its surface resembling the carvings on the east tower's archway.

The steel-eyed stranger cleared his throat, drawing Amarie's attention to the strong line of his stubbled jaw.

If I say no, he'll get in my way.

A cascading event spiral unwound in her imagination, ultimately resulting in her being unwelcome at the library, and prohibiting her from the text she sought. The first edition had been rewritten with massive redacted sections in all future volumes, eliminating the vital clauses she wanted to read. The tome was possibly the key to finding meaning within the most painful events in her life, but she might never know if she failed now.

"Caisus won't be gone long." She smirked. Her heart fluttered with mischievous excitement at the prospect of someone breaking the rules with her.

The stranger moved to the end of the bookcase and waited for her to catch up. His gaze turned towards the archway, allowing her a look at the defined shape of his chest and handsome features, which she shamelessly took a moment to appreciate. If fate forced her to have a partner in this endeavor, at least he was easy on the eyes.

For two people to pass with only one 'key,' they would need to be linked through physical touch. She doubted he even knew the barrier was there. Only those capable in the Art could feel it. She could use his ignorance later, should she need to leave him behind, assuming the stone would be necessary to leave the restricted tower.

She would have to risk that the barrier wasn't sensitive enough to detect two energies crossing together and the library's wards would remain dormant. Dark rumors about the guardians of the library made the entire experience all the more exhilarating.

Amarie joined him and grasped his hand.

His eyes darted down to their entwined hands and his warm grip tightened. "I would have thought holding hands might be more appropriate for our *second* felonious adventure together, but I'm not one to complain." When he gave her a sideways smile, her cheeks heated.

Her palm prickled.

He has the Art?

Amarie's soul shivered as it sensed an ability to manipulate energies running through his veins. It vibrated against her aura, which kept her own power hidden. As suddenly as she had felt the power within him, it ebbed away, slipping out of her awareness.

"Let's survive this one, first. Don't try to leave without me," she warned, dismissing what she felt. The adrenaline pulsed through her. She tugged him towards the restricted area of the Great Library.

They crossed through the arch, the energy of the barrier coalescing against them before it gave way with a satisfying pop, centered on the marble stone in her pocket. The barrier snapped back into place a moment later with a brief hum in the air.

They entered a space devoid of books but bearing the cracked mosaic of a crescent moon on the floor, the sister to the sun in the foyer. A wrought-iron spiral staircase rose from the center.

Amarie let go of his hand and hurried towards the stairs, taking them two at a time. Her hand sought the cold hilt of her sword rather than the banister, to keep it from smacking her in the legs as she made quick work of the curved steps.

The stranger's footfalls barely resounded on the metal behind her. The mystery of his quiet feet, soft hands, and tinge of ability for the Art made her glance back at his face again.

Who is this man?

In the moment's urgency, she decided not to dwell on it. Whatever tome he wanted was of little consequence to her. Once she had her first edition, she'd leave with or without him.

She bypassed the first landing, instinct telling her the book she sought wouldn't be so easily reached. She dared another backwards glance, hoping he'd heed her warning not to leave without her. If he did, he'd trigger the alarm, potentially trapping her within the tower.

He glanced around the first level, falling behind. Whether it was him coming to the same conclusion, or some other reason, he caught up to her as they climbed to the next landing.

She barely glanced at the second level, continuing up.

Each floor was approximately the same size, the spiral staircase offset from the center of the circular tower landings crammed with rare books. No walls within each landing obstructed her view, only low cases and shelves, providing ample opportunity to evaluate a floor without leaving the open iron staircase.

Pausing on the stairs to face him, her breath drawing somewhat faster, Amarie took a step backwards when he nearly ran into her. "Aren't you going to look for... whatever it is you came in here for?" She used the opportunity to catch her breath and study his face at the same time.

He heaved his own deep breath and gave her a puzzled look. "I am. Fairly certain it's farther up."

Amarie blinked at him, uncomfortably aware of his proximity only inches away. Goosebumps threatened to emerge at his vivid blue eyes exploring her face. His angular jaw and roguish, unshaven look drew her in, stealing away time she should have used to search.

His gaze narrowed, and she could have sworn his eyebrow rose ever so slightly in the prolonged moment.

Her eyes betrayed her, glancing at his chest.

"Did you need to go back down?" His voice pulled her out of her temporary trance.

"No." Tearing her vision away, Amarie continued up the stairs at a faster pace, shaking her head.

Focus. This isn't the time to be thinking about... whatever it is I'm thinking about.

Luckily, a glass case of tomes near the center of the room on the third level seized her attention. Grateful for the break from climbing stairs, she crossed the open floor to read the titles on the spines of the books within.

The handsome stranger gazed about the level, then continued up the stairs with a soft patter of his boots on metal steps.

Her eyes flickered to the stairs as he left. She shook her head again. "Just find the book," she whispered, returning to the titles in front of her. The top and sides of the case were made of single pane glass, held in place by an elegant carved frame. A velvet cushion held a collection of books with their spines facing upward, nestled between gold-leafed bookends. She tilted her head to read the titles and found the one she wanted with a gasp of excitement.

Amarie examined the frame, running her fingers along the edges, but found no obvious hinge. With a sigh, she plucked her dagger from her thigh and spun it in her fingers. Gripping it near the guard, she slammed the pommel down on the glass. The case shattered, a harsh disruption to the otherwise still air.

The glass broke into large, jagged shards. One of the razor-sharp pieces scraped over the bracer protecting her wrist and sank into her forearm.

She hissed as blood trickled forth, staining her white shirt. "Fuck."

Her temporary companion reappeared, his brow furrowed as he hopped over the final step to join her on the landing. "Everything all right?" His gaze lingered on the shattered case for only a moment before he veered to a rack of books on her right.

"Oh, just fantastic. No luck upstairs?"

He shook his head, running a finger over the leather-bound spines. His lips moved as he silently spoke the titles.

Amarie reached for the first edition text within the case, swiping shards from its spine. Gripping the worn leather, she lifted it. A shake rid it of further glass, causing a melodic clatter on the tiled floor. She stuffed the book, *Origins of Sundered Powers*, into an inside pocket of her cloak. Adjusting her right bracer higher on her arm, she pulled its laces tight to stem the bleeding.

Satisfied the makeshift bandage would do for the time being, she returned her dagger to the leather sheath at her thigh.

"You cut yourself." The man motioned to her with a dry smirk.

"I noticed, thanks." Amarie frowned at him.

"Need help?"

"No. It's nothing. Hurry up. I don't want to be here any longer than I have to be."

He hummed as he sidestepped along a row of books at the outer wall, the worn hem of his black cloak swaying at his ankles. Tracing his finger along more spines, he moved up to check the higher shelf.

Staying in the tower didn't sit well, yet she didn't abandon him like she should. As she stepped from the display case, pieces of glass crunched beneath her boots. "Perhaps I can help you."

He shook his head as he pulled a book from the shelf, but instead of pocketing it so they could be on their way, he flipped it open.

The pages rustled as he whipped through them.

"We have to go."

Now isn't the time to read the book.

She absently tapped her short sword while crossing to the staircase. Its tip clinked against the buckle on her boot.

"Impatient, aren't we?" He continued to thumb through the book.

Amarie ground her teeth. "No, of course not. Why would I be? It's not like I'm in a restricted section of the library with a stolen key and book or anything."

"Unaccustomed to thievery then?"

"Unaccustomed to getting caught."

"We won't get caught..." He paused, a finger sliding down the page before he snapped the volume shut and slipped it into a pocket of his cloak.

"No. *I* won't get caught. And you won't, either, if you keep up." As she made her way down the stairs, she didn't look back, able to hear his now heavier footsteps.

"Would now be a bad time to ask your name?"

Without turning to look at him, a brief laugh escaped her lips. "I thought you heard my conversation with Caisus?"

"Yes, I did. But Samitha is far too plain a name for you."

She swore she could hear the smirk on his lips. "Did you have a better suggestion for a name I can use next time the need arises?"

He chuckled as they came to the bottom of the stairs, both sets of boots echoing against the tiles. "I won't satisfy you with my suggestion until you give me your real name."

Amarie stopped and spun to face him.

His gaze met hers, the momentum of descending the staircase having left him near her again. He was taller by a fair margin, and she lifted her chin, a coy smile dancing on her face. "Then, I suppose you shall leave me unsatisfied for our first felonious adventure. Doesn't bode well for getting you a second. Much as I'd like to tell you it comes as a surprise..." She sighed. "Sadly, it doesn't."

In the closeness, his warmth radiated on her skin. His fingers slid between hers, and his grip caused a roll in the pit of her stomach as he returned her playful smile. "I'd much rather leave you satisfied. I wouldn't wish to create a habit of doing otherwise." The baritone of his voice sent a shiver up her spine.

Warnings flashed in her mind to run from the sensation.

She kept her voice low. "Then, perhaps you should first offer your name?" The removal of prized books could set off alarms, and she wouldn't see this man again once they exited the restricted section of the library, but learning his name still felt important.

He raised their hands together, bringing them to his chest. "My name's Kin." He lifted their hands as if to draw hers to his lips, causing her eyes to narrow. Diverting the movement at the last moment, he gestured towards the archway. "After you?" He used exaggerated eloquence, adding his sideways smile.

Taking a step back from him, but not releasing his hand, Amarie erased the playful attitude from her face with some effort.

This is business. Job is only half done. I still need to get out of here in one piece.

"It's likely these books aren't meant to leave, and someone will probably know as soon as we pass through the archway." She hoped he'd been paying enough attention earlier to understand her directions. "It'll be best if we split up after we're through the archway." She paused, thinking for a moment. "Take the door I entered the foyer from, while you were talking to Caisus. It leads to a service stairway and exits the library into an alley at the base of the hill."

Kin's face reflected the seriousness of the matter, and he nodded.

Giving away my own escape plan, brilliant. Time for the back-up route.

Turning towards the invisible barrier, she peered through at the rest of the library.

It remained peaceful. In case no alarm sounded, it would be best to walk through and act as if she'd done nothing wrong.

The buzz as she guided Kin through the barrier this time felt as if they were walking through a lightning storm, electric sparks prickling her skin with great intensity near the tome tucked in her cloak.

Damn.

Amarie smiled.

It's a good thing I enjoy a challenge.

She wasn't sure if Kin recognized the energy, his body offering no obvious sign. The focused jolt from the archway encouraged her to release his hand. "Go the way I told you."

Kin seemed to pause longer than necessary as he looked at her eyes. His expression was doubtful, with the same raised brow as before. "What about you?"

"I know another way out. This should be fun. Good luck, Kin."

Chapter 3

Fun?

Genuine excitement touched her tone.

Ancient Aueric Ley Lines and Myth: Volume Three weighed within Kin's cloak. His skin had buzzed with a jarring shock, emanating from the book, as he passed through the tangle of energy in the archway. He hadn't bothered to consider what Art-laden ward might protect the restricted section, but his accomplice had admitted to having a stolen key. Regardless, the possession didn't inhibit the books themselves from triggering the ward.

It'd felt odd to take the hand of a stranger at first, but the second time, it seemed more natural. He enjoyed the opportunity to tease a reaction from her ocean-blue eyes by drawing her close.

The spark of the barrier was enough to encourage him not to linger too long on how her fingers felt between his, and he released her hand once the vibration faded. His eyes darted to the doorway she'd told him about. His research hadn't included a study of the library's layout, and he'd have to trust she wasn't lying.

She enticed him with the idea she'd enjoy a dramatic exit. Her fleeing form held his attention longer than it should have.

Kin detested the idea of splitting up, but he had what he came for and needed to ensure he wasn't caught.

Her safety isn't my concern.

The barrier's disappearing energy pulsed as he took a step forward. At first, no sound followed, and he wondered if it was a silent alarm. A breath later, a long rumble of metal vibrated to life. Distant at first, as if from a ship within the port, the boom grew into a bone-rattling crescendo.

The ground shook with the increasing tempo as Kin's eyes turned upward. The exposed center of the tower housed the ancient mechanism. He'd seen it at the front of the largest of the library towers from the outside when he arrived.

On the exterior, the structure spun in a lazy cylinder with the face of a large mechanical monstrosity, clicking and whirring in a way Kin had never witnessed before.

Legend described the antique system of gears meant for tracking the passage of time. The race that built the complicated devices millennia before had become lost to the time they sought to track.

Those who desired to preserve history now maintained their creations.

Looking up, as if he were at the bottom of a well, Kin observed the clanking gears and chains roused from slumber at the release of the barrier. The spinning urged the once motionless beast of a bell, which would normally chime at designated times of day, to swing wide in fury. The tongue wailed in its collision within its steel housing. There would be no stopping it, and the tolling of the alarm wouldn't only be heard within the Great Library, but the entire city.

Well, that complicates matters.

The woman who'd been right next to him a moment before was now nowhere to be seen.

A curse found its way to his lips as he lunged forward, stirred to movement at the reverberation. His hand, skin humming with discomfort, clutched the vibrating iron door handle as he reached his destination. He yanked it open and plunged through the doorway.

I'll be a useful distraction for her if this is a dead end.

Kin flipped his cloak over his shoulder and reached for the cool hilt of his sword. He stepped into the new room, a cramped storage space.

An irritated mousing-cat leapt from one of the tall shelves with a dissatisfied mrowl. She turned, stalking through an open doorway between towering shelves to escape the screaming bell, made louder with the opened door.

The creature disappeared through a narrow hall which appeared to be the service exit Samitha had told him about.

He took a steadying breath as he moved to the top of the curved steps, peering into the shadowed descent.

As he released the leather hilt of his sword to grasp the handrail, he noticed the stickiness of Samitha's blood on his fingertips, left behind from when he'd gripped her hand to pass through the barrier. He rubbed the substance between his fingertips and wondered how she'd fare with the injury.

She should be the last thing on my mind.

The beams from artificial lights, spaced far enough apart to allow gaps of shadow between them, danced across the stone ceiling as Kin hustled down the stairs.

A yeowl from the cat came with shocking clarity over the chimes. He held in an exhale of surprise as the mouser rushed back up the stairs in a great flurry, invisible in shadow. The cat tangled around his boots, requiring him to brace himself against the narrow walls.

Kin's palm scraped against the rough stone, but he found balance enough to freeze and listen. His hand moved to his sword hilt as he heard a clamor from below rather than above.

The walls of the stairway vibrated with each toll. Mixed between chimes was the unmistakable beat of armored footfalls.

Muffled shouts came to Kin's ears. He could imagine at least four city guards rushing up the stairs at a winded pace.

Don't give in, yet. There will be another option for escape without using my Art.

No time for exhaustion, Kin climbed back up the stairs, skipping steps as he returned to the storage room at the top. As he passed through the open doorway, someone shouted behind him. His hands instinctively went to close the door before he remembered there was none at the stairwell entrance. Instead, his grip landed on the frame of a bookcase.

With a huff, Kin yanked to displace the shelf's weight and let gravity do the rest. Books scattered over the floor, the wood groaning in protest before the bookcase crashed to a stop against the shelf on the opposite side of the doorway, creating the barricade Kin needed. The fallen case pushed against the other wooden frame, forcing it to buckle and stoop forward as Kin ducked below, returning to where the rhythmic roar of the bell was loudest.

More shouts came, a banging of metal on wood as Kin pushed through the door back to the main foyer. The door hadn't settled before Kin looked in the direction Samitha had fled. He could either try to catch up to her or exit through the main entrance.

The dull light swayed, reflecting off the metal armor of a guard as he rounded a corner at the far end, likely pursuing Samitha. Needing to think of his own escape, he turned away and locked eyes with a distraught Caisus at his desk.

"Y-y-you!" Caisus pointed at Kin.

Kin couldn't help but smirk at the unguarded man.

Caisus scurried to block the exit as Kin lowered his head and barreled forward.

Kin's shoulder collided with the librarian's chest, and he pushed past him. He didn't wait to see where Caisus landed before he burst through the main door, greeted by spring sun. His steps thudded down the steep stairs leading from the front of the library as the tolling of the bell continued to cut through the peaceful seaside air. If he could get to the markets, he could disappear in the crowds before the guards realized Samitha had an accomplice.

Carved gargoyles, draconi-like creatures, rimmed the rooftops of the universities he passed, glaring as if they knew about his involvement.

With quick strides, he watched his feet to avoid slipping on the unevenness of where the stairs had worn with time.

The sound of shattering glass cut through the thunder of the bell when he was nearly halfway down the painfully long set of stairs. He ground to a halt, looking back.

The Great Library of Capul was Delkest's greatest monument. Stone pillars rose, stained at their edges with grime from the chimneys still billowing smoke. And now, it had a broken stained-glass eye with a woman tumbling from it, knees tucked to her chest in a graceful roll.

Colored glass jewels exploded from the window on the third floor of the west tower, sun reflecting off the armor of soldiers clustered within. They struggled to climb out the window, having widened the hazardous exit, but were less agile than the thief they pursued.

Samitha rose on the rooftop of the two-story building abutting the outer wall of the library.

One of her pursuers, possessing more agility than the rest, followed her out onto the roof. Landing a few feet from her, he drew his sword.

Instinct unexpectedly swelled in Kin, a desire to protect the woman. He paused when the guard and Samitha exchanged words. His mind had only a moment to consider why in Nymaera's name she bothered to talk to her pursuer. Negotiations were wasted on city guards.

Suddenly, she hopped back and drew her blade. Their voices rose, and while Kin could hear their unique timbres through the air, specific words were lost in the din of the alarm bell. But it wasn't a cordial conversation.

Their weapons clashed, her short sword moving swifter than his larger, two-handed blade. She jumped over a swing at her knees and smacked his lower back with the flat edge of her steel, causing him to stumble.

Kin's brows drew together.

She smiled. The lightly armored male guard appeared equally amused, judging by his facial expression, despite being unsuccessful in gaining an advantage.

She's distracting them. Keep moving and stop worrying about her.

He turned to continue down when a feminine yelp made him pause again. Against better judgment, he looked back.

Samitha was no longer visible, but the guard pointed his blade at the rooftop.

Kin's chest tightened.

The male guard collapsed, and the familiar head of dark-auburn hair rose again.

She disarmed him with a parry after he attempted a sloppy swing from his prone position, kicking his sword over the side of the building closest to Kin. When she sheathed her sword, Kin frowned.

Standing on the edge of the building, her eyes found Kin's, and she paused, straightening her spine. While she focused on Kin, the disarmed guard stood and advanced behind her.

Grappling her waist, he lifted her off her feet.

Samitha's elbow flew up with impressive speed. It collided with the side of his head, stunning him as he stumbled backward. She spun, the heels of her boots peeking over the side of the roof. She followed up her blow with a leap and roundhouse kick.

It knocked him onto the rooftop, an exclamation of pain leaving his lungs.

Precariously balanced on the edge, she glanced at Kin before running in the opposite direction of the remaining guards.

They dangled one at a time from the small window she'd shattered.

Kin suspected they were in no real hurry after seeing their comrade succumb to her kick. Challenging situations often brought out the laziness in Capul's lower-ranking city guards.

Samitha leapt to the neighboring building, similar in height. She passed over the narrow alley far below without hesitation.

He couldn't help but admire her feline grace as she progressed along the rooftops of the towering university buildings.

As she jumped another gap, Kin eyed the steep incline of the next roof and his breath caught. He rushed over the last steps, as if he could catch her if she fell. Bracing himself, he jumped over the short stone wall near the base of the stairs. He landed with bent knees to race forward again, but he was too late to help.

Her boots connected with the ground mere steps in front of him, but she didn't instantly crumple as he expected. She shifted her weight to roll, vaulting to her feet once more. She looked back at him with that same glimmer of mischief he'd seen just after passing through the archway.

She's enjoying this?

Kin couldn't suppress his smile, despite the advancing guards. "Fancy meeting you here." He used a charming tone reserved for special occasions at his parents' home. He hadn't seen many women fight and move like her.

Maybe she's from Ziona.

She panted as she looked at him, and he tried not to appreciate the way her chest rose. "You made it." Her mouth opened as if about to say more, but then shut. She raised her fingers to her mouth, blowing a sharp whistle. "What's your plan from here?"

A distant clattering stole her attention, and she turned, eyeing the alley's entrance behind her. In the time it took her to ask him the question, a muscled black Friesian horse rounded the corner, saddled and rider-less. As the horse approached her, Kin shook his head.

Her preparations for this heist surpass mine by a fair margin.

"The market." He gestured with a thumb. "I'll disappear into the crowds and lie low."

Guards shouted nearby, making their way onto the rooftops.

Ahead of them, a flash of sunlight on armor reflected at the end of the alley. He guessed the corner connected with the bottom entrance of the service stairwell he'd attempted to escape through. The guards who foiled his escape route had doubled back and were hurrying towards the shouts of their fellow guardsmen.

Kin drew his blade, its steel rasping against its scabbard.

Samitha looked past her horse to the approaching men and then back at Kin. Her eyes widened, her gaze falling on something behind him.

He whirled around, fixating on the guard now standing between them and the entrance to the alley, blocking the way.

It was the same blond guard she'd fought on the rooftop, and he'd recovered his sword. His right temple bled from where she kicked him, and a fresh bruise formed on his jaw.

He stared at Samitha, ignoring Kin. "Was kicking me *really* necessary?"

"You tried to throw me off the roof!"

"I was trying to keep you from falling!" He motioned with his drawn sword, but made no move to attack.

The plot thickens...

The clanking of the armored boots behind Samitha drew Kin's glance backward once more. He tried to evaluate who was the greater threat as he shifted the hilt of his sword within his palm, fingers grasping in anticipation. He remained between Samitha and the guard she appeared familiar with.

"And who in the hells is he?" The guard's voice rose considerably, and he gestured to Kin.

"None of your business, Gerard. But he's a protective lover and a better fighter than you, so move aside."

Not a power in Pantracia could stop Kin's eyebrow from rising. A foreign sensation passed through his chest, sudden pleasure at imagining wrapping his arms around her and kissing her neck. The thought made him eager to continue the ruse, even if to only keep her on his side.

Shaking away the daydream, Kin stepped forward to block the man's view of Samitha. "Clearly, you're not man enough for her."

"But Lilia..." Gerard leaned to look around Kin.

And thickens...

The woman didn't answer him and swung herself up onto the black beast, avoiding the close wall and moving with practiced ease. She stared down at Gerard once more. "Let us pass. You know what will happen if you don't." Her tone softened as she reached for Kin.

Kin hesitated, trying to predict the possible outcomes as his eyes lingered on her fingertips. He reasoned that a horse would be faster and less complicated than his other options.

Besides, now we have an appearance to maintain for poor, confused Gerard.

He deferred, once more, to his curiosity about the woman with multiple names.

The echo of armor clanking in the alley grew shrill in his ears.

Kin accepted her hand, awkwardly pulling himself onto the horse. He couldn't accomplish her grace even if he tried. His hands settled comfortably around her waist to maintain his balance, squeezing to alert her he was ready.

She needed no further encouragement, urging the big horse towards Gerard. With a shift of her hips and a tap from her heels, the beast leaned into a canter despite the close quarters.

Kin tightened his hold around her.

At first, Gerard didn't look as if he would move out of the way, but at the last moment he pressed himself against the alley wall to avoid being trampled.

They burst through the mouth of the alley, veering down the road Kin had climbed to the library. He glanced back to see Gerard running behind them before mounting a horse tied nearby.

Books and papers flew from the loaded arms of students and professors, who scrambled to clear the street.

Samitha cut down a second alleyway, avoiding the intricate iron gateway to the university district and the main square full of merchants. Then she banked to take another alleyway.

The route was precise. The horse knew exactly where to turn.

Hooves on stone couldn't drown out the continued toll of the bell, or the clatter of armor and weapons from somewhere unseen.

All this for some books?

Knowledge was revered in Delkest. It was still a young country, compared to the great warring nations at its borders, but the dedication to preserve wisdom attracted those willing to stand and protect it.

Too bad they hired lazy guards.

Samitha and Kin approached the main road leading towards the markets he originally planned as his means of escape.

Decadently adorned vendors lined the roads leading towards the capital city's ports. Kin had heard about them when he was a child. The banners and canopies of all imaginable colors were like a meadow of wildflowers. The people resembled ants after a hunk of bread. They clambered in an inexplicable rush to get to wherever they were going.

The alley widened as they neared the market square where throngs of people panicked and fled.

Before the black horse could leave the side road, a sluggish cart lumbered to a stop in front of them. The wagon blocked their path, with carts on either side of it and its driver in no hurry to move on.

Kin squeezed her waist to keep from being flung from the horse as Samitha leaned back, pulling on the reins.

"Damn it." She glanced behind them before pulling her sword.

The cart, full of liquor, was hitched to two horses standing obediently still.

"Grab my arm." Edging her horse closer, Samitha leaned to the side.

He gripped her bicep without question while holding the saddle with his other hand to counterbalance her sudden movement. While he supported her weight, she angled off the horse with only one boot still in a stirrup.

"Lower." She wriggled her arm in his grip, reaching with her sword towards the cart's hitch.

Kin grunted. "You're not as light as you look." He let his grip slip and tightened his hold again on her forearm.

She laughed, locking her own grip on his forearm, and he marveled at her blind trust. Using the tip of her drawn blade, she pried free the pin securing cart to carriage. The pin clattered to the cobblestone, but the cart remained in place despite the slight incline of the street.

Straining, he hauled her back into the saddle, and she met his eyes as she let go of him. Her lips twitched.

When she turned her horse alongside the cart, it seemed a waste to ignore his convenient proximity to the bottles in the back.

We might celebrate later, and what's celebration without a drink?

He leaned over and plucked the glass neck of one of the corked bottles, 'rescuing' it from the coming plummet down the hill.

Samitha grabbed one of the corner posts of the cart and pulled with a huff. It lurched backward, wood groaning. Slow at first, but its speed increased as it met the steep hill.

Pedestrians wailed as the rattle of glass bottles and squeak of wheels hurtled towards them.

A battalion of guards rounded a corner down the street just in time to see the oncoming liquor wagon. They scattered, armor clattering as they dove out of the way onto the cobblestone street. The cart jostled as it bounced over a guard, unable to get out of the way in time. Bottles flew from their cases onto the streets and shattered on the stone. The cart slowed only temporarily, before continuing towards the colorful market stalls.

With the guards and townsfolk thoroughly distracted and her path now clear, Samitha returned her sword to its sheath. They raced across the unblocked street and entered another narrow side road. The horse moved with surprising agility down shallow, wide steps, and then under an overhead walkway as they galloped on a path Kin didn't know existed.

Rounding another turn, Kin gaped at a drop ahead of them. "Watch out!"

"Hang on."

The horse hopped down to a lower portion of cobblestone, leaving Kin's stomach somewhere behind them. They entered a dried-out waterway, an ancient drainage tunnel long abandoned.

Samitha glanced at him. "Never tried that with a second rider in the test run."

The stomp of the horse startled a poor beggar curled up against the drain wall, napping.

"How many times did you practice this?" Kin leaned over her shoulder to catch her eye.

She chuckled, tilting her head to look him in the eye. "Once, and at a *slightly* slower pace."

He frowned. "Fooled me. I thought a professional thief like you would practice at least twice."

She let go of the reins with one hand and touched his chin with her thumb. "Guess I fooled you there, too."

Not a thief? Then what knowledge was worth becoming a criminal for?

As if reading his thoughts, she smiled before facing forward again.

Kin listened for the sound of guards pursuing them over the distant alarm bell and their horse's hooves, but none came. None patrolled this part of Capul. Not a waterway that could flood at high tide.

The horse galloped faster, the stretch of sand-coated stone ahead of them long and straight. The walls on either side tapered down until they dissipated, the sand of the beach muting the horse's hooves.

Samitha looked back before her shoulders relaxed, and she allowed her horse to run free.

Kin followed her gaze, watching the sleepy form of the city walls grow distant. He welcomed the gradual diminishing of the bell's thrum, turning to the whisper of waves kissing the beach.

No one pursued them.

A sense of calm pervaded his body. His chest slumped against Samitha's back, feeling her warmth permeating through the layers of fabric between them. He resisted the temptation to bury his face among the sweet aroma of her hair as it whipped beside his face. Her scent mingled pleasantly with the salt air of the waves rolling in. That, coupled with relief as the adrenaline faded, led to a smile at his lips.

"So..." His mouth played near her ear. "Seeing as I know your name isn't Samitha and likely not Lilia either, have I earned your true one yet?"

Chapter 4

Blood seeped down Amarie's wrist, escaping her tightened bracer. The slash stung, the material of her shirt pulling and reigniting the pain every time she moved. Reaching with her sword to detach the liquor wagon had reopened the wound. It needed to be cleaned and wrapped properly, but at a more opportune time.

The encounter with Gerard, now the commander of the guard battalion, surprised her. She hadn't expected to see a familiar face pursuing her.

Apparently, he'd been transferred to Capul after the last time their paths crossed in Haven Port, where he'd been stationed previously. Granted, their romance hadn't exactly ended in ideal circumstances.

I doubt he even cares about the book. He just wants to interrogate me.

She needed to use more force than she would've liked to get away. Handsome men were a weakness, leading to the foolish choice to involve Kin in the lie she told Gerard to dissuade him from pursuing her. She tried not to dwell on the decision, or the distracting circumstances it caused during their escape through the city.

She resisted the urge to rub her arm where Kin had held her weight, and looked down at his hands with a smile, feeling oddly comfortable with them around her.

Once they slowed to a canter on the beach, Kin asked for her name again and this time she couldn't lie. He'd been quick to give her his. Something about the way he said it confirmed its authenticity.

"Amarie." She turned to look at him. "My name is Amarie, and this is Viento." She motioned to her horse.

Hopefully, I don't regret this.

His eyes met hers, and heat rushed through her at the tenderness in his unique steel-blue eyes.

Damn, I'm in trouble.

Kin broke eye contact first. "Well, Amarie and Viento." He loosened his grip on her waist as they slowed to a more comfortable pace. "You have my gratitude for your assistance."

Gazing at the shoreline, she took a deep breath of fresh seaside air. If she were intelligent, she would stop Viento right there and dump Kin off to find his own way.

Partnerships were better short-lived since they usually ended in disaster.

Curiosity burned in her, willing her to continue to humor the unexpected alliance.

Despite the screaming protest from her brain to avoid complications like another good-looking man, her tongue moved to further engage him. "Are you referring to my assistance in helping you into the east tower?" She didn't wait for an answer before continuing. "Or do you mean in distracting the guards while you escaped? Or perhaps you're referring to providing you with a speedy exit from Capul..."

A chuckle rumbled through his chest against her upper back. "All the above? Though I snagged this to convey my appreciation." He thrust his hand from his cloak and shook a full bottle of amber liquid in front of her, evidently liberated from the doomed cart in the city.

A short laugh came from her lips. "Are you trying to pay me with stolen liquor?"

"I apologize, I'd assumed you didn't have a problem with unlawfully acquired goods, considering the circumstances." He shifted back from her, the bottle leaving her vision. In the corner of her eye, he turned towards the city.

Is he worried about someone pursuing us, or does he need to return?

Viento slowed, responding to the subtle tension on the reins.

"I don't. I've just never been paid with alcohol before." Amarie paused. "Should I have dropped you off close to the city?" She stopped Viento and quirked an eyebrow at him. "I feel like I'm kidnapping you."

"No." He shifted in the saddle. "I got what I came to Capul for. I'm a willing victim if you're kidnapping me."

Amarie scoffed and nudged her horse to move again. "Adding to my criminal repertoire. I knew I should've left you in that tower."

He chuckled, leaning a little harder against her back. "Why didn't you?"

Because you're my kind of trouble.

She rolled her eyes at herself. "Because I'm an idiot. Why did you get on my horse?"

"Curiosity. Besides, you claimed me to be a protective lover. I merely played my part."

Amarie looked back at him again and bit her lip. "Our audience is gone now, and you're still here. That excited to share a bottle of liquor?"

"Delkest spirits are the best in Pantracia. I'm no fool." He leaned away, leaving a gap between them and her back cooled, despite the cloak. "How much longer do you think we should ride?"

Preferably until I get some sense and leave you somewhere.

"I'll stop when the sun gets too low." Amarie wanted to get as far from Capul as they could to avoid the possibility of Gerard finding her.

She occupied her thoughts with those of the stolen book, hoping the rare tome in her cloak held answers. So few had come from other sources. She was desperate for something useful that could shed light on her and her family's origin.

No hum of energy emanated from the book, nor from the one hidden within Kin's cloak, so she felt confident the authorities couldn't track them. She steered Viento towards the wet sand of the shore, letting his hoof prints get swept away by the waves.

Comfortable silence prevailed for the rest of the ride.

She glanced at her injured forearm. The bleeding appeared to have stopped again, but stains marred the sleeve of her white shirt nearly to the elbow with dark, drying blood.

Her lifestyle attracted the occasional hazardous incident, but her current situation felt different.

Even Viento ran with unusual nervousness, acknowledging the discomfort of a second rider. The luxury of friends and lovers belonged to other people. Even short-lived physical relationships were never with her real name.

Gerard included.

He merely hadn't realized his purpose.

Her only comfort was that the man behind her was merely a last-minute accomplice, who looked nothing like a common thief.

She wondered which book he'd stolen, but if she asked, he'd ask her the same thing. Giving him that information was out of the question, regardless of how much she enjoyed the banter during their escapades.

No one needed to know her personal interest. The Berylian Key. Too many were already intrigued by it.

As the sun dipped lower in the sky, the coast curved, hiding the city of Capul from the horizon.

Viento slowed at her urging, and she ventured farther from the water to avoid a rising tide in the middle of the night. They stopped just before the sand transitioned to tall grass in a shallow meadow, rimmed with craggy shelves of black rock offering shelter from the wind.

Kin dismounted Viento quickly, dropping to the sand with an exhale and stretching his legs.

Chuckling, she dropped to the sand beside him. "Not a rider?" As she removed Viento's saddle, she could feel Kin's eyes on her and a shiver ran down her spine.

"That obvious?"

She left the horse's bridle in place, patting his neck to send him to graze. "You're walking like your legs aren't straight anymore. How do you get around if not by horse?"

Kin shrugged, the thick black cloak around his shoulders accentuating the action. He tugged at the hem and turned away, looking about as if considering a place to sit. "Going to be a chilly night."

She narrowed her eyes at the redirection.

Choosing a spot in front of a large piece of driftwood, he sat against the old cottonwood gnarled over time by the wrath of the sea. He withdrew the liquor bottle once more and twisted it into the sand beside him. "Join me?"

Amarie huffed. "Should make a fire before that bottle gets opened, or we might freeze solid overnight." The chill of winter still crept in during the night, especially near the sea.

"Is that a good idea?"

Amarie looked back towards Capul.

The sun cast long shadows in twilight, halfway beneath the horizon. A ghostly, low-hanging fog hovered within the trees just off the sand, threatening to blanket the beach in the night.

She shook her head. "It should be fine. With how far away we are and the weather, I doubt their soldiers would come this distance for two books."

Kin drew his feet beneath him. "I'll gather some wood, then."

Amarie looked from him to her belongings and back again. She traveled light, with only the simplest of supplies her horse could carry, yet here he was in just a cloak. "All right."

He left the bottle nestled in the sand, disappearing into the sparse woods.

When he returned a short time later, he crouched with obvious soreness to place driftwood and sticks next to her dug-out circle of stone. "Ahria."

Amarie looked at him. "Excuse me?"

"You asked for a better-suited name and that's the one I've decided on. Ahria."

She smiled and shook her head.

Has a nice ring to it.

Kin unfastened his cloak's button at his shoulder before spreading it like a blanket to sit on, little lumps near the edges suggesting it held more than just the book. He turned his back to Amarie, and she eyed his fine-crafted tunic, which would have been expensive.

Not something a thief would spend his coin on.

Amarie crossed to her saddle, which she'd draped over the end of the driftwood log, drew a piece of flint from a pocket and returned to kneel by the fire pit. The fire started easily, and she fed it enough wood to burn for hours without further attention.

Settling into the space meant for her against the log, she looked at Kin with the fire warming her face. "And I thought I traveled light."

"It has its advantages and disadvantages." He smirked. "However, the biggest disadvantage, at this moment, is that I have nothing to clean that with." He motioned towards her blood-stained sleeve. "Do you? I could help you take care of it. I still owe you a thank you."

"And if you didn't owe me, you'd let me bleed out?"

He laughed. "Are you always so literal? You're right-handed, it'll be easier if you let me do it."

Narrowing her eyes at him, she pursed her lips. "I could be left-handed."

"With a dagger on your right thigh, and your sword on your left?"

Her expression melted into a smile, and she laughed. "All right, all right. Please help me, I'm doomed without you." Turning, she dug into her saddle bag and retrieved a roll of gauze, a small cloth, and a little bottle of clear liquid she used for sterilizing.

He rolled his eyes with an exaggerated sigh and held out his open hand. "Why do I suspect you are always this fiercely independent?"

She handed him the items and grinned. "You're obviously a terrible judge of character." Unfastening her right bracer, she slid it off with a wince before offering her injured arm to Kin.

"I'm not so sure." Setting the supplies in his lap, Kin took her hand. He rolled her sleeve up to her elbow. "So, what information is worth all the effort you put in as Samitha? Caisus seemed rather familiar with you." He let go of her to pour solution from the bottle onto a cloth.

Amarie raised an eyebrow. "Oh, you know. Just blueprints of draconi breeding grounds in Feyor. I hear they're due to receive a shipment of eggs, and I thought one might make a fantastic pet."

An unrestrained laugh erupted from Kin as he took her wrist in his free hand, turning it to get a better view of her wound in the firelight. The cut ran in a straight, shallow line down the underside of her forearm.

"Why does a pet dragon sound incredibly appropriate for you? Perhaps you could give it multiple aliases to match your own?" He didn't look from the injury, and his touch only confirmed what Amarie noticed before.

Soft hands, but a strong grip. Like a noble.

"I shall name him Kin, in your honor." She smirked.

"And will Kin be your protector or your mount?" His eyes glimmered with a mischievous glance towards her.

Amarie laughed. "We'll see." She shook her head. "I suppose it depends how obedient he is."

His sideways smirk broadened. "I guess only time will tell, then." He showed no hesitation as he cleaned her wound, pressing the cloth down to give her a moment to feel the sting.

The pain made her cringe, distracting her from asking him if they were still talking about the draconi.

A flick of his eyes to her lips gave away his awareness of her half-formed words. He continued to clean, moving from the wound itself to her unmarred skin.

"Yes?" He elongated the word.

Amarie thought of something else. "You didn't take the service exit I told you about."

"I guess I'm not very obedient." His charming tone brought a grin to her face. He let the question linger as he unrolled part of the gauze to wrap around the wound. "I started to, but some guards cut me off before I got all the way down. Luckily, a cat warned me before I ran headlong into them."

Amarie frowned. "I didn't know they'd enter from there. It was my original escape route before I gave it to you." She studied his features while he worked.

He appeared earnest, a strange quality for a noble-turned-thief. Handsome, that much was obvious, but something about his face drew her in.

Those piercing blue eyes, maybe.

The shadow of a future beard dusted his jaw. He looked rugged, masculine, and she hadn't missed the broad shoulders or muscled appearance of his torso even if it had been shrouded with a tunic.

Admitting the thoughts to herself made her stomach turn over.

Kin shrugged and finished wrapping her injury, tucking the end of the gauze within the bandage to keep it in place. A breath passed before he released her. When he offered the supplies back, she returned them to the satchel they'd come from. "I'm sure I don't have to tell you how to maintain that from infection. I have a feeling it's not your first flesh wound."

Smiling, she tilted her head. "You might be onto something."

"Well, Amarie." Kin leaned against the driftwood. "You are a woman of mystery. Familiar with injuries, apparent combat skills, multiple names, jilted lovers, pet dragons..." He gave her an inquisitive look.

Her eyes narrowed, but a smile played on her lips. "Says the man who travels with nothing but a cloak and the rather expensive clothes on his back." Her lips traveled around each word deliberately as she watched his face for a reaction but found none.

"I find I rarely need much else. There are many ways to travel. Perhaps I'm a mercenary who markets myself out to trading caravans?"

That's possible. But I don't buy it.

The sword at his side supported the story, and mercenaries made decent wages. They often rode on the wagons, which would account for his lack of riding experience.

Yet, even the best-paid mercenaries wouldn't spend their money on fine clothes. And there was still the matter of the low buzz of his ability in the Art.

"Something tells me if that were true, you wouldn't have told me. You also wouldn't be sitting here with me."

"Fair points." He gave her a lopsided smile which added to his charm. His eyes lingered on hers, stirring a distant temptation. "While my choices in how to travel are curious, I find it far more interesting to consider you. Why would a seemingly intelligent and practiced thief steal within the city where an ex-lover is commander of the guard?"

A short laugh came to her lips, and she shook her head with more conviction than necessary. "I didn't know he was stationed in Capul. The last I knew, he was in Haven Port. And who said anything about him being an ex-lover?"

"He seemed to have that impression. Is he not your type then?"

"You always so curious? Maybe I prefer my men stealing alongside me," she quipped before her mind had the good sense not to.

Kin's smile broadened in a way that flipped her stomach again.

"Gerard's line of work... interfered with mine, but I'm not a thief. Not usually."

"I see." Kin's gaze flickered over her, but she couldn't tell exactly where he looked before his gaze returned to her face. "Then, I'll consider it a blessing from the gods that our goals perfectly aligned today. I owe you a most thorough thank you."

Amarie never took her eyes off him, even while her mind screamed at her to stop venturing down such a dangerous line of thought. Something about the adrenaline of the day and the attractive man beside her caused her logic to wane. "You've already said thank you. What exactly does a *thorough* thank you entail?"

"Like traveling, there are many ways to do it." Kin's hand drifted closer.

A wave of anticipation coursed through Amarie, wanting to feel his touch again. But it didn't come. At the last moment, his hand diverted towards the bottle in the sand beside them.

"For example." A pop broke the still air when his fingers wrenched the cork free. "Ladies first."

With a coy smile, she took the offered bottle. Shifting to her side to face him, she leaned against the driftwood. "What is it? Whisky?" She brought it to her nose before moving it away with a shake of her head. "Rum!" After taking a sip, she offered it back to him as the smooth liquid coated her throat.

"To unlikely partners?" Kin lifted the bottle in a toast as the firelight danced across his face.

"To unlikely partners." Her voice was barely audible over the sound of the ocean waves and crackling fire.

Temporary partners.

Lifting the bottle to his mouth, he took a generous drink, reacting to the alcohol as it hit the back of his throat. He crossed his feet beneath him and mirrored her turn. "More?"

"Are you trying to get me drunk?" This time, she drank deeply and couldn't hide the wince the burn elicited. She bit her bottom lip and held out the bottle to him. "Because it might work."

 Chapter 5

Fire rushed through him, too early to blame the rum.

He stared at her mouth.

She's doing that on purpose.

The barely visible pearl of her front teeth on the perfect curve of a full lower lip made him clench his jaw. It complimented her smooth skin and soft, high cheekbones.

Kin fell into a haze, far faster than alcohol could accomplish alone.

The sound of the surf, and the fog over the beach, only added to the cozy atmosphere provided by the fire.

He couldn't help thinking about caressing her where the warm light bounced off her exposed collarbone. Where her deep-auburn hair curled on her neck.

The allure already surpassed the physical.

She had a strength, a confidence Kin gravitated to. Never had he been so immediately enthralled, but he couldn't find words.

He sought distraction in the bottle. His gulp of the warm amber liquid was slow, perhaps too slow to hide its purpose as an excuse not to talk. Forcing his eyes closed in a feigned reaction to the burn, Kin tried to get his wits together. He blindly offered the bottle to her.

Amarie.

A pretty name.

He hoped it was her true one.

A delicate hand accepted the bottle from him, her fingers brushing against his and prompting his eyes to open.

He valiantly fought the desire to look directly at her.

She didn't drink from the rum right away, watching him before releasing her bottom lip.

Kin regained his ability to look at her without instantly wanting to kiss her. The need felt like a primal fury warring within him. He offered a smile and leaned sideways against the driftwood.

He wanted to prolong the experience with her beyond a single night.

Contemplating his words, he raised a hand to comb through the straight locks of his thick, brown hair. "I have a distinct feeling that even if I wanted to get you drunk, you'd find another way to surprise me."

He liked her unpredictability. Anything to distract from the monotony his life had become. Simple retrieval quests. He felt like a dog playing fetch.

Amarie eyed the bottle, swirling its contents. "Is that a terrible thing?"

He hesitated, eyes betraying him by surveying the curve of her neck. "I'm open to further surprises."

"Did you have something in mind, Kin?" She used his name again, speaking it slower, as if she knew it would send a shiver up his spine.

Can she read me so easily?

He managed to smile. "Perhaps..."

The mischievous grin returned to her features, and she took a swig of rum without breaking eye contact.

The sun cast shades of pink and red across the sky over the water, and as Amarie turned to gaze at it, the colors reflected in her eyes. Mingling with the blue, it turned her irises a vibrant shade of purple.

The temptation of her defeated his restraint, and he reached for her chin. His fingertips grazed her soft skin, and he leaned closer. Their mouths met in a sudden fiery kiss.

Her lips moved against his with a sharp inhale, and she touched his face before breaking away.

Heart pounding, he met her eyes. "Too presumptuous?"

"No." Her voice breathy, she kept her hand on his cheek and licked her bottom lip. "You just surprised me."

"It was my turn, then." He traced his fingertips back across her jaw.

Running her thumb over his chin, she rolled her lips together and smiled. "You're not like other men."

"Is that a compliment?"

"Maybe." Her eyes narrowed. "Depends how much trouble you cause me."

His brows knitted together as his hand ventured into her hair, touching the back of her neck. "How much trouble were you hoping for?"

Lifting her hand from him, she held her index finger and thumb less than an inch apart. "No more than this much."

He smiled as he took the hand she gestured with and pulled it to his lips, trailing kisses along her knuckles. "How much trouble is this?"

Amarie shook her head, eyes locked on his. "A manageable amount."

He turned her hand in his, kissing the inside of her wrist, feeling her pulse against his lips. "And this?"

The muscle at the side of her jaw flexed. "I'm totally unaffected."

He chuckled, kissing her again, flicking his tongue to taste the salty sweetness of her skin.

Amarie sucked in a breath and pulled her hand from his grasp. "Definitely trouble. Are you hungry?" She averted her gaze, shifting her hips where she sat, drawing his attention down her body again.

"Hungry? For food?" His elated mind tried to comprehend the question that no longer matched what his body demanded.

"Yes, Kin. Food. If I don't eat something, this rum will go straight to my head, and you're *definitely* not helping." She turned to a bag on the other side of her saddle. Dragging it to the front of the log, she nestled it into the sand opposite of where he sat.

Kin still tasted the sweetness of her on his tongue, mind buzzing. The lingering adrenaline from the robbery fueled his forwardness, but he suspected the attraction would have been there, regardless. "I already owe you for all you did for me today, and now you're offering to feed me? Be careful, or you may never get rid of me."

A slow smile spread across her face. "I don't think that'll be a problem."

Without thinking, he shifted closer. "Where did you learn to move and fight like that, anyway?"

"I practice?" She pulled a cloth from her bag and unwrapped it between them.

Fresh bread accompanied by cubed cheeses and dried meats.

"My uncle taught me to fight." She tore off a chunk of bread. "Help yourself."

Kin couldn't deny the rumble of hunger in his stomach. He popped a cube of cheese into his mouth, returning to the spread as he tore off a piece of bread with some meat.

He dared a glance at her and found her eyes on him. "Thank you." He couldn't recall the last time he'd eaten fresh cheese.

The lump of the book beneath his leg urged him to stop wasting time and get back to his original purpose.

He was eager to complete his task, even if another would follow.

But a drawn-out evening near Capul won't be noticeable in the greater scheme.

Amarie was a worthy excuse for a brief delay. It had been some time since he'd allowed himself to spend time with a woman.

As their fingers touched in the bottle's passing, another undeniable wave of desire for more raged through him, his shoulders tightening. He looked towards the food for more cheese to distract from his rising tension.

Amarie lifted an eyebrow, swirling the half-full bottle of rum before taking another gulp. She leaned forward and pushed it into the sand between them before removing her cloak, laying the dark blue garment over the driftwood.

Kin gained a less restricted view of her form, hugged by a black leather vest that did well to accentuate her curves. He no longer hid his lingering look. "May I kiss you again?"

She paused and stared at him for a moment. "Are you always so forward?"

"Not always. Would you rather I wasn't?"

Amarie hesitated, but then shifted onto his cloak with him. "It's not a complaint, but I can't tell if you're naturally good at it, or if you're just *well practiced*." She tilted her head, eyes intent on his.

She was close enough now that he could catch the sweet scent of her hair over the smoke of the campfire.

He touched her side, slipping his arm around her. "Does it matter?"

Turning away from him briefly, her exposed neck beckoned him. Before he succumbed to the allure of her skin, she offered him the rum.

She swirled it under his chin, mixing its sharp spice with her lovely scent. "I suppose not, if your actions are genuine, but I am no one's conquest." Her tone lowered, but she maintained eye contact.

He took the bottle and instigated the touch between their fingers as he did. "It's been awhile since I've kissed someone, but I'd like to remedy that with you further, if I may?" He held the half-full bottle, but forgot its purpose.

She pulled the food closer, and he glanced again at the exposed skin near her collarbone, curving towards her chest. He imagined kissing it, and the feel of her body against his.

"Because it's been awhile?" Her eyes flashed a playful gleam as she twisted a cube of cheese within her fingertips and raised it to his mouth, where her gaze lingered.

The unmistakable look caused an exaggerated response. It started in his chest and passed downward. He could have blamed it on the rum, but the alcohol had nothing to do with it.

He hesitated, his mind trying to navigate the possible pathways leading to and from this moment. Sheer desire urged him to lean towards her offer and take the cheese. His lips closed on her fingertips, wanting to taste them, too.

Her gaze faltered, and she bit her lower lip again.

"No. It's something about you. Because that kiss rocked me deeper than anything has in a long time. I'm dying to know if it's a repeatable phenomenon." Kin's left arm tightened around her waist, reminding him of their ride.

Everything within him tensed, starkly aware of her reaction. His original hope to avoid an unwanted attachment succumbed to his more insistent cravings.

Amarie's eyes narrowed, and she touched his chin with her thumb again. "Well practiced," she whispered, but her tone lacked any hint of her thoughts.

Kin lifted the bottle with his woefully unhindered arm to offer her a drink. "On the contrary, I don't believe I've ever said that to anyone before."

After taking a long swig, Amarie set the bottle down, this time opposite of Kin but not out of his reach. "You should write it down for later use. It'll be effective then, too, I'm sure." She smiled, lowering her hand from his face.

He frowned, shifting to look at her face more directly. "Why make light of it like that? Can't it be just for you?"

Her brows twitched. "Are you telling me it can?"

He touched her cheek, guiding her lips to be only an inch from his. "It's just us on this beach. So yes, it's only for you."

Amarie's hand covered his, moving it from her face. His doubt dared show itself, but she didn't let it go, bringing it close.

Eyes still on his face, she kissed his knuckles. "You're a dangerous kind of trouble, aren't you?"

His mind spun, banishing any hope for logical thought.

The feel of her lips intoxicated him far beyond the rum.

Primal attraction ran vigorously through his core. His breath caught in his throat as he watched her lips press to his skin again. Then his eyes locked on hers.

A coy smile spread across her face as she separated her lips from his hand. Her teeth again idly chewed her bottom lip.

A half-formed response died on his tongue, breath ceasing when her teeth pressed down on her lip. The crushing desire to be that pressure on her lip shook him.

Taking her fingers between his, he aligned his chest with hers. Her exhale tickled his bottom lip as he drew her in, and his eyes shut to allow the rest of his senses to take over. He listened to her soft breath, felt the heat of her as he hovered agonizingly close, still expecting her mind to snap to some logic which would pull her from him.

As he paused, her free hand touched his face, running over the stubble on his cheek before sliding to the side of his neck at the base of his hairline.

Her breathing came quicker than before, and she squeezed his hand.

Their mouths met, and the same shudder of perfection passed through him. Each fervent kiss led to another.

Kin's hand slid from hers to brush through her hair. An exhilarated inhale brought the sweet scent he'd so briefly experienced before. He pulled Amarie onto his lap, and she straddled his hips. He explored the curve of her lower back while she drew her hands through his hair.

The almost-empty bottle of rum remained off to the side, long forgotten in the night air.

 Chapter 6

Kin tasted like rum, the movement of his lips matching hers in a tangle of passion impossible to feign.

Amarie lost herself to him, forgetting anything else. Even if she'd failed to obtain the first edition text she sought at the library, the whole adventure would have been worth it to feel his mouth against hers.

During a moment of conscious thought, she kissed him softer, easing the affection to a gentle conclusion. She tilted her head, hesitant to part.

He touched his forehead to hers, his hands on her hips.

"You have a stupid amount of power over me." She kept her eyes closed.

A deep laugh rippled from his chest. He kissed her lower lip. "In this case, you hold the power."

Her stomach lurched, taken aback by how openly he spoke. The buzz from the liquor, long gone, left nothing for an excuse. Tilting her head again, she kissed him with hard, passionate intent and an inhale through her nose.

The way his body pressed into hers invited her to enter a timeless place with no need for secrets or clothing.

With him.

But her mind fought hard to bring her back to the real world. A world of danger and shattered lives.

Parting her mouth from his with a reluctant sigh, she bit his bottom lip, pulling before releasing it as she moved away.

A rumble came from his throat, causing her jaw to tighten and her hips to shift.

Encounters like this, with such fire and emotion, rarely happened to her. She made a habit of avoiding any kind of connection with someone sensitive to the Art.

But Kin.

He'd drawn her in with his tender caresses, heated affection, and his words.

And, oh, the things he said.

Kin gradually opened his eyes to meet hers. The steel-blue looked darker in the dying light of the fire trying to cling to life before them. His hands moved through her hair, twisting pieces around his fingers.

Silence lingered, as if they both knew if they didn't stop now, they wouldn't.

And I can't let that happen...

A part of her wanted to let go, but a stronger instinct refused. Certain things hidden within her were sensitive to the rise of emotions already too close to the surface.

Memories of days long passed flickered into her mind. Days before her hiding aura was well established. Horrified faces acknowledging her power with fear and greed. It made her shudder.

If things were different...

"Perhaps..." Her chest slowed as her breathing normalized. "Sleep... might be a good idea?" It was possibly the only solution to fend off her desire to be closer to him. Sleep, at least for him.

"Sleep." His breath evened as he nodded. "All right. Though perhaps you'll allow me to selfishly hope you won't leave my arms tonight."

A wide smile crossed her lips at his request, even though her heart sank. "I don't think it's considered selfish if I share your preference."

No need to make empty promises.

Her hand drifted to rest on his chest where she could feel his heart beating, and it brought a comfort she wished she could enjoy longer.

Together, they used his cloak as a barrier from the sand, and Kin lay his head at the base of the driftwood log. His arms welcomed Amarie, where she found a comfortable spot in the crook of his shoulder.

His hand rested over hers when she traced the laces of his tunic.

"Kin?"

"Hmm?" He opened one eye to look at her, his lips forming a kiss on the top of her head.

"I'll never forget tonight."

He hummed, squeezing her closer to his chest. "Neither will I."

Insensible time passed before Kin's breathing steadied beneath her hand, his lips near her hair.

Amarie didn't allow herself the same relaxation. Her mind whirled through the series of events leading to this moment.

Despite the comfort Kin's embrace brought her, it couldn't last. There would come a time, soon or in the future, when he would look at her the same way others before him had. His vague link to the Art only complicated things further.

It's better we go back to being strangers, even if I won't ever forget.

The thought was harder to process than she expected.

It was better for both of them, even if she couldn't explain why to him.

The hidden part of herself was beyond dangerous.

Lives had already been stolen because of her curse, and her heart already weighed heavy with guilt. If she could go back and walk away from those people before they got too close, she would.

The best courtesy she could grant Kin was her absence.

I can't give him an opportunity to talk me out of it.

Breathing in his scent a final time, she enjoyed it before carefully rising.

His breathing remained deep. With the activity of the day and added rum, he'd likely sleep through a storm.

Her movements agile, she pulled on her cloak and lifted her saddle to Viento's back.

Occasionally, she glanced at Kin to ensure he was still sound asleep and found him unmoving each time.

Once ready, a quiet sigh of resignation escaped her lips, and she lifted herself onto her horse. She patted the pocket of her cloak, checking for the book. Tapping her fingers against its leather spine to draw strength, she tore her eyes from Kin.

The answers are in the text. Not with him.

The book was only a piece of her puzzle, and she would read it while she tracked down another false idol of power. Delkest's Great Library had been a convenient stop while she made her way north to Feyor.

Gathering more Berylian Key shards was the only way she could continue to guarantee her own safety. And she had to do whatever necessary to find every piece she could.

Including riding away.

Six months later...
Autumn, 2610 R.T.

The shard looked like a broken piece of dirty rose glass, etched with veins of navy and amethyst. Forced into the constraints of a gold setting, it hung from a thick chain.

Amarie's heart leapt.

"Ahria." Coltin called her again, and she nearly jumped as he gestured towards the garish woman approaching, the shard around her neck. "You haven't met my wonderful Aunt Deliah yet."

The woman gave Amarie a grin, clearly having heard about Coltin's Ahria, but Amarie had never heard of Aunt Deliah.

She wore a dress not nearly as daring as Amarie's, cinched at a waistline no longer youthfully small. Her hair was done up in complicated twists, prohibiting it from falling to her ample bosom, squished by a frilled neckline matching the lace of her lilac skirt. Her neckline displayed the gaudy piece of jewelry, which had Amarie's undivided attention.

In the months following her departure from Capul and Kin, Amarie had refocused her attention where it should have been all along.

The book she acquired from the Great Library in Capul turned out to be as informative as she hoped.

The ancient Aueric legend told of a crystal, known as the Berylian Keystone. It once acted as the conduit for the rivers of life-giving energies flowing through Pantracia long before the Sundering shattered the land.

Whether they were physical rivers, or if the legends spoke in metaphor, Amarie didn't know.

Humans recorded little about the world before the ground shook and broke to reshape the land. After thousands of years, the current seven human-ruled countries had formed. Many common folks didn't even know a great shattering of the continent occurred before Recorded Time.

The knowledge of the Sundering lived with the auer, an elusive race Amarie had plenty of experience with. With darker skin, vibrant eyes, and angular features, the auer stood out on the rare occasions they left their island. Eralas was a place few humans tread, but Amarie had spent several months there.

The auer had answers to her questions about the Berylian Key. They lived long enough that there were some still alive who'd seen the time of the Sundering and probably knew truths about the Berylian Key. Human records weren't reliable, and the auer were stingy with sharing their knowledge.

The first-edition text she stole from the Great Library of Capul six months prior was the closest she'd come to the actual truth.

When the ley lines were contained, the Keystone existed as the intersection between five points of power, and surged with all the potential of those ley lines. When the Sundering destroyed Pantracia, and the ley lines ruptured, the Keystone shattered. Human legend believed the shards held a portion of the power that once coursed through the intact stone.

While she didn't believe such rumors, Amarie had been pursuing the shards all of her adult life. In recent months, she learned the location of another. As usual, she thoroughly planned every step required to secure the shard without incident.

The Delphi estate was lavish compared to the modest fields, stable, and oversized kennels on the actual property. The Delphi family had risen to power within the Feyorian military through their progressive breeding techniques, leading to the rapid growth of the dire wolf population used within the country's armies.

Such breeding rarely happened within view of the sprawling, single-story mansion anymore. The current generation of Delphi didn't have the slightest clue what went into raising one of the monstrous war machines. Instead, all the Delphis were known for now was expensive parties and overzealous spending on Delkest wine.

Amarie arrived at the property that summer, and after two months of patient research, she learned much about the younger generation living on the estate. Fracine, the youngest at fifteen years old, and her two brothers, Wintham, nineteen, and Coltin, the eldest at twenty-three. Given her own age of twenty-two, she pegged Coltin as her best target.

To assume the role of a wealthy socialite new to the city, she changed her appearance, wearing dresses, fine shoes, and hair decorations, all foreign and uncomfortable.

Coltin became quickly smitten with her.

Amarie merely had to act indifferent at first to gain his attention. Girls he met usually swooned over him, stroking his already impressive ego but providing him no challenge.

She paid a steep fee to have her stallion properly cared for at a Jaspa inn. It was well worth it to keep him away from the estate and any complications that might arise from her scheme.

Amarie spent most of her time on the estate, getting to know Coltin and his family. Keeping the amount of affection she showed

Coltin conservative, she never made him any promises on their long walks around the lake. Physical affection was kept equally modest, never succeeding in speeding her heart even if she feigned it for his benefit. She kept a habit of returning to her room at the inn every evening, limiting the young heir's presumptions.

The character she'd adopted became so ingrained that the falsehoods flowed effortlessly. Her image of herself blurred between reality and her newest alias, Ahria.

She'd arrived at the estate in the morning to help prepare for the evening's party, and the day had dragged painfully long. It was to be a modest gathering, which for the Delphis meant at least twenty guests. They sought to celebrate the latest addition to their collection. A tooth from an actual dragon, lost centuries ago.

While she could appreciate the rarity of such a piece, it held no interest for her.

Amarie's dark-blue gown shimmered with jewels encrusting the plunging neckline and the hem of the sleeves covering her arms to her elbows. The cuffs opened, and fabric flowed down beside her waist. Buttons up the back hugged the dress to her hips before it cascaded to the floor, hiding her boots beneath.

Amarie knew not to protest the delicate fabrics despite how exposed the style made her feel. Most of Pantracia favored multiple layers and thick materials, but this family enjoyed the fashions of the auer. And she couldn't refuse a gift from the man publicly courting her without earning suspicion.

For her own sanity, she wore cut-off breeches beneath the dress and a small blade at the inside of her thigh. She also fit a thin, sleeveless tunic under the outfit, positioned to be undetectable. The extra layer helped battle the autumn chill auer styles didn't take into consideration. She had to arrange the materials carefully to hide the creases at her waistline and hips, but it was worth the effort.

Her hair, loosely curled, flowed down over her shoulder. A gem-studded comb she'd never have chosen for herself pinned one side above her ear.

"Ahria!" Coltin had called from the main hall near the entrance to the mansion at Aunt Deliah's arrival, ushering her towards him with a beaming smile as he opened the front door.

I should have used Samitha again. This name just makes me think of him.

A carriage pulled into the gravel drive and the door swung wide as Amarie stopped beside Coltin.

A shrill laugh escaped the confines of the carriage as the woman stepped out in extravagant shoes.

Resisting the urge to make a face, Amarie looked up at Coltin.

He gazed at her dress and grinned furiously. His dark-brown eyes were kind with the naivety of youth. She couldn't fault his personality, given his spoiled upbringing. He had an honest heart, and his features were charming, in a boyish way.

In moments of intimate conversation or closeness, Amarie often imagined him with steel-blue eyes to enhance the believability of her performance.

"I told you the dress would be perfect. You look stunning." Coltin offered his arm in a practiced motion before turning his attention to the woman from the carriage.

Aunt Deliah.

Of all the places that shard could have been, she'd never expected to see it used as jewelry.

I need that necklace. Tonight.

Chapter 7

Kin stood perfectly still, pressing his back against the wide base of an aspen. He tugged at his cloak to keep it around him, hiding within the shadow cast by the monstrous tree as the sun set in the distance. He couldn't draw any closer to the mansion until nightfall. As an uninvited guest, he doubted they'd take kindly to him joining the festivities.

When he'd arrived in the small city on Feyor's west coast, the Delphi family was a hot topic for gossip. They served as entertainment for the residents and visitors of the docks, which served the country's capital, Jaspa, further inland.

Kin had slid an iron mark across the tavern bar and bought an ale for a local, learning all he needed to plan his journey to the estate. The family no longer kept hounds on the property, easing his fears. The war wolves were the only thing that might detect him.

Kin's drinking companion confirmed the Delphis tendency to pay too much for things holding no value for those without the Art.

But only one artifact led him to lurk in the shadows outside their mansion.

Kin hoped his eight months of searching were about to end. The first two months hadn't been awful. The second had ended with an advantageous trip to the Great Library and an evening he wouldn't soon forget, even though he tried. The vision of firelight dancing on Amarie's skin still warmed his memory.

Pre-Sundering Aueric Ley Lines and Myth, Volume Three, which he retrieved from the library, was extremely helpful in narrowing his search. It wasn't the Aueric legend he needed, but the detailed record of who was believed to own the objects mentioned in the tales. Skimming through his book's pages, he'd seen the name of the Delphi family next to many artifacts, though originally not next to the one he sought. Cross-checking the list of names had been a tedious process and sent Kin zigzagging across the southern part of the continent, each name leading to a dead end.

A rare goods dealer in Kiek finally pointed him back to the Delphi family. It was the one solid lead Kin had obtained.

Never be seen in Feyor. The warning lingered in the back of Kin's mind, even though he wasn't sure why. He guessed his benefactor had ties to the country, complicating matters if Kin were caught.

I just won't get caught.

His hood draped over his hair, left to grow over the past six months. It nearly reached behind his ear to his stubbled jaw. He watched as a carriage crunched up the narrow drive, noting the first of the guests arriving.

An obnoxious laugh radiated from one carriage as the door swung open, eliciting a grimace from Kin. The laugh, accompanied by the squeak of a carriage door, reminded Kin of the occasional parties of his youth.

The extravagant Delphi estate reeked with overindulgence, unlike where Kin grew up. While large, each part of Kin's old home had a distinct purpose. Not like the gaudy sculptures and architecture of the Delphi estate.

Yet, with all the advantages of a life like that, I still ended up here. In the shadows.

The front door of the mansion opened, cascading lamplight over the gravel drive. At first, he could only make out the silhouetted form of a young man until another shape manifested, encouraging his attention to linger on a slender feminine figure. A physique with enticing proportions, wearing a form-fitting gown.

Kin paused, entranced, before forcing himself to remember the last time he got distracted by the lure of a woman. It may have been an enjoyable evening by a campfire, but morning left him cold and alone.

Not long after the trio disappeared inside, the sun vanished behind the horizon and night enveloped the estate grounds.

The party noise emanated from the south side of the mansion, so Kin inspected the north wings first.

His boots crunched briefly on the drive before he slipped back into the aspen grove. The damp, leaf-covered ground silenced his steps. He gave the line of carriages and their napping coachmen a wide berth as he crept from window to window.

Each peek inside dissatisfied him.

Kin found only ostentatious bedrooms and a study through the uncovered windows. The room that held the most promise had its curtains drawn. A tickle of manipulated energy hovered in the air.

He dared only a little of his own power to sense it.

Despite his certainty the room was the one he sought, experience insisted he survey the rest of the mansion before trying to enter.

He rounded the southeast side of the mansion, keeping to the shadows cast by the wooden pergola where ivy dangled above the porch overlooking the lakeside.

Snow-capped mountains, lit by a crescent moon, backdropped the mirrored surface of the lake. Silver and pink leaves dappled the shore, looking like crystal in the moonlight.

Kin would have stopped to admire the view if laughter hadn't drawn his attention to the mansion's back doors. It originated from inside the dining space, reverberating closer to where he stood.

He tugged on his hood, then skulked across the expansive patio along the walls towards a window. He neared his destination when a flicker of movement made him freeze. Dangerously close to the source, he eyed the set of glass doors. He waited in a crouch between the exterior wall of the mansion and a column of the pergola.

The doors flung open, and two inhabitants of the estate stumbled out onto the patio in a flurry of laughter. It was the young man, still accompanied by the enticing woman he'd seen at the front door.

"Ahria." The man's gleeful voice sounded out of breath.

The name paralyzed Kin.

The two figures walked farther out onto the patio, hand in hand, and the man spoke again. "You look gorgeous. Please tell me you'll stay here with me tonight?" His tone, slurred by alcohol, held uncertainty.

She nodded and turned to face him instead of the lake.

Kin studied the profile of her face outlined by the moonlight. It cast similar shadows as the firelight had the night they shared on the beach. He couldn't forget the lips he'd savored until he fell asleep with her in his arms.

"Coltin..." She touched his upper arm, her voice smooth. "I'd love to."

The young man leaned in quickly, pressing his lips to hers.

Disgust rumbled deep within Kin, something he didn't fully recognize.

Amarie pulled away from the kiss and smiled at her escort. "But I'd like a moment in the fresh air. I'll be back inside shortly, if that's all right?" Her well composed words were distinctly sober.

"Yes, of course, my sweet. I'll go prepare another drink for when you return." He lifted her hand to his lips and planted a formal kiss before returning inside, leaving her alone.

Kin waited until he heard the doors click shut before he shifted to get a better view of the woman he'd stolen books with in Capul.

Is this, perhaps, who Amarie really is?

Yet, the use of her alias, an alias he gave her, suggested otherwise.

Why is she here? She's not after the same artifact, is she? No, it's impossible.

The chances were too remote. So few put stock in old Aueric legends.

A smile crossed his lips at the memory of following her down spiral stairs, insisting the name Samitha was too plain for a woman such as her. It held even more truth now with the delicate dress and noble appearance.

Amarie turned to face the lake, her body stilling. The moonlight caressed the exposed skin at her upper back, framed by her hair, black in the night.

Glancing back to the door she and Coltin used to exit the house, her face held no remnants of the tipsy smile from only moments before. She walked from the patio towards the lake, her shoes tapping on the stairs. Lit only by the moon, she glided over the well-manicured lawn and onto the platform of the white gazebo near the water. The small structure had eight pillars and short sets of stairs on opposite sides.

Kin admired her gait and the sway of her hips. Her curves were alluring, and the dress accentuated them even more.

He took a step forward without meaning to, then froze. Revealing himself was a risk, no matter how much he wanted to trust her.

What if I'm wrong, and Amarie is also a lie?

The reeling of his stomach returned as he considered Coltin might be someone Amarie truly cared for, and his feet moved again.

She owes me an explanation.

Dropping off the side of the patio in near silence, he crossed below the stairs in a crouched run towards the gazebo. Glancing at the house, he noted the pergola perfectly obscured the windows to the dining hall and, subsequently, the guests.

He slipped into the shadows within the gazebo, planting his feet beneath him as he rose to his full height a few steps behind her. He assumed she carried a hidden blade, considering her previous habits. The realization evoked playful thoughts and a wandering gaze to explore where she might have stowed it.

Kin's lips quirked into an ironic smile as he drew his hood back for the first time that evening. He hoped she'd recognize his voice before stabbing him. "Fancy meeting you here."

Chapter 8

Amarie's breath caught in her throat.

Impossible.

Spinning on her heels, she didn't hide the disbelief on her face as her gaze settled on the steel-blue eyes she never thought she'd see again. Even in that moment of recognition, her heart thudded its response.

She thought it'd been Coltin coming up behind her, encouraged to try something daring by the evening's drinks. But Kin's voice sent a shiver down her spine. Swallowing, she took a single step in the direction of the man who still haunted her thoughts. The yearning to feel his arms engulf her wasn't something she could indulge, not with her current charade.

"Kin." She breathed his name in an exhale, tucking a loose strand of hair behind her ear. "What are you doing here?" She skimmed his appearance with wide eyes, but his black clothes blended into shadow.

His gaze steady on hers, he took a silent step forward. "I could ask you the same thing. And I was right, Ahria is a much better alias for you." A charming sideways smirk followed.

Her eyes darted briefly to the estate house. "It's nice to have your approval."

"I doubt approval is the right word." His eyes fluttered down to admire the Aueric dress, and her cheeks heated. "But it suits you, especially considering how gorgeous you look." His tone mimicked Coltin's from when he complimented her only moments before.

How long has he been watching us?

"Perhaps this atmosphere mirrors your actual life, since you wear it so comfortably?"

Amarie raised an eyebrow. "I'm glad my acting is convincing enough to fool you. Or could it be that you're jealous?" She attempted to keep her voice smooth, trying to piece together his presence at the Delphi estate.

His eyes narrowed, and he took another step closer.

He's dressed like a thief.

If Kin was at the estate intending to perform a robbery, he'd become a liability depending on what he planned to steal.

"Should I be jealous?" His tone was too simple for a question with so much potential complexity. "Perhaps you didn't enjoy my affection the last time we were together, after all." His smile vanished, and his brow twitched.

Amarie swallowed hard at his words, knowing how cold her exit must have felt. "Quite the contrary." She wished she could tell him how she hadn't wanted to leave, explain to him her lack of choice, but she couldn't form the words in a way that didn't sound trite.

Kin shook his head at her vague contradiction and turned from her. A chuckle rose to his chest, twisting her heart.

Is he toying with me?

"Don't worry." He leaned against the gazebo railing. "I'm not here for you. But it would be remiss of me if I didn't at least say hello."

His words brought a swell of disappointment.

She found her voice again as she took another step towards him. "Why risk being seen if you believe me so indifferent? Just to say hello?" Her tone softened as she drew closer.

His eyes dropped to her feet, irises almost silver in the moonlight. "Perhaps the hello is more for me than you. I never had the chance to say goodbye."

She took another step over the raised deck of the gazebo. Finally within arm's reach, she reached to touch him before her mind took over and redirected her hand to tuck the stubborn piece of hair behind her ear again.

I'm so close.

The Berylian Key shards meant far more to her than she could explain, and certainly not to Kin. It wasn't about power. Her own safety depended on keeping the truth of them hidden.

Kin's presence proved a greater distraction than she'd ever imagined.

"I didn't want to leave you like I did." Her heart beat faster.

"No?" A curl returned to the side of his mouth. He didn't close the gap between them, even if she wished he would. "Then what was your plan? Why did you leave the way you did?" His voice grew strained.

"I had no plan." She wrapped her arms around herself to prevent them from moving towards him. "You... You caught me off guard, and I feared that if I didn't leave, I'd lose the nerve come dawn." She absently bit her bottom lip.

Kin stared at her mouth, his jaw tightening beneath a thick layer of stubble. His hand moved in the corner of her vision, reaching up towards her, and her stomach fluttered.

He stopped, halfway to her face, and formed a fist before he thrust it back to his side, knuckles popping. "And here I was, thinking you were the one who always had a plan." He spoke through a clenched jaw, as if in pain. "You didn't consider speaking with me about it? Or asking me about my feelings or situation instead of just your own?"

She winced when his words stabbed in their truth. "I had no choice. If I allowed myself to sleep in your arms, it would've been too difficult to walk away the next day. From you. I knew you would have weakened my resolve if I waited until morning."

"So finite," Kin muttered, breaking away from her. He pushed from the railing and stepped around her towards the dreamy landscape of the lake, fists still clenched at his sides. "Why would you need to leave? I posed no threat to you. I'd never hurt you." He kept his back to her.

Amarie's pulse thudded in her ears, the truth burning in her throat. But it was too risky. Not only for herself, but for him. And if she cared for him, why expose him to the danger surrounding the

Berylian Key and those who sought the shards?

"What if I posed a threat to you?" She closed the distance between them as a tentative hand touched his shoulder. "Would you still have wanted me to stay?"

His head turned ever so slightly towards her hand before the warmth of his closed over it. A deep inhale caused his chest to rise as he turned to face her, taking her hand. "You're no threat to me. You never would be."

Her eyes lingered on his, the surety of his statement pervasive in her thoughts. He was wrong, but she wasn't interested in proving it. He knew so little about her.

The grip of his hand reminded her of the strength of his enveloping arms.

Desire to feel it again almost defeated her determination. She reminded herself of her need for urgency and set her jaw in resolution, delaying the emotional craving. He'd need to wait until the next day. Her prize, and the freedom to meet him somewhere without the risk of prying eyes, was more important.

But should I meet him? Did fate reunite us for a reason? Just not here, not now.

Every moment he stayed posed a greater threat to her plans.

"Why are you here?"

He hesitated and his gaze fell from hers, looking at where his thumb ran over her wrist. "An object. Collected by the family."

She let out a brief sigh.

The Delphi family were eclectic collectors, and the chances of him being after the same object as she were slim. No harm would come from letting him keep his secret as long as he agreed to leave.

"You jeopardize me by being here. The estate will be much the same if you return tomorrow night instead."

"I can't wait." Kin shook his head. "There's no party tomorrow. This is the distraction I need to find what I'm looking for. I have to make my move tonight."

Her jaw tightened. "A few hours, then, please?"

"I'll be fast. And I won't get caught. They won't notice it's gone." Kin squeezed her hand. "The family won't even know I'm here. We can both walk away tonight."

Amarie ground her teeth.

A ward protected the collection room, and while she could nullify its powers of detection, she doubted Kin noticed it. Crafted to be practically invisible to those with sensitivity to the Art, even she wouldn't have noticed if Coltin hadn't bragged about it.

It wasn't as simple as telling Kin about the ward. If she did, she'd reveal the existence of her power and her awareness of his. Those were details she wasn't ready to share with him. Practitioners of the Art rarely hid their abilities as fully as she did. She'd learned at a young age to keep her power secret and was determined to continue.

"If you go in there, they'll not only catch you, but everything I've done will be destroyed. I can't let you do that." She yanked her hand from his.

Kin gave a slow, sideways smile, and a sparkle of amusement danced in his eyes. He leaned back on the gazebo railing, his hands behind him. "No? What? Will you call the guards on me yourself?"

"I will." She backed up a step. "You can't ruin this."

Kin opened his mouth to respond but stopped, turning to the patio outside the mansion. He sidestepped into the shadows and pulled his hood back over his head.

"Ahria!" Coltin's concerned voice rang from the patio above as he looked at the gazebo.

Amarie jumped and whirled to face the house.

Kin stood, barely visible, in the shadows next to her.

"You've been out here for ages, are you all right?" Coltin tilted his head.

Amarie stared at Kin as she contemplated her options. The pale blue of his eyes playfully dared her to follow through with her threat.

She let out a low growl and grit her teeth. In a practiced move, she changed her expression and turned to face the patio. "Yes, I'm fine, Coltin!"

Coltin descended the stairs and shuffled across the grass towards her.

In her peripheral vision, shadows shifted as Kin hopped over the railing. He didn't make a sound as he dropped below the raised platform of the gazebo, disappearing from sight.

She crossed to the short rise of stairs just as Coltin arrived and plastered a wide smile on her face to match his giddy, drunken one.

"I miss you, won't you accompany me back to civility? The lake is boring..." His voice trailed off as he looked out over the water and then back to her. "Unless, of course, one has such a captivating woman to share it with."

Amarie credited his newfound smoothness to the wine in his belly, since he wasn't usually so bold.

Starkly aware of Kin's presence nearby and needing to get rid of Coltin as quickly as possible, she tried to think of an excuse to encourage him back inside. Kin might use her distraction as his opportunity to make his way to the collection room. She couldn't allow him to reach it before she disarmed it.

"Perhaps we can share the view later. Just the two of us, once all the guests have left?" Amarie granted him her most charming smile.

Coltin eyed her mouth, his feet propelling him another step towards her. He clumsily wrapped his arms around her waist, urging her closer.

This is what I get for agreeing to spend the night.

"Cole," she cooed, placing her hands firmly against his chest. "Your guests will miss you."

It didn't work. His mouth met hers in a sloppy attempt at passion. He tasted of the Delkest wine and liquor the family was known to indulge in, forcing her to fight an overwhelming instinctual response to shove him away.

Her mind whirled with how to end the demanding affection, as his tongue bravely pried open her teeth.

She endured it for another moment before pressing harder on his chest.

Thankfully, he released her.

She grinned at him. "Later. When we can be alone." Her eyes darted back to the patio as if she were afraid someone would see.

Coltin tried to move in to kiss her, but her hand against his chest held him back. She added a vapid giggle to counteract her use of force.

He seemed to accept it as teasing, loosening his grip at her waist, and nodded with a glint in his eyes which made her stomach turn. "Later. Come back inside with me?"

She shook her head. "In a moment, I promise." She dared not show her relief as he slid from her and started towards the mansion.

"Don't be long." He turned at the top of the steps, sounding pleased with himself. "Aunt Deliah wants to chat with you more."

Forcing the smile to remain on her face, Amarie said nothing else as the young bachelor rejoined the party inside. She released her breath and looked in the direction Kin had gone.

Shadows fluttered near the base of the railing as a crouched figure stood, leaning against the wood. A heavy weight formed in her stomach.

Tentatively, she stepped towards the lakeside of the gazebo and descended the three stairs to the grass before rounding the corner to look at Kin.

He stood gnawing on his lip, his arms crossed beneath his cloak. He didn't look at her, his eyes reflecting the serenity of the shore.

I owe him no explanation.

He had no claim over her, but it didn't stop the ache of perceived betrayal.

"A few hours, please?" She dared a step towards him.

Kin's eyes darkened as he raised a hand between them, his palm out to her. "A few hours for what?" His voice sounded hollow. "So you can go to Coltin's bed tonight?" His body seemed to shake beneath his cloak, enveloping him as he drew an unsteady breath.

"Kin." The shift in his demeanor left little room for negotiation, but she at least needed to warn him about the ward. "You don't understand, you can't go in there. Cole told me—"

"Cole?" Kin spat the name. "Forget it. I didn't come here for you, so stay out of my way." He slipped sideways against the gazebo, tugging on the hem of his cloak. Hunched forward, he rushed towards the mansion. His shadow disappeared into the darkness beneath the wooden deck and pergola.

Amarie opened her mouth to speak, but he was too far away. She pulled up the skirt of her dress and raced for the house.

I need to disarm the ward before he triggers it and ruins everything.

Chapter 9

Kin emerged from the shadows at the north edge of the mansion, moving towards the heavily draped windows. He urged himself to focus, but his blood ran hot. It didn't seem natural for Amarie to hold so much sway over his emotions.

How could she claim to feel anything for him, when she desired her evening with Coltin? She'd surely been lying to him when she insisted the entire thing was an act. Otherwise, why would she have allowed such affection from the rich bachelor?

Kin's imagination treated him to repeated images of Amarie in the young heir's arms, returning kisses Kin desired for himself. His mind sought to cool the fire within him with a logical defense.

I hold no claim over her.

All they'd shared was an evening on a beach six months prior, with nothing more than kisses. He felt naïve in his hope to continue what began there. She'd disappeared from his arms while he slept. He'd wanted to believe her statement of not wanting to depart the way she had.

Kin tried to find delight in imagining Coltin's face if Kin, a mysterious thief, wooed and swept his Ahria away from him.

He allowed the thoughts to run rampant for only another moment before he examined the closed, sideways-swinging window. A new haste echoed deep within him to get what he came for and leave.

Remember your task.

It was foolish to even make his presence known to Amarie.

How could he have been so callow?

The locked window stood as tall as Kin, wide enough for his broad shoulders without turning sideways. He used a whisper of the Art, and the latch made a satisfying click as it fell loose. The window opened, obeying his prying fingers.

In his hurry, Kin forgot the possibility of wards around the room, but he felt only the dissipation of his own energy as it flowed back into him, where it belonged.

He hopped over the low sill to land silently within the darkness. The curtains rustled, but his hands quieted them and closed the window behind him. He left it ajar an inch, so he could exit quickly if he needed to.

Stillness blanketed the room, and a dull hum of the Art buzzed against his skin from the objects within. A strange glow came from a case near a side doorway, the only light source in the room.

Kin's eyes lingered on it before he realized it was a large transparent glass vase. Corked, it contained a licking blue and white flame. The fire danced as if alive, swirling within its container and casting ghostly shadows as its light passed over the other objects in the room.

Stepping forward, Kin was grateful for the intricate carpet silencing his boot falls as he moved past the cases. Nothing within them held his interest. He approached the shelves at the far wall, willing his eyes to adjust to the dim light.

The door near the case with the odd flame opened.

Kin flung himself to the floor, breaking his fall and slinking low. He hoped the shadow of a nearby display case would obscure him enough from whoever entered. With a breath, he prepared himself to reach for the Art as a figure slid into the dark room, shut the door, and leaned on it with an exhale.

"Damn it, Kin." Amarie's whisper broke the silence. "Get up!"

A thousand curses came to mind as Kin debated obeying. She might not actually know he was there, but the tone of her voice urged him to stand.

He grumbled before he pushed himself up, his hands beneath his chest, and crossed the room towards her. Frustration tangled with the fear of her bringing someone else into the room, intentionally or not. He didn't wait for her reaction before he moved against her. Placing his hand on the door beside her head where she leaned, he glared at her.

She stood her ground as his face leaned close to hers with a hiss.

"Go away, Amarie." His voice deepened. He didn't need the distraction. Not now, when he was so close.

No trace of fear touched her eyes. Instead, she stood straighter and lifted her chin.

Gods, she's infuriating.

His blood ran hotter.

"You have no command over me. Tell me, and tell me now, what you are searching for that couldn't possibly wait a few hours longer. Or I swear to the gods, I'll have the guards in here within seconds."

A shadow rose in Kin, fueled by irritation at her stubbornness not to drop the subject he'd already said too much about. It wasn't any concern of hers, so why did she keep asking? She couldn't possibly understand the urgency to complete his task. The importance. Besides, a deep part of him rationalized the knowledge of his task wasn't his to tell.

A growl rumbled in his chest while he pinned Amarie to the door, anger masking his desire for her. His eyes darted down her, the thin fabric of her dress doing little to conceal the shape of her body. The view threatened his conviction.

He forced a deep breath, furrowing his brow and trying to gauge if she would call the entire guard down on his head.

But she didn't give me away to Coltin at the gazebo.

The thought of the young man caused Kin's chest to constrict, another rumble passing through him.

Her mouth tight in defiance, Amarie's chest rose against him with each breath, her skin pale in the strange blue glow.

Kin's anger evolved to provocative thoughts, and he turned his eyes back to hers. He smiled, though didn't know why, with his lips hovering close to hers. "You won't call them," he whispered. "You can't."

Her eyes narrowed. She took a sudden inhale, opening her mouth to shout, and his heart leapt.

Kin found the fastest way to stop her mouth. His lips met hers in a hard kiss, pressing the back of her head against the door to stop the call she might have made.

Her mouth, forced to pause in its shout, emitted a barely audible whimper. She touched his sides, and her mouth moved with his.

The vibration against his lips, along with the motion to return the kiss, propelled him deeper into abrupt passion. The need, first discovered months before, reignited with ferocity as their lips moved in rhythm to rediscover what had been lost.

Don't lose focus. But gods, how I missed this...

After a brief tangle of tongues, Kin pulled away with a gasp. He kept his hand pressed on the door beside her head, his body tight against hers. "Please. Don't."

Much to Kin's relief, Amarie made no move to yell, breathing hard.

Her blue eyes stared at him, filled with uncertainty and something else he couldn't decipher. "Kin, you don't understand." She lifted her chin just enough to brush his bottom lip with the hint of a kiss.

His breath caught, and he almost returned it before he stopped himself. He shook his head and leaned his forehead against hers. "Then help me understand." He caressed her neck, her soft skin warm beneath his fingertips.

"I've been here for months. If anyone can find something here, it's me, but I need you to wait." Her eyes flickered to his mouth.

Kin pulled away, doubt reclaiming his thoughts.

Her hands flexed against his sides, prohibiting his retreat and pulling him close. "And don't you dare accuse me of wishing for a night in his bed."

It caught him off guard, but he was more than willing to remain close to her. He shifted from leaning with his hand on the door to his elbow, her breath wisping past his neck.

"Then what do you wish for?" He growled, pressing his mouth near her jaw.

Her lips close to his ear, he heard the pleasing sound of her breath catch, sending shivers through his entire being.

Kin's eyes closed when her mouth pressed against his neck under his earlobe.

She squeezed his sides as she trailed a second damp kiss lower.

A desperate little sound escaped his lips before he could contain it, resonating in a response to the heat surging through him. As much as his body demanded more, a cynical voice told him Amarie was trying to manipulate him. Trying to spur an answer he hadn't yet given.

"I wish for many things," she whispered against his skin and then paused. Moving her face back from his neck, the tip of her nose trailed over his cheek.

For a breath, he thought she intended to kiss him, but her mouth hovered near his without touching.

"Many things, including a few more hours to finish my purpose here, and then I can help you acquire whatever it is you seek. If you would just trust me and tell me..." Her voice trailed off, eyes flicking up to meet his. Not a trace of dishonesty touched her face, and, gods damn him, he believed her.

Against all better judgment, he wanted to give her the time she requested. His task had already waited eight months. What was one more night? And with Amarie's help...

Eagerly, his head moved towards hers, the solid surface of the door prohibiting her from pulling away from a fiery kiss.

Amarie melted against him, and her hand touched his face. The softness of her fingertips trailed over the rough stubble on his jaw.

He tried to untangle whatever thoughts were on his tongue by moving it against hers. The arm not supporting his weight slid down her side, exploring the curves he'd not had such open access to before.

Everything within him burned for nothing but her. He'd give her anything she asked for. As long as he could taste her like this, he'd wrap up the world and present it to her in a stained-glass box.

He forced the break after an obnoxious laugh reverberated through the walls from wherever the guests were being entertained. Air gasped into his lungs, mirrored by her own breath, as a hand wrapped around her waist.

"You've probably never heard of it." He couldn't wait for his heart to slow, in case he lost the nerve to tell her the truth. "It's a shard. Looks like glass or a gem. Red, with veins of purple through it. I know the family acquired it roughly two years ago from a tradesman in Kiek." It all came out in a rush, his mind still craving her instead of focusing on his task. His lips found her neck in his desperation for more, trailing towards her shoulder.

When she exhaled, he realized she'd held her breath through his description.

She knows the object I'm looking for?

She didn't respond immediately, tilting her head to give him better access to her neck, and he indulged. "I know where it is."

Kin's heart pounded, and he completed a slow kiss before he pulled away. Touching her jaw, he smiled. "Good. Then you can help me get it tomorrow." A calm finally settled within him. Perhaps he could take Amarie with him and continue exploring whatever about her intoxicated him so. He encouraged her lips near his again, but she didn't close the distance.

"I can't."

His body tensed, shock pulling him from her.

Before he could respond, she continued. "It won't be here tomorrow." Her eyes followed his as he moved away, but she did not try to force him to return.

"What?" The new emotions starkly clashed with the ones Amarie brought out in him, quenching the growing fire with moderate panic. "Where will it be?"

"I don't know. But you must take it tonight. One of the guests is

74

wearing it around her neck, but she'll leave once the party is over."

A familiar growl came to his chest, new frustrations pulling him fully from her.

Amarie let out a sigh as he stepped back.

Tugging at his hair, Kin paced across the lavish carpets. His mind ran through possible solutions to his new problem. He'd have to corner the guest and separate her from the rest somehow to get the object from her.

Perhaps I can use Amarie to...

His thoughts trailed off as he looked back at her. "What about what you're after?"

Amarie watched him and stepped away from the door to follow. "I'll find another way. But getting what you're after might be a little difficult."

"Who has it?" Kin glanced towards the door behind her as she drew close to him again. He reached for her without even thinking. "I saw all the guests arrive, I just need to know what she was wearing so I know who I'm looking for."

She slipped into his arms again. "Coltin's aunt."

His stomach rolled at the sound of the young man's name on Amarie's lips.

"Aunt Deliah, the large woman in the lilac—" Amarie stiffened and stopped short at the sound of footsteps in the hallway beyond the door she'd entered through.

Kin's hand went to his side, falling on the hilt of his sword within his cloak.

"I'm not supposed to be in here," she hissed.

Kin couldn't help the sideways smile at her sudden concern and ran a hand along her jaw. "Good thing you're only in here because a handsome thief coerced you."

Her dark eyes flashed, and her lower lip found itself pinned in the habit which threatened every ounce of his self-control.

Holding her chin between his fingers, he drew her against him, granting himself the pleasure of gently biting her lower lip.

She inhaled sharply, her body responding as he caressed her side, urging her to face the opposite direction.

His mouth released hers to allow the turn, only to seek the soft skin of her neck, forcing her head aside to grant him greater access with his tongue. He drew her partially exposed back against him, his dominant left hand slipping down her abdomen, while his right awkwardly withdrew his sword.

Her hand moved atop his, nails biting into the back of his hand as she held it against herself.

"Ahria?" Coltin's voice came from the other side of the door, though it was a directionless call.

Kin trailed his kisses up her neck, suckling beneath her earlobe. "How do you feel about screaming?" He shifted his sword to his other hand. "We can put your acting skills to the test?" His fingers closed around the leather-wrapped hilt, its weight balanced in his grasp.

Amarie took the cue and gasped out a rather convincing sob, followed by the sharp cry of her voice. The sound almost made Kin let go, but she held his arm tight to her waist, denying his movement to release her.

"Coltin!"

Her terrified timbre threatened Kin's nerve to follow through with the ruse he'd suggested.

She's acting. Only pretending to be afraid of me.

His whole body tensed at the mere thought of her fear being genuine, though she wouldn't have been the first to feel so. He didn't want her to know how natural the action felt as he turned his sword against her, lifting it parallel to the ground.

Kin took a calming inhale. He didn't particularly need the complication of the man seeing him, but saw no other option to get what he came for and escape with Amarie. He temporarily released his hold on her so he could yank his hood over his head, and then he pulled her back.

Coltin's voice came again. "Ahria!"

This might just work.

Kin placed a kiss on Amarie's temple. "Trust me?"

She nodded. "I trust you."

The words sent ripples of relief through him, certain now he hadn't misinterpreted her compliance.

He allowed himself a moment to enjoy Amarie's sweet scent against him before willing his expression to twist into a deadly one. He reached towards the wickedness within him, a side of him Amarie hadn't yet seen.

"Ahria? Where are you?" Coltin's voice came louder than before.

The door knob twisted as Kin brought his blade up around Amarie's slender form. He positioned the steel under her chin, while his other hand held her waist tight against him.

Her body tensed, and he heard the shaky inhale of her breath.

Only acting.

Kin took a step back as the door swung open, his hip bumping against one of the display cases. He shifted to avoid it, pulling Amarie with him.

The glimmer from the strange translucent vase containing fire highlighted Coltin's features as he squinted into the dim room. His feet stilled as his eyes widened.

The heartfelt fear in his brown eyes made Kin's stomach sour with deep-seated dislike. The man's care for Ahria made him wonder if any part of it was reciprocal.

Could she have remained Ahria and lived a comfortable, wealthy life as a Delphi?

Regardless of the tormenting thoughts, Kin held the sword steady while he dared the sharpened blade closer to Amarie's neck.

"Cole." Amarie's voice came again in a gasp, and she grabbed Kin's forearm, pulling it with a feigned amount of strength.

Coltin's mouth opened to answer, but Kin spoke instead.

"Hello, Coltin." His tone shifted to be far more sinister than he once believed possible. He gripped Amarie tighter, forcing her to squirm within his arms. "Might I have a word?" A wet drop hit his wrist, encouraging a glance down at his victim.

Amarie's eyes brimmed with tears as she looked at the young heir before her.

Another wave of panic coursed through Kin, but he swallowed it. He ignored any doubts and kept his hand steady and his gaze locked on the dumbstruck nobleman before him.

Coltin stood stone still. His face paled in the flickering blue light, eyes wild and pinned on the blade at Amarie's throat. "Don't hurt her, please." His gaze shifted to her captor. "I'll give you whatever you want, I swear."

Kin eyed Coltin and twisted the hilt of his blade, rocking it under Amarie's chin for extra effect. He leaned forward, pressing his temple against hers, and listened to the rasp as the edge of steel grazed over her skin.

She pressed harder against him, freeing her other hand to clasp a fistful of his tunic at his side.

Coltin rocked forward, but caught himself before he lunged forward when Kin twitched in response. Carefully, the bachelor took a step back, seeming to realize his helplessness.

"That's a good boy." Kin drew his lips near Amarie's ear.

A little squirm interrupted Coltin's stance.

Kin reveled in his discomfort, but there was business to take care of. "The great purple creature out there..." He kept his chin low. "She has a fancy necklace I'd like you to fetch for me."

"Please, Coltin." Amarie's voice shook.

Another tear hit Kin's skin and rolled down his wrist.

Coltin nodded vigorously. "Of course, the necklace. Just, please, don't hurt her." He didn't turn to leave, despite his understanding. He stared, encouraging Kin to further torment him.

He turned his head into Amarie's hair, taking a long inhale for Coltin's benefit.

Amarie's eyes closed with an added whimper of fear.

"I tend to get impatient." Kin pulled Amarie farther back into the room. "So, I'd be quick, boy." He squeezed her waist, lifting her from the ground.

Amarie's foot caught on the lavish fringe of the rug, jerking her in his arms. His grip tightened to stabilize her, and she hissed.

Blue and white light reflected off the flat of his sword, glinting across Coltin's face, forcing the nobleman to blink and turn his eyes away. Without another word, he hurled himself back through the doorway.

As soon as the door closed to nothing but a crack in Coltin's hasty exit, Kin's arm relaxed. It fell to his side, sword pommel thunking against a display case.

What kind of monster have I become for this to feel natural?

He couldn't drop the act for long, Coltin would be back soon.

Hopefully, with the necklace.

He didn't release Amarie's waist, drawing in a steadying inhale. "Sorry," he whispered, leaning against the display case.

She relaxed back onto his shoulder, making no move to distance herself. Touching the soft underside of her chin near her throat, she hissed. "I think you cut me." She drew her hand in front of their vision.

Blood ran down her fingertips, black in the dim light.

Kin cringed, and a regretful groan escaped his lips. Letting go of her waist, he lifted her chin to the side so he could see the accidental laceration.

A wide stream of red ran down her throat.

He'd never intended to cut her and, although the wound was superficial, it would require attention. His heart thudded harder in his chest as he fought to keep control of all his emotions. "Is your Coltin intelligent enough not to complicate this?" Kin kept his vision focused at the door, in case Coltin returned quicker than expected.

"*My* Coltin isn't smooth enough to keep this simple."

Kin appreciated the sarcasm, and it brought some comfort.

Her affections for him aren't real.

She'd been fast to forget the heir in the rampant heat of desire just moments before he arrived.

"This might get a little messier." Kin gave a disappointed huff. He doubted he'd frightened Coltin sufficiently to avoid the appearance of the family's personal guard. Considering the direct connection between the family and the Feyorian military, their guards would have formal training.

Kin's hand slipped back into place at Amarie's waist as he urged his mind to think clearly despite the distraction at such an inopportune moment. His body still buzzed with his desire for her.

Amarie pressed her backside against him, as if to torment him, and glanced at him. "Don't let him catch you looking at me like that." She tilted her chin up, but didn't close the distance between them.

Kin couldn't prevent a smile from reaching his lips. Excitement fueled the steadily growing attraction overwhelming him. A groan came to his lips as he moved his head back, lips brushing against her ear to share just how difficult what she said was.

Amarie exhaled through her mouth in an act of visible self-control.

Damn, she's going to make everything more complicated.

Kin forced his eyes towards the door, sword arm tense and ready for whatever might come.

Boot steps echoed from the hall. More than one set.

He returned the sword to Amarie's throat, placing it higher to avoid the life-giving arteries.

The door opened, and Kin's grasp tightened at Amarie's waist.

As expected, the man who came through the doorway first wasn't Coltin. The guard's eyes tracked to where Kin and Amarie were with no hint of surprise.

The burly, older man's greying auburn beard and slicked-back hair gave him the appearance of an angry bear. He raised his hands beside his head as he moved past the door frame, making it clear he was unarmed.

Considering the guard's muscled arms, he wouldn't require weapons to be dangerous.

Holding tightly to Amarie, a sudden desire to put space between himself and the unknown man overcame him. He moved sideways around the case, tugging Amarie towards the side of the room close to the window from which he'd entered.

Amarie stumbled as Kin pulled her with him, and the muscles in his arm protested, but he lifted her struggling body upright.

She found tears again, her body quivering as they fell from her eyes in slow streams. "Killian." Amarie gasped, her voice trembling. "Where's Coltin?"

Kin suspected Killian was a well-paid mercenary by the quality of his clothing.

Her knowledge of the guard's name piqued his curiosity about just how deeply engrossed she'd become in the Delphi family.

While Kin might have put on a convincing show for Coltin, he needed to establish control all over again to Killian.

Following Amarie's words, Kin moved the blade flat against her chin to force her head up as his mouth moved near her ear. He gave an exaggerated shushing sound not meant for her alone.

Glancing at the doorway, he verified it was still empty behind Killian, then locked eyes with the newcomer. "I hope you have what I asked for."

Killian stepped from the doorway, leaving it ajar to a hallway patterned with gaudy purple and gold wallpaper.

Additional streams of light rushed in, and Kin lowered his head to elongate the shadow of his hood.

Killian withdrew something from the front pocket of his tunic and lifted his fist. He opened his hand, and a gold chain dangled towards the ground. At the bottom glittered a semi-opaque, deep burgundy crystal shard, which reflected the hall light behind it. Small pink orbs of light danced into the collection room, flickering across its walls and carpets.

Kin couldn't help the anxious rise of his chin.

That's it. A Berylian Key shard.

"No one needs to get hurt." Killian's calm, gruff voice held a practiced air. "You can let the girl go. I have the necklace you want."

His gaze remained solidly on Kin's, as if trying to judge how much of a threat he truly was to the woman he held.

A foreboding smile curled the edge of Kin's lips. A wickedly distorted expression he'd mastered before meeting Amarie, born of the shadow infesting his soul so long ago. He watched Killian, no longer retreating.

"I could, but I'm not quite comfortable enough." Kin's right hand slid up Amarie's ribs, moving to her throat. His fingers closed below his sword, wrapping around the front of her windpipe. He was careful to keep from squeezing more than necessary, just enough to look convincing to the guard.

Amarie's hands returned to his forearm, fighting his grip as he lowered his sword. She breathed hard and let out a whimper.

Kin's upper arm tensed to make it appear as if he pushed harder on her throat. He hissed another shush for her to be silent. Raising his sword, he pointed it at Killian. His eyes traveled from the man's gaze to the necklace, to his sword tip, then back to the guard's eyes again. "If you please, sir. I'd appreciate your cooperation in handing over that trinket."

Killian's shoulders pulled back, straining the fabric of his uniform. He held the necklace towards the sword, in what Kin guessed was an attempt to establish good faith. "Can you give me your assurance you'll let her go without harming her?"

Kin heaved a tired sigh and rolled his eyes. "I give my word." He smirked, bobbing the tip of the sword in a silent demand.

In the pause that followed, Kin squeezed harder on Amarie's neck, pressing her into his chest while gritting his teeth. His grip brought a short squeak from Amarie, and she clawed at his arm.

"All right." Killian dragged the word out. He took another step forward, draping the chain of the necklace over the tip of Kin's sword, and let it go.

The twang of the metal chain on the steel blade sounded melodic in Kin's ears as he tilted his sword upward. The necklace tumbled down its length before he lifted his fingers from the hilt to grip the pendant. He spun the sword in his hand to reestablish his grip on the leather hilt and drew it back to his side.

"Much obliged." Kin pulled Amarie back with him against the drawn curtains. His sword hand grasped at the material and tugged. It didn't take much strength to tear the fabric free of its rungs, and they tumbled into a pile at their feet, exposing the large window frames facing the mountains.

He stepped over it, pushing his back to the cold glass, even as Amarie continued to struggle against him. He spotted the window he'd entered from to his right, just barely open.

"Let Ahria go. You don't need her anymore." The guard stood still, but his jaw flexed.

Kin's eyes narrowed.

He cares, too.

Coltin leapt into the room.

The guard reached out for him in a quick reaction, trying to stop him, but Coltin slipped through his grasp.

Kin stiffened behind Amarie, his hand loosening on her neck as he focused on the new threat.

Coltin, armed with a short sword, ran without hesitation towards Kin and the woman he sought to protect. "Let her go!"

Kin's sword rose at an angle in front of him. Using the hand still grasped around Amarie's throat, he yanked her to the side, away from the fight. Their hips maintained contact, but the last thing he wanted was her accidentally getting hurt.

Again.

Coltin's blade arced up to clash with Kin's, smacking it to the side in well-practiced form. Privileged man or not, he'd been taught to use a blade.

Kin turned the movement into a swift return of the blade, bringing it back to a new resting position near Amarie's abdomen. The curtain between them on the floor made the reach awkward for Coltin and forced him to pause. Kin gave Amarie's neck a quick squeeze, urging her to react.

Amarie cried out as he gripped her throat. Tears raced down her face, dribbling onto his wrist. She shook her head at Coltin. "Cole, no. He'll kill you," she sobbed, bringing hesitation to the young man's attack.

"If you hurt her." The adrenaline and alcohol coursing through Coltin's veins undoubtedly gave him extra courage. "I will kill you."

The threat brought a strange thrill to Kin's mind, making him curious to see what the man could do. He raised an eyebrow at Coltin, finding the cut he'd accidentally caused on Amarie's neck. He ran a finger over its fresh opening to elicit another trickle of blood, which he drew down her neck.

Amarie growled and dug her nails into his forearm, breaking his skin.

He answered the rage in Coltin's eyes with an amused smile. "Oops?" Kin pulled the blade closer to Amarie, pressing it against her stomach. The chain hanging against his pommel jangled. "Careful, Coltin. This situation can become much worse." His heel found the bottom of the windowsill, and he pushed the glass open with the sole of his boot, watching the two men. He balanced on the raised edge, lifting Amarie with him as he wrapped his sword arm around her entirely.

She let out a convincing squeak of surprise and struggled against his grip.

Kin's hood, displaced during the exchange with Coltin, fell back against his shoulders.

Killian, wide-eyed, approached Coltin from behind and spoke quietly while placing a hand on the young man's shoulder.

Coltin didn't move forward, but the fury remained on his face.

Kin focused on the fire in Coltin's eyes as he forcefully spun Amarie by the waist to face him, then hopped backwards off the window ledge onto the grass below. He found his footing and yanked on Amarie before she had any time to protest as either herself or Ahria.

With the added height and the strength of his now free sword arm, Kin lifted her over his right shoulder. He carried her easily, even though her body was much denser with muscle than it looked in the fragile gown.

She let out a gasp as her abdomen bent over his shoulder, and Kin squeezed her thigh to keep her in place.

He ran for the trees in the distance with his accomplice hostage.

Chapter 10

This isn't how I imagined his arms around me.

Amarie endured Kin carrying her over his shoulder because Killian and Coltin stood at the window watching their escape. She beat at his shoulders, kicking enough to maintain the appearance of a struggle without making it too difficult on him. The sooner he reached the trees, the sooner she could get down.

When they entered the darkness beneath the aspens, he didn't immediately release her.

She gritted her teeth, waiting a few extra breaths before snapping her knee forward to impact his ribs. Hard enough to get the message across.

An exhalation of breath led to a stumbling stop. Momentum slid her off his shoulder in front of him. As she dropped to the ground, she caught herself upright despite the awkwardness of it.

Kin rubbed at his middle, narrowing his eyes at her. He slid his sword back into its scabbard, the shard necklace wrapped around his knuckles. "What was *that* for?"

"I can use my own feet, thank you very much."

They looked back the way they'd come.

The guards would be gathering to pursue them, but there was still time.

Her immediate concern was retaining a shred of dignity and some control. When she looked at Kin again, he examined her, but not her face. His gaze trailed down over her body, and she resisted the instinct to frown.

"I'd like to see you keep up with me wearing that." Kin gestured to the long silky skirt touching the ground and hugging her form.

Amarie rolled her eyes and turned her back to him. "Then unbutton me."

"Is now really the time?" Kin teased, his voice devoid of the evil it held before.

It caused her negative emotions to pause, reminding her of the rum they drank and his embrace as they sat in the firelight.

He sounded so convincing as the villain.

"This, most certainly, *is* the time."

He hesitated for only a moment before he unbuttoned the gown, his breath coming quickly. A chuckle rumbled from him as the dress fell loose enough to expose her sleeveless shirt, the straps pushed to the side to accommodate the wide neckline of the dress.

Once he got enough of the buttons undone, she twisted her hips and pulled the dress off the rest of the way, tucking it under her arm. Grabbing the strap holding the small dagger in place over her cut off breeches, she adjusted the blade to the outside of her thigh.

Kin took in her new appearance briefly before his hand closed around the jagged shard. "Now you look more like how I remember you." He untangled the chain, thrusting it over his head and dropping it beneath his collar. His fingers lingered at his chest, pressing the slight bulge in the fabric against his sternum. A satisfied sigh passed through him before he moved away to offer her his hand. A soft, crooked smile crossed his lips. "Will you come with me? I'd rather not be apart again."

Her eyes moved to the offered hand and then back to his steel-blue irises. She'd imagined this for months, especially when forced to show affection to Coltin.

"Me neither." She wanted to know more about what was growing between them. But she also needed to get the shard without earning his anger.

His hand warmed hers as they raced through the forest, towards the boundary of the estate.

"Where do you want to go?" Amarie slowed as they reached uneven terrain, pulling on Kin's hand.

They crossed into the looming shadows of massive kennels, long since abandoned. They crumbled at the outskirts of a field nature had reclaimed. Failing fences and housing for the dire wolves, no longer allowed on the property, promised effective hiding places. They'd always been a potential part of Amarie's escape plan.

Kin turned to her, glancing behind them.

Distant shouting echoed, but far enough away to earn a moment to stop and catch their breath.

"Safest thing is to make our way back to the port city. Find a boat to get out of Feyor." Kin sucked in steadying breaths of the frigid air. His eyes fell to her bare shoulders with a furrowed brow. He unfastened his cloak, and before she could protest, wrapped it around her.

Amarie hadn't noticed how cold her skin was until his warm cloak draped over her. She smiled as she looked up at him. Taking a deep inhale through her nose, she caught his earthy scent within the cloak. It weighed heavier than she expected, more than just the cloth. "Thank you."

He gave a nod before he took a step towards her. Touching her chin, he encouraged her to lift her head so he could check the injury he'd reopened. Remorse clouded his expression, and he reached inside the cloak wrapped at her shoulders. He withdrew a cloth from one pocket, which he raised to clean her skin. "I'm sorry."

Amarie's heart softened further at his tone, and the previous irritation she'd felt towards him diminished. "You really don't like him." She watched for his reaction. It was Coltin who'd caused Kin to get overzealous in his acting.

He ran the cloth over the skin beneath her chin, his thumb rubbing her jaw, far from the injury. "I got carried away."

"Why?" Her word was a mere breath, and her pulse quickened so close to him again.

"Has anyone ever told you that you oversimplify tough

questions?" Kin gave her a small, teasing smile. The hand with the cloth moved from her chin, but the other remained, tracing her jaw.

"No one's ever been around long enough to complain." Inwardly, disappointment stung at his subtle refusal to be open with her.

"Then, I suppose I'll be grateful. For two reasons. The first being I've been around long enough to tell you, and the second reason will have to wait as we are about to be rudely interrupted." He finished his sentence with a tip of his head towards the woods they'd come from.

A glow shimmered within the aspens.

Torches.

A search party looking for them, or at least for her, getting closer.

"Now's your chance." Kin's hands dropped from her. "To go back."

Amarie's brow furrowed. "Go back?"

"To live the life of a Delphi. I wouldn't blame you if you wanted it. It's far more elegant than what I can offer you."

Shaking her head, Amarie gaped at him. "I don't want the life of a Delphi. That was never the plan. Even if you hadn't shown up."

Someone shouted, pulling both their gazes to the woods.

Amarie sighed, taking his hand. "I'll take hiding in musty kennels with you every day over living another minute as Coltin's Ahria."

He squeezed her hand, a flash of a smile crossing his features. Moving closer, he brushed his hand against her side to stow the cloth before he looked towards the kennels nearby.

"We can hide until they move on. Go." Letting go of his hand, she pushed the bundle of her dress into his arms. "I will make sure they look in the wrong direction. I'll find you after."

Kin's eyes narrowed. "Don't be long."

"I'll be as quick as I can." Amarie turned on her heels and ran the opposite way from the kennels. She would cross the road the search party was coming down if she kept moving west. If they stayed on the road, it would lead them away from the kennels.

Her feet carried her quickly through the crisp night air. She didn't pause, arcing wide around the searching guards. She pushed herself onward until she was far enough ahead to avoid them seeing her approach the road.

Grateful for Kin's black cloak, she pulled the hood over her face as she reached the edge of the gravel road. Pulling the glittering comb from her hair, she threw it into the middle of the path. The gems covering it sparkled in the darkening moonlight and would catch the eye of whoever walked past.

Gloomy clouds rolled in above, blanketing the stars from view with only the moon peeking through to the east.

She slipped back into the forest and ran towards the spot she left Kin only a short while before.

It occurred to her, in a bitter realization of her own naivety, he might not have risked waiting in the kennels. He could have pushed on to wherever he wanted to go. It was entirely possible the plan he told her was untrue, and he'd simply waited for an opportunity to be free of her.

Her detour inadvertently created such an ideal opportunity for him, except she still wore his cloak.

Would he be willing to leave that behind?

Amarie crouched through a break in the rundown fence around the dog runs. She started off towards a long row of abandoned kennels, farther in from the fence line.

Kin had some kind of sensitivity for the Art, though she wasn't sure to what extent. But it didn't feel like other practitioners she'd encountered. While she admitted the physical and emotional effect he had on her, she also needed to address the potential danger he posed to her.

And the danger I pose to him.

Based on his secretive attitude, she doubted he'd display his abilities in front of her. She'd need to force him to expose his power before she could allow herself to become attached. She slowed her pace to step carefully over the less-manicured terrain, giving her mind time to reel through possibilities of how to accomplish it.

A drop of rain hit her nose, and she looked up, more speckling her cheeks. Taking a deep breath, she enjoyed the scent.

Rain will help if they use the tracking hounds.

Lowering her gaze, Amarie noticed a kennel in better shape than the others surrounding it. Its roof was still firmly in place, and the outer walls remained covered. She paused in her steps and eyed it for a moment, unable to see within.

Is this the one he chose?

Kin's form appeared at the crumbling doorway, and she released a sigh of relief. He didn't speak, vanishing inside after she saw him.

Amarie entered the kennel, waiting for her eyes to adjust to the shadows.

The moonlight couldn't reach the depths of the kennel, and rain pattered on the tin roof.

She held Kin's cloak tightly around her, feeling the cold more now with her normalized pulse. She used the inside of it to dry her face. The adrenaline had worn off, but her mind was far from drowsy.

An old pile of dried-out hay occupied a corner. Perhaps once a wolf's bed, it lay empty, her dress folded in a bundle by the wall. Nearby, large rimmed barrels collected dripping rainwater from the cracks in the forgotten roof. Her eyes caught a metallic glimmer nestled in the other corner. The partially rusted chains might have been used to restrain the beasts within their kennels. With each link as large as one of her palms, the chains sat coiled like a sleeping snake waiting for an opportunity to rouse.

She found a spot against the wall near the doorway and leaned against it.

Kin moved farther into the kennel. He took a deep breath with his back towards her, his hand at his chest.

He's touching the shard.

A rock formed in her gut.

Why does he cherish it like that?

He ran a hand through his hair, longer than the last time she'd seen him, before he turned towards her. Leaning against a partially fallen beam across from her, he watched the entrance of the kennel. His form, in the depths of the night's shadows, was difficult to make out. But remnants of moonlight reflected from deep within his pale eyes like an animal's. "Not the worst place I've had to hide in."

"I'm not surprised." Her gaze returned to the entrance, fearing her eyes would betray her thoughts.

The silence that fell between them felt awkward for the first time.

Amarie wanted to explore their connection, but wasn't sure how if he couldn't find the nerve to answer a hard question honestly.

"It might seem silly." Kin's whisper broke through the silence, catching her off guard enough to elicit a flinch. "But you're right. I don't like Coltin." He took a deep breath. "After what happened at the gazebo... I was jealous and got carried away in the moment. I'm sorry."

She smiled. Between the sarcasm and the quips, she was never sure what he meant and what he didn't. In hindsight, she felt foolish for not considering he might be embarrassed. "You were jealous? You don't need to be. You'd be much too pleased to learn my methods for enduring moments similar to the one you witnessed at the gazebo."

"Methods?" He paused, but continued when she didn't explain. "You can't offer something like that and not elaborate."

Keeping her gaze steady on his, she shrugged. "I imagined he was you."

His eyes widened, mouth parted in surprise. His feet shuffled in place. "And after tonight? Would your method still be effective?"

Standing, Amarie walked to him, the smile lingering on her face. She took a breath, understanding his doubt. "I dare say it would." She touched his face, and only a moment passed before he leaned into her palm. "I'm fine. Perhaps the threat was necessary to ensure he didn't try anything further. We both did what we needed to get out of there." Of course, getting away hadn't been a concern of hers. She would have been safe there.

But he wasn't.

He smiled. "You're quite the actor." He placed his hand over hers on his cheek. "Though, helplessness doesn't suit you."

Her smile broadened. "That's because—and don't take this personally—but you were never *actually* in control of me."

Her smirk brought a chuckle to Kin's lips, but he didn't counter her suggestion.

She sighed. "Honestly, I've been acting nonstop for the past month. That scene with you was at least exciting."

"Sounds exhausting." His hand traced hers where it still touched his jaw. His fingers were light on her skin, going to her wrist. "You are far more dedicated than I could ever be. I'm rather accustomed to bursting in without a plan. It's worked well for me so far, especially when I run into you."

"You do thoroughly enjoy hijacking my plans, don't you?" She tried to resist the brightness of his eyes and think about instigating her new plan.

"It's unintentional. I hope I didn't mess things up too badly this time. Perhaps we can still get what you were there for?"

Amarie smiled at his offer. "I'm sure we can." Disappointment lingered within her thoughts, centered on what would come next.

He needs to reveal what his power is.

His hand closed around her wrist to draw her hand towards his lips. His soft kisses fell on top of her fingertips. "I promise I'll make up for the extra effort and time it takes you to reach your goal." His voice deepened as he continued kissing her knuckles.

Her heart thudded in her ears at the warmth of his mouth, blocking out the growing storm. It would have been easier if he kept silent and secretive.

Taking one last moment to show her true feelings, she moved her hand away from his lips to touch his neck. Her body shifted closer, and her lips found his. She kissed him, and he returned it, drawing it out with her eyes blissfully closed.

When she pulled away from him, it was with a reluctant step. "Unfortunately, I think this will make us even."

With her final word, a rattling snap echoed within the kennel.

She'd noticed a fortuitous chain cuff near his unoccupied right arm, and it had required only the slightest movement for her to close the ring, meant to attach to a dire wolf's collar, around his wrist.

Kin's head jerked back, though he couldn't move far.

The chain chimed against the cuff at his wrist.

He pulled at the metal with his free hand, but the lock held tight. "What are you doing?" Urgency tainted his tone, tugging at her heartstrings.

Amarie crouched, picking up a second cuff. No haste accompanied her movements, feeling no threat from him. It was strange when he didn't resist her, almost as if he accepted the entrapment.

He doesn't fear chains, because he can free himself.

She lifted the second cuff as she stood, delicately taking his free hand into hers.

He gripped her hand and squeezed.

With a bite of her bottom lip, she snapped the second cuff closed. The chains pulled Kin's wrists towards the floor with their weight.

Confusion, and a fear which didn't suit him, leapt into Kin's eyes as his arms tensed against the strain "Amarie?" He struggled, yanking on the left chain, but the bolt anchoring it to the rocky ground beneath the hay held strong.

She lingered close to him, yet he made no move of violence against her. Her hand moved to rest on his face.

Kin only watched her, slowing his struggle and lowering the chains to the ground.

Her stomach knotted. It would be no easy feat to free himself and, undoubtedly, he'd use whatever power he had access to.

With the intensity of emotion he evoked in her, Amarie feared losing control of the aura that kept her power hidden from other practitioners of the Art. It would be simpler if Kin held no ability. He would be oblivious to hers if she faltered, and she'd be safe. They'd both be safe.

"Please believe me when I tell you I'm sorry. You simply interfered in something you didn't understand." Her shoulders drooped, and she let her hand slide from his face. She touched the delicate chain that stuck out at the sides of his neck and pulled the shard pendant free from within his clothing. "I worked too hard for this. I can't let you have it." Using both hands, she removed the necklace over his head and placed it around her neck.

Kin's head tilted as his jaw tightened, and his eyes begged her to stop. His expression lost the edge of anger and now held only shock in his wide eyes. "Wait." The chains rattled as he tugged against their weight, his muscles straining. "Please."

"I could wait." Amarie rested her hands on his chest and shook her head. "But I can't give it back to you..."

Kin leaned forward, touching his forehead against hers as they had before, his eyes closing. "Why not?"

Her heart thudded hard with regret. She had no reason to keep telling him things, but a part of her wanted him to know she meant it. "You draw a reaction from me, which I swear to you, no one else ever has."

He didn't move as he listened, eyes still closed.

"If I don't do this now, I'll forever lose my nerve." Her voice came softly, and his eyes opened, looking down towards the shard.

"Like before? When you left me on the beach?"

Amarie winced. "I wish I could explain." In a typical moment of absent thinking, she bit her bottom lip as Kin's gaze slid up her face.

The moment his penetrating eyes saw her lips, they closed again, his jaw tightening.

Lying to him left her throat raw. This wasn't necessarily about the shard, it was about him. She could imagine giving him the shard of her own free will. Perhaps she would, depending on how the rest of the night unfolded.

His eyes opened again to meet hers. "Please." His voice sounded weaker than ever before, rasping against the back of his throat as his eyes shifted in a forlorn plea. "Don't go."

Amarie let out a rueful sigh and released her bottom lip in the motion. She tilted her chin, feeling the power he held over her, and her lips nearly touched his. She paused, feeling it would be an abuse of power, her hand still on the side of his neck.

Kin didn't close the distance, and her intention faded. Her touch slipped from his neck, and she stepped back, feeling exposed even though she held the power.

She removed his cloak from her shoulders, folding it carefully so the contents didn't spill from their pockets, and placed it near him. She swallowed hard as she knelt.

"Amarie." Her name no longer came as a question, but drawn out from his mouth as he looked at her while leaning against the pull of the chains. He didn't struggle. He didn't look at his cloak, or at anything but her. His eyes didn't even flick to the crystal.

She waited to see if he had something more to say. When he remained silent, she walked to the entrance of the kennel. She looked back at him.

This is for the best, even if he doesn't understand what's happening yet.

If, by chance, he couldn't free himself, she'd return for him. The ease of his escape, and whether he could find her, would help her understand the extent of his power. It was more important than the pain tugging at her heart at the betrayal in his eyes.

Her mouth opened, but she closed it. Finally, she turned from him and ran into the rain. The frigid night air and water numbed her skin as she made her way through the shadows towards Jaspa.

Chapter 11

Well, this is a fun situation. Can't say I've ever been chained up in a doghouse before.

Grievously alone, he tugged on the chains secured at his wrists, looking back to trace their origin in the shadows of the dire wolf kennel. They disappeared beneath the moldy pile of hay, and he looked towards the doorway as the rain slowed.

Maybe this is a joke, and she will come back.

An unnatural stillness filled him, his eyes lingering on the frozen shadows outside.

Any second...

Kin sighed, jerking his hand to the side to make the chains clatter.

Fuck.

He'd let his guard down with her, and that stung the most. Opening up was never a strength of Kin's, even before his life dropped into Nymaera's deepest hell. Against all better judgment, he admitted his feelings to her, albeit in a roundabout way. His jealousy of Coltin might have been unfounded, but the root behind it wasn't.

This woman made Kin forget everything else. His responsibilities, duties, and task were all forgotten. There was only her, and the feeling left him shaken.

The urge to rub at a developing headache encouraged Kin to raise his hand, only to find it still firmly restrained by the weight of the chains. The chains Amarie had snapped into place.

The most important question lingered in Kin's mind.

Why, in the sanctified names of the ancient gods, is she after the Berylian Key shard?

His body burned with frustration from the loss of the necklace, mixed with the heat Amarie aroused.

Suddenly, he was glad his cloak was at his feet and not on his shoulders.

Kin forced himself to stand still, trying to ignore the cold metal on his skin and regain control of his emotions.

It was better he wasn't immediately free from the chains. He questioned what he would do if he were.

When I catch up to her, do I kiss her... or kill her to get the shard back?

The horrible thought of her death passed through his mind. It made him sick to his stomach. There was no way he could end her life. Yet, if she stayed stubbornly attached to the Berylian Key shard, another might cause her death.

Danger followed that object. It followed him.

Kin's purpose melted into a desire to live two separate lives. One with Amarie, and the one forced on him.

Regardless of what he did when he caught up to her, first he needed to find her. He needed the shard and hoped he could convince her to abandon it. Only then could she truly be safe. From *him*.

She's just getting farther and farther away.

He'd already blown it and been seen by Coltin and his guard within the estate, defying the instruction to never be seen in Feyor. He was in too deep with no turning back.

The realization drove him to inhale a steadying breath as he reached into the darkest crevices of his soul. The gloom-riddled rivers flowed through him, their waters destroying all they touched.

Kin drew power from a lethargic snake in its den, a fern growing against the back of the kennel, the blades of grass. He dipped into the pulsing energy. It reminded him of submerging entirely in deep, fathomless water with no respite in sight. Closing his eyes, he put himself there with an icy exhale from his lips.

He found the depths strangely comforting, like a mother's arms, as his physical body dissolved into the darkness surrounding him. The energy, arranged like weaves of fabric, ebbed against what had been his skin as it devolved to shadow.

Kin never fully understood where his consciousness went while he became shadow, though he remained in control of each subtle movement.

The chains crashed to the ground, his solid form gone from their grasp. The pool of ink coalesced towards the floor, rolling like lava.

His shadow devoured the cloak on the ground, then flowed towards the doorway. Bubbling like oil on creeping vines, he pulled his way across the slick, dilapidated wood of the kennel. He escaped into the night, crossing into moonlight as no natural shadow could.

Clouds still dappled the sky, but the rain ceased.

The fern outside the doorway of the kennel shriveled, crumbling to dust. The surrounding grass fell limp and turned a sickly pale brown as he scrambled against the wood panels. He clawed his way but left no marks behind except the withered flora.

Kin shifted his oozing mass over the wall to pull himself onto the failing roof, having no weight to break it. One way existed for him to catch up with Amarie, and he didn't look forward to it. While shadow was easy enough, he felt the drain on his soul each time.

In desperation, he attempted the change he'd only accomplished once before.

Breathing wasn't the same while in shadow, but the concept was.

Kin exhaled and urged his mind to calm. The blackness stilled before it stirred once more, shaped by his will. Shadow moved, pushing together as if being squeezed between a giant's hands, vibrating before it peeled away. Flakes of onyx snow fell to the wind.

A midnight-feathered wing erupted first, struggling from the shadows as they twisted to form a raven's body, darkness seeping away from a sudden molting of feathers and skin. An eternity passed, but it was only a few breaths before he shook the body he wasn't accustomed to.

He quelled the caw of triumph, using the elation of success to push from the roof and catch the updraft of cold autumn air blowing from the sea towards the mountains. The roof crumbled, devoid of any remnants of life clinging to the ancient wood. Its coating of moss decayed to dust and drifted away.

Specks of shadow flung like water from his feathers with a beat of his wings.

Spotting Amarie running through the thick of the forest from high above happened faster than he thought. She approached the sleeping city of Jaspa, with sunrise still some time off.

The air rippled his neck feathers as he shook his head in displeasure.

The city means more people to avoid.

He glared down to keep careful watch as he flew faster.

Jaspa. The jewel of Feyor. It hid within the umbra of the mountains, the moon shining through the clouds above it. The streets all led to one place, the royal palace, which dominated the mountain's rocky crags. The terrain itself was carved to accommodate the plethora of streets, shops, and homes within the city. They clung to the rock like mountain goats, built precariously of wood and stone.

As Kin flew over, the city resembled a disease on the flesh of the mountainside. The arching, stone-grey towers of the palace were the worst offenders. The entire city looked and smelled of smoke, which made Kin's eyes burn as he grew closer.

Amarie entered through the front gate, but he lost her among the alleys. He circled until he caught a glimpse of her hurrying through the streets.

She moved with determination, familiar with the route.

Kin followed her from his height in the sky.

Smoke billowed from the chimney of the building she approached as cooks prepared food for the day, despite the early hour. Once she disappeared inside, he waited a few moments before swooping down and reading the sign out front.

Swann's Inn.

Banking tightly around a corner, he landed. Talons skittered along the ground within the shadows of a dirty alley beside the inn. Scanning the space around him, Kin tapped once more into the folds of the Art. Accessing the energy was harder in the city. Humans were beyond his reach, their wills denying access to their life source. But he found strength within the rats and an unfortunate stray cat, returning to his true form.

The change back came easier, his body shifting first to shadow, then to stand as if he'd merely knelt on the ground. His cloak enveloped his body, the shadow melting into it and dripping from its hem to the stone road.

He pulled on a lock of his hair until he felt a twinge of pain.

Can't waste time.

Tugging his cloak around his shoulders and lifting its hood over his head, he walked down the alleyway towards the inn.

A clerk at the front desk of the inn seemed unlikely so early before dawn. And, even if there was, no innkeeper in their right mind would direct an unknown man dressed in black to the room of a lone woman.

Kin entered the stable attached to the inn, confident he could recognize her horse if he was there.

Sure enough, Kin found the familiar black Friesian quickly and rested his hand on the gate of his stall.

Viento snorted and shook his mane with a stomp.

Glancing to the side of the stall, a sign hung from the hook holding Viento's bridle. It bore a scrawled number six.

A slight smile came to his lips, but a brief thought caused him to pause.

Did she mean for it to be this easy?

Mentally preparing for a trap, he made his way back to the inn's main entrance. After a glance through the window to confirm the front desk was unoccupied, he opened the door. His hand shot to silence the small bells adorning the top.

Closing it behind him with the same care, he crossed the room and climbed the first set of stairs. His hood still shielded his face when he came to the door marked six.

Kin hesitated. His hand hovered over the doorknob as he debated his options. He should knock, but the need for politeness dimmed within him the moment she left him chained in the kennel. His heart still wanted to believe the words she'd said were earnest, refusing to succumb to the fear she was acting all along.

The possibilities of what lay on the other side of the door whirled in his mind, torturing him with images of her and Coltin enjoying their victory over the thief who nearly got away with the Berylian Key shard.

Fueled by the rage the image caused him, his hand closed on the cold brass knob and he shoved the unlocked door open. He strode in but halted at what he saw.

Amarie's eyes flickered from the book in her hands to the door. Brief surprise widened her eyes as she closed the book, setting it aside on a table and standing.

What the... Was she just sitting here, waiting for me?

His gaze went to her neck, seeking the trinket he tried to convince himself was the only reason he'd come after her.

The shard necklace was nowhere in sight.

Relief flooded the back of his mind when his glance around the room also confirmed she was alone.

He grasped the edge of the door to close it behind him. Out of habit, with a twist of fingers, he secured the lock she'd so blatantly left undone.

The light from several candles reflected off the water in a cleaning basin, with a stack of linen cloths next to it. Her bags were on the floor near one of the two chairs, along with her short sword, leaving her mostly unarmed.

She always has that dagger on her thigh.

"That was fast." Her voice held something akin to admiration.

He stood his ground, trying to process what was happening.

I hate games.

"Oh, I apologize. Should I have remained chained like a dog longer?" He couldn't help the harsh tone.

Regret followed almost immediately when her gaze dropped to the floor. Her jaw worked, but he kept his mouth shut rather than take back the words he still felt she deserved.

Her gaze returned to him a breath later, her expression difficult to read. No fear showed in her eyes as she looked at him. "How did you free yourself?" Something in her voice suggested that she already knew the answer.

He hesitated, striving to find a plausible lie to appease her, but couldn't come up with anything.

"So, you do have the Art."

It wasn't a question.

She considered the information as he opened his mouth to deny it. Again, she spoke before he could form words. "I am sorry, but I needed to know if you were merely sensitive or could use your gift."

Up to this moment, he'd given no indication he had the ability. He wondered what made her suspicious in the first place.

She has the Art and she can feel it from me.

He'd never felt such a thing from her, and the laws of the Art dictated he should have. He wasn't sure if denying it would help, since he still had no way to explain how he escaped the steel chains she left him in.

Amarie turned, a sheepish smile touching her lips. When she did, he noticed the sheen on her throat. Her cut must have reopened during her run to Jaspa.

"You can come in, if you like." She motioned to the chair angled towards the one she previously occupied. The candlelight shimmering off her skin steadily weakened his resolve.

Sighing, his anger faded, even as he tried to maintain it. She looked too perfect amid the candlelight, drawing him towards her. He decided it would be better not to confirm or deny her suggestions of his access to the fabric of Pantracia, and instead, focus on the injury he'd accidentally caused.

Kin turned from her, going to the basin of water and linens. "Sit." His voice was soft but urging as he gestured to her chair.

Providing no protest, for once, Amarie sat.

He loosened his sleeves and rolled them up. He stopped the roll at the middle of his forearm, unwilling to fully display the tattoo on his skin, even to himself.

The black ink drew Amarie's attention before he turned it from her vision and lifted the basin in his other hand. Taking up the linens, he knelt on the floor before her.

Kin dropped one strip into the water and settled the rest on Amarie's lap.

She reached for him, tentatively pushing his hood back to reveal his face.

The simple action made his heart pound, and he ground his jaw. Moving slowly but deliberately, he wrung out the water-soaked cloth and lifted it to her neck. His right hand stabilized himself on the outside of her knee.

Amarie's hand rested on the back of his. Her gaze remained on him, with only a momentary flick to their touching skin.

Or my tattoo.

His throat tightened at the sensation of her touch, and the rapidly growing anxiousness she always seemed to elicit. He forced his nerves to calm so he could focus on caring for her wound.

A few breaths passed as he cleaned the drying blood from her skin. He reminded himself she was his priority at the moment. Once she was patched up, he would think about the shard again. Spending time growing more attached was foolish, but he couldn't resist.

"This room of yours..." Kin sought to fill the silence. "Have you actually used it before? I assumed you slept at the estate."

Coltin asked her to stay the night... But that doesn't mean she hadn't agreed previously.

Amarie shot him an incredulous look, which transformed into a smile. She laughed and shook her head. "You *are* jealous." Relief laced her voice. "Kin, I used this room, *alone*, every single night."

He couldn't deny the wave of joy.

"So, am I in trouble?" She tilted her head to catch his gaze.

His hand paused between the basin and her neck. "Horrible trouble. I'm not entirely sure how you'll make it up to me." Satisfied her wound was finally clean, he dropped the cloth into the basin and pushed it towards the wall. He lifted a new clean cloth to her neck and dabbed her skin dry. "Why do I have a feeling this is becoming a habit? Cleaning your wounds."

Kin looked away from her as he put the final cloth beside the basin on the floor, satisfied he'd done what he could. He didn't move from where he knelt, but pulled his hand from hers to rest them on his knees.

"Why are you being so kind to someone who left you chained in a doghouse?"

Kin chuckled. "That's a good question. I suppose it has something to do with all the things you said before you left, even though you didn't have to."

"I meant them." Her voice dropped to a whisper.

He'd asked himself a million times while he was flying after her, why he still wanted to be near her. It was strange when he thought about what it meant. Despite everything else in his life and everything involving that damn crystal shard, she held him in her control. He'd told her the first night they met she was the one who held power over him. He hadn't realized how true it would become.

"I know." The smile on his face faded, but a curl remained at the edge of his lips. "And I know how hard it is to admit that to someone. Every time I try to tell you the same thing, I can't find the words."

Her expression softened. "Maybe you should keep trying."

Kin returned his right hand to her knee, while the other touched the soft skin of her jaw.

Amarie made him feel like a lovesick schoolboy who'd never been with a woman before. He didn't know how to say the words without sounding like an utter fool. Perhaps it was his pride that kept him from admitting the truth.

His lips turned as the thought slipped through his mind, and he brushed his fingertips across her face. Keeping his breathing steady, he silently thanked her for her patience during the lengthy silence.

"Amarie." Her name tasted sweet, like the smell of her hair against the wind. "I'm not exactly in touch with my emotions most of the time. I've learned to ignore them out of necessity. But there's something about you." His hand cupped her cheek, and her head tilted into it, riveting encouragement through him. "You make everything I've tried to seal away come crashing through the walls I've built. You're the only person who's ever done this to me. You're the only woman to make me question everything about myself. You make me want to change."

Amarie said nothing, but her light smile lingered. Biting her lip, her gaze flickered to his mouth before back to his eyes. Her hand at her side moved, but only minimally before it paused.

He dared to take the initiative she struggled with. Sliding his hand up her knee, he found her fingers. The touch sparked fire through his veins, even with just their fingers entwining. He'd held her hand before, but somehow this was different now.

"I can't help but follow this tugging in my chest." Kin squeezed her hand. "I know it's pulling me to you, and only you."

Amarie leaned forward in the chair, her head at the same height as his, and placed her free hand on his chest as she touched her forehead to his.

He lifted his chin, barely regaining control before their lips could meet. His head whirled with questions and fears.

"You don't have to resist it." Her voice, barely a whisper, quieted the noise in his head.

Kin wasn't entirely sure how he heard her over the thundering of his heart. His body and mind screamed as one.

I need her. Kiss her.

He closed the space between their mouths, eager to taste her once more. His hand slid back, stroking the base of her neck and tangling in her soft hair.

Her arms draped around him as he sank into her.

The kisses came naturally between them, fevered and hungry.

Kin shifted closer, wrapping his arms around her waist and encouraging her to leave the chair.

Amarie slid down and settled on his lap. Her knees came to either side of him in a position he remembered well from the beach.

His hand found the small of her back and traced the edge of her breeches while his other maintained its gentle grip within her hair. He tilted his head to gain greater access to her mouth, and the beautiful tangle of passion rose between them.

Lips parted from each other only briefly for a heated breath before reuniting.

Kin wanted more, to know just how fiercely they were drawn to each other.

He trailed kisses along her jaw, her skin sweet. His mouth played there, pressing over her skin and working to evoke more of the soft gasps echoing near his ear. His hand at her back dared to explore, slipping along her side to caress up towards the bottom of her ribs before making its way down across her waist and hip.

Kin's hand passed over a sharp bulge within her side pocket, his fingertips vibrating at the remnant of power beneath them. His mind leapt to overpower his body and an internal struggle ensued. He urged his hand to continue its path downward.

Praying his lips distracted Amarie from noticing the pause, he moved his mouth up her neck to find her lips, making him nearly forget the Berylian Key shard in her pocket.

Chapter 12

Kin's lips felt hot on her neck, and Amarie closed her eyes as her back arched on the bed.

Her mind warred against her heart.

She played with the bottom of his shirt, his bent elbow supporting him above her. Venturing beneath the material, she touched his skin as her blood raced. The heat of his mouth, as it played along her neck, urged her to seek more access to his body. Reluctantly abandoning the bare skin at his waist to glide up the front of his tunic, she unfastened the black buttons.

He smiled against her neck, his teeth grazing her skin.

When the tunic fell open, she pushed at it near his shoulders to rid him of it completely.

Kin leaned back on his knees, one pressed against the outside of her right hip, the other nestled between her thighs.

Amarie's neck cooled in his absence, but his new position gave her the opportunity to enjoy the sight of him. She flashed him a coy smile before biting her lower lip.

Pretty sure that affects him.

He paused, watching her with a glimmer of desire. His abdominal muscles flexed with each breath, the definition growing more prominent towards his chest. Olive skin boasted a slight tan, partially obscured by a trail of dark hair dusting his chest and vanishing beneath his breeches.

Amarie's heart pounded in her ears as she watched him.

His hands trailed down her sides as he straightened his back, following the curve of her body towards her hips. He rolled his shoulders, displacing the thick tunic from his broad frame. It slid from him, dropping off the bed with a soft thud.

The intricate tattoo on his right forearm stole her attention again. The geometric shapes formed a pattern she could discern no meaning from, but Kin's earlier shyness about it was gone.

He leaned forward, lowering himself to her as his hand pressed to the bed at her hip.

The sound of delicate metal cascaded through the pounding of her heart.

Kin paused and straightened, sitting up again. His right hand rose with the chain bearing the shard tangled between his fingers.

Amarie's stomach flopped.

The deep red shard swung like a lazy pendulum beneath his palm, reflecting in his eyes.

She searched his face, waiting to see what he would do, and released her lip. Time temporarily suspended with her held breath.

Did he purposely distract me so he could find it?

She gulped but didn't reach for it. Amid everything, she would rather he take it and leave than live in uncertainty. She never expected a person to become more important to her than a Berylian Key shard. The emotions Kin evoked in her brought a refreshing component to her turbulent life. She couldn't help the desire to see where it led once she learned the truth of his priorities.

If it came at the cost of a shard, she would pay that price.

Kin hesitated, his eyes locked on the object for a time before they shifted back to Amarie. He absently twisted the chain around his fingertips. His chest heaved like hers, seeking the breath their passion stole.

He shifted, though not in the way Amarie expected. Leaning forward, he reached past the side of her head. The stone thunked onto the wooden surface of the side table, followed by the slow cadence of the chain dropping around it.

Kin's empty hand moved to her jaw. He traced a line towards her lips with his fingertips, lowering his own once more to hers, giving his answer.

Amarie breathed a sigh of relief, which turned into a whimper against his lips.

His mouth pressed hard as their kisses deepened. His tongue responded with each touch of her hands. The tips of his fingers caressed over the thin material of her shirt, touching her ribs before playing at the bottom hem. They slipped beneath to touch her bare waist.

He pressed his palm against her side before sliding it up, leaving a trail of fire in its wake.

Amarie's knee rose, pressing against the outside of his hip, and she pushed his chest. She tucked his arm in with hers and, with no resistance from Kin, rolled them so she laid on him.

Moving her lips from his, she caught her breath, smiling. She sat back, straddling him. The firmness of his desire caused a deep stir within her as she gazed at him. With much more ease than his shirt had been, she pulled off her sleeveless tunic, aware as his eyes shifted down to watch the slow exposure of her skin.

Tossing her shirt to the opposite side of the bed as his, she watched his gaze travel over her. It paused at her toned midsection, where a straight scar marred the right side of her abdomen. She wore a simple, fitted, cropped chemise over her breasts made of soft, dark linen. Thin straps secured her chemise over her shoulders, and three small buttons at the front kept it in place.

Kin's thumb caressed the long white scar before his hands wrapped around her. Reaching, he guided her lips back to his.

The feeling of his skin only encouraged the weight of her body on his. Her eyes slid closed again as her mouth lingered on his before moving to his jaw and leaving a trail of damp kisses against his stubbled jaw. While one arm supported her, her other hand tangled with his hair. Her lips ventured down his neck, enjoying his taste.

His head tilted to give her access, followed by a soft inhale. A quiet moan echoed in her ear as his hips rocked against hers.

Her breath quivered, and her mouth paused against his neck with a gasp. Trailing her hands down his sides, she hovered above him, her mouth tracing his collarbone. Before her mind could step in and stop her, she flicked her fingers at the top of his breeches and released the first button.

Amarie's heart skipped a beat as she struggled to keep control over her hiding aura, now begging to engulf him.

I can't let him know.

His hands explored over her backside and pulled her against him.

Amarie closed her eyes, her pulse racing and her mind spinning even faster. She returned her mouth to his with a sharp inhale as her inner struggle ensued. His hands moved to the fastener of her own breeches, and her breath caught again.

She parted her mouth from his to breathe. Her entire body stilled, and Kin's hands paused on her hips.

His scent, the feel of his skin against her, everything screamed at her to blindly trust him and let her aura falter.

But he seeks the shards.

Biting her bottom lip, she lifted herself higher to look at his face. Her hand supported her on the bed, and the other rested on his chest.

Kin's eyes swam with a stormy grey, holding a softness she wanted to put faith in. "Too fast?" His voice had dropped even lower. He lifted his hand towards her cheek, caressing her jawline.

"Kin, I... I want to be with you, but I'm..."

His fingers brushed down her chin. "I want that too, but if you want to wait..."

"I don't *want* to wait." Amarie laughed and kissed him. "But I can't rush this... There's too much..." She shook her head, biting her tongue.

His chest heaved with a deep breath, and he nodded. "Then we'll wait. I don't want you to have any doubts." He slid his hand down her arm and took her hand. Lifting her knuckles to his lips, he kissed them. "Do you want to talk about it?"

Amarie lowered herself, nuzzling her face into the side of his neck. "Talking is boring." His skin muffled her words, and she kissed him. Her body shook with the low rumble of a laugh in his chest.

"Well, we can agree on that." He brushed his fingers through her hair. "Kiss me, then." He guided her chin up, lifting his head briefly to pull her into another fiery kiss. His lips moved slowly against hers, deeply, encouraging her to sink back into him.

When her tongue met his, and she didn't feel her hiding aura weaken, she smiled and tilted her hips.

He moaned, his grip around her tightening and kisses growing harder.

Maybe it won't fail if we...

Amarie paused, taking a deep breath and searching for her aura.

It's not there.

Yet, Kin didn't react to sensing her Art.

She lifted her lips from his and touched both sides of his face, seeking the vibration of the Art she always felt within him.

Why can't I sense it?

His brow furrowed. "What's wrong?"

Delving into herself, she found her power but it lay dormant. She tested it by trickling a tiny amount of energy into Kin, but it wouldn't flow.

He didn't react, only studying her with his pale eyes.

She sat up, a chill rushing through her veins. "Can you feel your Art?"

Kin tensed, pushing his elbows beneath him. He glanced at his forearm, the muscles beneath his tattoo flexing. "No. It's gone."

A rush of fear filled her. "Something's wrong. We should—" Her focus shifted, and she turned her head to listen to the squeak of wood outside her room. Her heart sank. "We have company." Slipping off the bed, she reached for her sleeveless tunic and yanked it over her head.

"Do the Delphis have the resources to have found us so quickly?" Kin moved the opposite way, his boots thumping to the ground near the bedside table where the shard lay.

Amarie shook her head. "No, but they know where I'm staying."

With a heave of breath, he grabbed his tunic, pulling it over his shoulders. As his fingers fastened the buttons, the sounds of booted feet and metal armor grew closer.

They made their way up the stairs towards her room, whoever they were.

Her eyes darted to the necklace, too far from her reach. "Kin, take it. If they found out I'm not who I said..."

He nodded and grasped the shard, thrusting it into the pocket of his breeches.

She followed his gaze to the other side of the room where his sword rested against the desk.

He'll never get to it in time.

Amarie rushed to the window and pushed it open, heaving her pack over her shoulder.

Kin crossed the room to grab his cloak off where it draped over a chair.

"Come on." She motioned to the window.

He only made it halfway to her before the door splintered from its frame.

As the first intruder came through the door, candlelight glinted off the emblem at his shoulder.

The Feyorian royal crest?

His armor looked battle-worn, unpolished like the city guards who offered decoration rather than actual security.

Feyorian military? Why would they come for me?

The soldier wielded a stocky club. In the flowing action of crossing the threshold of the room, he swung it towards Kin's legs.

Kin jumped back, clear of the swing, and another soldier circled towards the bed.

Neither of the soldiers paid attention to her, both fixated on Kin.

They still think I'm the innocent hostage. They're here for him, but Coltin's family doesn't have soldiers on their payroll.

She made a rapid choice. Play the victim and walk out unscathed or take part in Kin's defense. Running to her sword, she pulled the blade from its sheath.

Another soldier joined the fray, pushing past his companion, who backed Kin farther from Amarie towards the corner with the chairs.

Kin snatched his sword while backing past it, but she doubted he'd have enough space to draw it. Before he could make an attempt, the soldier who initially attacked roared and swung his club up, catching Kin's hand.

A pained yell escaped Kin's lips, and he used the sheathed steel to push against a soldier who grasped for it. A kick propelled the attacker back on his heels, but the man took Kin's blade with him.

Grabbing the back of a chair, Kin spun it around his body, pulling his cloak free as the piece of furniture crashed into the club-wielder hard enough to throw him off his feet.

Amarie charged from the other side of the room, sword raised and aimed for the club-wielder's neck.

Another soldier clambered through the door in time to protect his compatriot. His armored forearm blocked Amarie's blow, shoving her back, and he withdrew a short blade to meet her renewed attack.

Clashing steel and grinding furniture blocked out any other sounds except her breathing. Her muscles strained with the effort of defending herself, unable to make enough ground to aid Kin while he faced three soldiers alone.

Hopelessness reared in the back of her mind, granting her fear at the futility of their efforts.

Her yell mixed with others, breath expelled as she pushed off another strike.

Kin cried out, pinned against the wall by the heavy desk, held in place by a soldier.

He needs me.

With a roar of frustration, Amarie swung her sword against the man in front of her. He met her blade, but the force was enough to distract him while she lifted a booted foot and kicked him in the gut.

She met Kin's gaze across the room, but he didn't pause as he grabbed a fistful of a soldier's hair and slammed his attacker's head into the desk. When he looked up again, his eyes mirrored her emotions.

Gritting her teeth, she refocused, spinning her sword in a diagonal slash, which the soldier could only partially deflect. He fell back as her sword sliced through an opening in his armor.

Amarie yanked her dagger from her thigh and plunged it into the exposed collar of the staggering soldier.

He gurgled and choked as she withdrew it.

Before she could step towards a new target, brawny arms encircled her from a fifth soldier.

"Murderous bitch." He gripped her upper body in a vice, then hurled her across the room.

Breath forcefully escaped her lungs as she crashed into a bedside table, splintering it.

The sound of wood grinding against the floor came again as Kin kicked the desk into a soldier. He reached across the table, wrapping his cloak around the man's head. With a sharp jerk, he crushed the soldier's head against the desk. The man fell away, dazed, and took the cloak with him.

The soldier wielding the club inched between Kin and the wall, wrapped the club around his neck, and yanked back.

Kin's feet lifted off the ground. He arched his back, and his boots caught the edge of the table, pushing it away. He grappled at the club to lessen the pressure on his throat. His boots found leverage against the table as it caught on an imperfection in the floor, and Kin rammed his body back into the man who held him.

With a grunt, the club-wielder lost his grip, and Kin pushed off to stand on the desk, his chest heaving.

The soldier who threw Amarie came at her with his sword, pinning her against the wall where she sat. She growled and locked her sword with the guard of his, her muscles shaking.

A sickening crack reverberated through the room, and Amarie's wide eyes darted to Kin.

Kin released his victim's head, and the body crumbled to the floor.

A raging bellow exploded from the club-wielding soldier as he struck with surprising speed at the back of Kin's leg.

Amarie huffed, the soldier's blade inching closer to her torso as her arms weakened. She realized gradually, and with painful certainty, what would happen. She saw no escape this time.

The tip of his sword sank into the flesh of her left shoulder.

She cried out at the searing pain as the sword delved deeper with each breath of her failing strength.

In an attempt at self-preservation, she kicked with all her might, hitting him solidly between the legs.

He crumpled to the ground, withdrawing the blade from her shoulder.

Warm blood soaked her collar, threatening to drain the rest of her strength.

The convulsing soldier vomited to the side, granting Amarie an opportunity to rise to her feet, bracing herself against the wall.

A loud grunt came from Kin's direction as the soldiers flung his body atop the desk. They pulled his feet out from under him and wrenched his arms against his back, the club held behind his neck. Steel shackles clacked around his wrists.

Kin looked at Amarie, his eyes glazed. His lips formed a pleading word to her.

Run.

It broke her heart, knowing she could do nothing more.

She never ran from a fight. From many things, yes, but not a fight. Her breath heaved, and she seized Kin's cloak from the floor, her other hand snagging her pack. Pain shot through her shoulder in protest.

As she ran to the window, she dared a glance back at Kin.

He only mouthed the silent plea again. *Run.*

He hardly fought, exhaustion overtaking him. The club crammed his face against the solid oak desk.

She cursed before ducking and diving out the window. She rolled with her head tucked into her chest as she landed on the ground. The impact knocked the air from her lungs, and she rose to her feet with an agonizing breath. With Kin's cloak secured around her shoulders, she ran down the alley towards the stable.

The sun peeked over the horizon, rousing the city from slumber. The sky danced with the golds and oranges of sunrise.

It took only moments to tack her horse, attach her pack, and escape to a nearby alley. She tried to spark energy from her fingers to her horse, but her power wouldn't respond.

How did they do this?

She closed her eyes, swallowing the discomfort it stirred in her stomach.

Will it stay dormant forever now?

Opening her eyes, a part of her hoped it would. Her life would be immeasurably less complicated. She'd never imagined being free of the curse of her Art, but a knot in her gut told her this was temporary. One place existed in Pantracia capable of nullifying the Art, and she guessed Feyor had succeeded in weaponizing the phenomenon dominating their northern region.

Out of fear, practitioners avoided Lungaz. The soldiers must have been sent from there, with some kind of mobile conductor of the area's effect on the fabric of the Art.

Amarie watched from the darkness, pushing a bandage to her shoulder to stop the bleeding.

Locals hovered around the inn until soldiers streamed out the front and shooed them away. More soldiers went in, some came out. All their armor displayed the royal crest of Feyor.

Why would the crown arrest Kin?

A pair of dire wolves, as large as horses, paced and sniffed at the ground outside the front door. Their thickly muscled forms of mouse-grey fur shimmered in the morning light.

Aren't war beasts a little extreme?

Kin emerged, roughly escorted with a dark linen bag over his head. He moved on his own feet, even with his hands manacled behind his back and his steps uncertain.

The wolves sniffed the air as he passed them before being tossed inside waiting transport. The shrouded carriage, not typical for prisoners, hid whoever was inside.

A high-pitched whistle caused the beasts' ears to swivel forward. They followed behind the carriage as it lurched towards the entrance of the city.

Amarie waited after they left, allowing the crudely applied bandage time to stop the bleeding from her left shoulder. The carriage would be easy to track, especially with such an escort.

Her connection to the fabric of the Art gradually strengthened, reinstating her need for her hiding aura. Breathing a sigh of resignation, she used her good hand to pull Kin's hood over her head and nudged Viento out into the streets.

Making her way to the spot she'd landed after rolling out the window, she waited and listened for any sounds inside the second-story room.

Viento stood perfectly still as she climbed up to stand on his back, reaching to the open window with her uninjured arm. With the help of her Art's energy, she pulled herself into the room.

The scene inside looked much like it had when she left, though the bodies had been removed. A giant red smear marked where she'd downed the first soldier.

Amarie scanned for the necklace or anything else left behind. Collecting the sheath for her sword, she strapped it to her waist. She found Kin's sword under the bed, still within its scabbard. Seeing nothing else, she moved back to the window and dropped onto her waiting horse.

Securing Kin's blade to the saddlebags, she sheathed her own at her side. Careful to avoid city guards, she made a quick stop for supplies and to send a letter.

Coltin,

I've escaped my captor. I'm safe. You were so brave in

*my defense, but I fear I am not brave enough to
return to the estate. I hope you find all you are
searching for. Please don't look for me. You deserve
better.*

Ahria

While tracking the carriage, Amarie kept her distance. The disruption to her hiding aura whenever she got too close made her scramble to reaffirm it every time she reconnected to the fabric of Pantracia.

After going through the process a third time, she took a brief break and changed into warmer clothes from her pack.

It would have been faster if she didn't have to work around her injured shoulder, careful not to cause further bleeding. She didn't bother removing the stained sleeveless tunic, covering it with a long-sleeved shirt before securing her vest again. More than once, she lifted her arm too high and gasped.

Shivering, she retrieved a small black pelt from her pack and secured it over the shoulders of her cloak. Pulling gloves on, she wracked her brain for knowledge of the area she rode through.

In the hills ahead stood a military outpost, and she dared the disconnected void to get close enough to see what was happening. Lacking her ability to use the power still flowing in her veins made her nauseous, but she pushed the feeling away.

I hardly know how to use it, anyway.

Amarie dismounted as the trees thinned and continued on foot, crouching within the brush to spy on the outpost. The shrouded carriage waited outside with its door ajar, empty.

The hexagonal outpost had no roof in the middle, the center courtyards used for training with open access to the elements of the sky.

She kept her breathing controlled, despite the ache of the wound she couldn't heal. Her connection to the fabrics didn't work for mending, even without the void.

Of all the different conceptions of the Art, human belief forced them into categories of good and evil. She preferred to think about life-giving versus destructive, though energy could never truly be destroyed. Either method could be equally capable of an array of moral implications.

The auer, secluded on their island, condemned the 'corrupted,' destructive practices of humans. It was the easier of the two. In the Art, destruction involved spending the energy and pushing it away rather than repurposing it.

Amarie had never pursued learning to control the forces inside her.

Facing an attack on a military outpost, she hoped her sword would be enough. It would be less complicated if she could get to Kin before they took him to Feyor's largest prison in Lungaz.

Assuming that's where they're going.

A deafening bellow shattered the air, interrupting Amarie's thoughts. Like a human shriek and a lion's roar wrapped into one. The hairs on the back of her neck stood up as she searched for the source of the monstrous sound. As she comprehended what it could be, it blasted again.

A dull-orange blur lifted from the opening in front of the morning sun, light reflecting off its scales. A large wyvern with passengers on its back.

"Shit." Amarie gaped, a knot forming in her stomach as she backed up. "They have a damn draconi?" She'd seen depictions of the winged beasts used by Feyor, but had never seen one, despite her jokes with Kin on the beach.

How can I keep up with that?

The giant reptilian body was lean everywhere but its massive shoulders, which sloped into an impressive wingspan. The bat-like wings beat thunderously against the air swirling beneath the creature, redirecting the flags and banners surrounding the outpost.

As its wings spread, they could have easily spanned the entire training ground from tip to tip. She couldn't see how many were on its back, the figures difficult to distinguish as she squinted against the sun, but suspected the beast could carry at least four.

And I bet Kin is one of them.

Heading north, its long-horned tail lashed as a guide within the winds as it rose. With a gasp, Amarie scrambled to get back to Viento.

As the beast rose higher in the sky, she prepared her hiding aura for the dissipation of the block. As soon as the wyvern parted the clouds, her connection snapped back into place along with her aura.

At least there's something I'm good at.

She whispered Aueric words of speed to Viento, and they took off north.

With a breath of concentration, she tapped into the expanse of power she rarely needed. It was a part of her she denied, ever since she was young. The very source of her trouble with trust.

While she wasn't practiced in manifesting the Art, she could harness it in a different way. She pulled it to the surface of her blood and continued the flow into Viento. It flooded him with strength, allowing him the speed and stamina she demanded of him.

His hooves barely touched the ground as his empowered muscles maintained the pace Amarie urged him to.

Her surroundings blurred, the momentum of their travel pushing her hood back from her face. Whipping free, her dark-auburn hair lashed out behind her.

Forcing herself to take short sleep breaks along the way was hard but necessary. As much as the unnaturally fast travel didn't affect Viento, they both still needed to sleep and eat, and she tried to time her breaks to match those riding the draconi.

She became less aware of the days passing. Sometimes, when she rode, it was daylight. Other times, it was by the light of the moon, following the drumbeat of the wyvern's wings.

They pressed north, confirming her suspicions of heading to Lungaz, which only meant one thing.

A time would come in which she could no longer aid Viento with the well of Art within her.

The approach to Lungaz was easy to miss at first, but it became impossible to ignore. A stillness descended on the pine forest around her. A definitive lack of life. The wildlife had abandoned the area, instinct encouraging them to never return. The natural buzz of the forest died away. Not even a fly for Viento to flick his tail at.

As Amarie raced further into the desolation, the grass soon disappeared.

The natural green clinging to the ground, even in the autumn, withered and died.

She rode over the stark boundary. Simultaneously, her energy grew more difficult to access and subsequently share, though it still lingered.

Further in, the heartier pines became misshapen and barren of their needles. No foliage dappled the ground, having disintegrated in the rip of wind tearing through from the sea somewhere beyond. Wraiths of trees grasped at the sky, their trunks cracked and withered, before they, too, disappeared.

They ended as blatantly as the grass, a distinct line where they ceased to exist. And at the tree line came a tighter restriction on her access to her Art.

The curved border of Lungaz, under control of the Feyorian government, formed a perfect circular curve. The line ran all the way to both sides of the peninsula, which was the tip of the country. From where she stood, it was only possible to discern a slight curve, the dead land too wide to see where the barren expanse ended. The center of the circle was somewhere to the north, lost in the grey horizon.

The ground beyond the trees faded to the color of sun-bleached bone. The land still had natural hills and valleys which might have once been covered in forest and life. What was once dirt now formed rigid rock, as if the terrain had melted and quickly refrozen to produce the permanent shape.

The jagged rocks whistled in the breeze. Deep grooves ran over the distant hills, worn over time by those crazy enough to venture into its ashen lands. The stones, blanketed with utter stillness, echoed with ghostly cries of the wind still lamenting the cataclysmic loss of what was once there.

The terrain reverberated with the distant screech of the wyvern, confirming its flight into the sickening void.

Life could enter Lungaz, the corrosive power of whatever destroyed the land having dissipated after hundreds of years, but only humans were stupid enough to do so.

Viento decelerated at her urging, falling into a steady gallop. As his hooves crossed the border of death, he balked. He snorted with distaste, and Amarie tried to soothe him as he stomped at the ground. Guiding him north, Viento protested again and wheeled to face the direction they'd come.

"Come on, boy." Amarie gritted her teeth, circling him around another time. "I don't like how it feels either, but we need to get to Kin."

Viento huffed, tugging his head around in blatant disagreement.

She patted his neck, letting him come to a stop. "Please don't make me walk."

As her horse finally obliged her request, Amarie thought of the great beasts Feyor used in their war-seeking habits.

If the void of Lungaz was truly mobile, even Helgath's grand battle artisans wouldn't stand a chance. But if animals distrusted whatever aura the unnatural land created, it would affect Feyor's favored war beasts. An animal less trained than Viento might have reacted violently to avoid crossing the Lungaz border.

The wyvern must have gone through extensive training, along with the dire wolves in front of the inn. Amarie wondered how many trainers were dismembered in the early attempts at desensitizing the animals.

That's a lot of effort to capture a thief. Who is he to them?

Her entire body ached with exhaustion, the wound at her shoulder burning in protest of each movement. But every moment counted and could mean the difference between finding Kin alive or dead.

The unnatural silence, broken only by the sound of Viento's hooves, gave her nothing to do but withdraw into thoughts she'd tried to avoid.

She undoubtedly played a role in his capture, even if she wasn't sure what it was. Guilt plagued her, imagining what they were doing to him because of her.

She'd been so close to letting him in.

I can't. If he learns who I am, he'll never look at me the same again. And that's the best-case scenario.

When the first outpost for the prison came into view, she looked down at her black horse, sticking out like a beacon against the ash ground. She kept behind a swell of hills to avoid the view of any sentries and left Viento shrouded by a jagged rise of stone.

Keeping low, she crawled forward to spy over a ridge of pale stone. She could hear the occasional cries from the wyvern grow louder the closer she crept. The screeches overlapped, and she paused.

Two wyverns?

Eager to remain out of sight, Amarie paused at a steep outcropping a hundred feet from the outpost.

At least Kin hadn't been taken to the prison proper, which would have proven far more difficult to infiltrate and much farther north into Lungaz. The outpost could be a temporary stop, which compelled her to act quickly.

A single sentry stood near a deep-set doorway. Otherwise, the outpost appeared surprisingly unmanned, the watchtowers at either end of the outpost empty.

The structure, built within the rolling terrain, had its main floor deep in the ground so only the tops of the exterior walls were visible. They were made of large stones, as were the pathways running between the sparsely placed outbuildings.

Amarie took a calming breath as she watched the armored head of the sentry turn towards another wyvern howl. She threw herself across the terrain and slid on her side to drop onto the lower pathway of the outpost. Skulking behind the sentry into the outpost, she touched the dagger strapped to her thigh.

Chapter 13

Garbled noise filled the air when Kin regained awareness of his surroundings. His head drooped, floating in a disoriented haze.

He remembered the inn and the events there, at least mostly. Flashes in his vision and echoes in his ears. In all the chaos, pieces were missing.

He'd heard Amarie cry out in pain, the glint of a blade sinking into her torso.

His entire being fell into numbness at the thought of her death before his mind recalled another moment—Amarie disappearing through the window. But the room he'd invited himself into was on the second floor. The fall wouldn't have been easy.

At least she ran.

Something he could be grateful for, and it left him with hope.

The bag over his head, which strained his breathing, had been removed at some point. His wrists stung from the biting clasp of metal cuffs and his unsuccessful attempts to break free of them.

No matter how he prodded, Kin couldn't reach a single strand of the Art. It felt buried under impenetrable stone. Only one place caused such an absence of the fabric.

The steady beat of a war drum had lulled him back and forth from unconsciousness during the journey, aided by a foul concoction they occasionally forced down his throat.

His eyelids weighed and refused to open, neck twinging as his head rolled to the side. A moan, unbidden, reverberated through his cracked lips.

Kin urged his eyes to open and saw the blurry outline of his boot thrust out in front of him. His rear was sore from whatever hard surface he sat on. It was a brutal confirmation he was in his human form, regardless of how his head swam.

Throat raw, he choked in an effort to swallow. He pressed his tongue against the top of his mouth and bit down on its sides to rouse himself further from whatever dream state he lingered in.

Kin's stomach ached, and his lungs wheezed for more air. He wanted to wrap his arms around himself and shiver. Attempting the unattainable desire, he realized they bound his wrists above him and no longer behind his back. A surface of unforgiving stone kept his spine painfully straight.

The sound of metal against stone sounded like thunder within the mix of voices, and he winced.

His knees howled when he tried to bend and pull them towards his chest. He ground his teeth and tucked his feet beneath him.

Leaning heavily on the wall to maintain his balance, the corners of his vision flashed. He refused to lose consciousness again, huffing with each movement. He focused on the sound of air passing through his nose.

Stand.

The pressure of the chains slackened at his wrist after utilizing them to pull himself upward, bringing relief to torn skin.

Someone walked towards him.

"The resemblance is rather uncanny, really." A baritone voice bounced off the stone walls. "Though I'm amazed I didn't know about him until today. I'm glad you came directly to me." His voice grated with irritation, becoming deeper and reminding Kin of his own.

"Do you suppose this is some ploy of your father to distract you, my lord?" A gruffer bass voice. It was older and worn with years of use.

I've heard that voice before.

The baritone chuckled. "I don't know if I'd put that much faith in my father's foresight."

Kin tried to open his eyes again. They focused on the ground, a pallid shade of light grey that made his black boots stand out.

Another pair of boots occupied the space ahead of him, rich brown leather which he imagined belonged to one of the men who spoke. A third pair of well-worn boots stood farther back.

Kin blinked several times, trying to get his eyes to focus.

The owner of the expensive footwear shifted closer to him, as if aware he watched. Before Kin could lift his head, someone else did it for him.

Kin's eyes shut, and a reactionary hiss came to his lips. A fist gripped the roots of his hair, forcing his head up, and his neck shot with pain. He tried to reach towards the attacker, but the chains held his hands back, clanking beside him. His wrists burned as metal cut into open wounds.

Getting sick of chains.

It took a moment for Kin's vision to clear as he met a set of steel-blue eyes staring into his. He tried to take in the man's features, but his brain struggled to translate the information it received.

Am I looking in a mirror?

Kin gazed on his own face. Or nearly his own, for it bore subtle differences.

The shape was the same, an angular jaw framing a slightly rounded chin. This chin had no beard, clean of all the dark hair Kin hadn't shaven from his face in weeks.

The man's lips followed the same curve his own did. A straight nose set between vibrant blue eyes with thick, black lashes. His mirror's right brow had a scar running over its tip, which Kin didn't recall ever seeing before.

A glorious numbness overtook him, allowing him to hover in shock.

The sideways smirk sharpened at the corners of the stranger's mouth. "So nice of you to finally join us."

He even has my voice.

"My lord Jarac!" A new voice echoed from somewhere else,

followed by the rhythmic stomp of metal-tipped boots on stone and a clatter of armor.

A guard bounded down stairs roughly carved into the terrain of Lungaz itself, confirming they were below ground level.

"We found the armorer unconscious and several things missing from the hold. We're looking for the infiltrator." The man attempted a salute as he spat out his news.

His twin pulled back on Kin's hair again, then released it and walked away. Jarac's hair was longer, falling past his shoulders.

With his head finally free, Kin shook it to clear his vision and his mind. He leaned against the wall, pressing his head to the cold stone as he comprehended his situation.

Since when do I share my face with another?

Kin grew up as an only child. "Who..."

The other figure in the room stepped forward, and Kin immediately recognized the greying red beard and burly features of the personal guard he encountered at the Delphi estate.

"Nymaera's breath," Kin spat.

Killian's ruddy complexion rounded with a glimmer of white beneath his mustache, but he didn't speak.

Jarac tugged on the hem of his expensive nobleman's vest as he crossed to the guard who'd run to the base of the stairs. He gave pointed orders in a hushed voice, to which the guard nodded before rushing back up the stairs.

Jarac chuckled. "Useless." Sauntering towards Kin, he twisted a garish ring on his right hand, his pale-blue eyes distant. "I know you're not using the Art to look like me." His eyes narrowed at Kin. "Or it would have dissipated the moment my men came for you. So I find myself with several questions."

Kin snorted. "You and me both." His voice grated in his parched throat.

"Trust nothing he says, Lord Jarac." Killian shook his head, and displeasure flashed in Jarac's eyes, his head twitching to the side. "He's a monster. The girl he kidnapped from the Delphi estate wasn't found. She's likely dead, along with my two men he killed during his arrest."

Even with his memories jumbled, Kin only remembered killing one man for certain. Amarie must have done in the other, though he hadn't seen it happen.

Did the soldiers lie to Killian about a woman's involvement?

Jarac's hand shot forward and grabbed Kin's jaw, forcing his head up. "Are you working for my father?"

Kin shook his head, both in answer and to free his face.

Jarac grabbed him again. "Who are you?" His voice lowered to a sinister whisper Kin struggled to hear through the pounding of his head.

Even in his compromised state, Kin had little patience for the man's questions. His body tensed, granting him the energy to push from the wall. While he acted as if he was pulling his head away, he shifted his weight and slammed his head forward.

Jarac's fingers released as Kin's forehead crunched into his nose. "Son of a bitch!" He recoiled, lifting a hand to catch the blood streaming over his lips. He glowered, then struck Kin's face with the back of his hand, swinging with the full force of his upper body.

Dazed, Kin slumped against the stone wall behind him. He struggled to find his feet as the room spun.

A crimson stain glimmered on the gold signet ring on Jarac's left hand, and he reached for a handkerchief. "Bastard." He pressed the white cloth beneath his nose. "Killian, please persuade our friend here to tell us where he comes from."

Killian nodded, his knuckles cracking as they gripped into fists.

Kin sought refuge in the darkest places of his mind. Despite his recent adversity to the forlorn parts of his soul, the indifference made the agony more bearable. Killian's methods of persuasion made it far harder to keep his eyes open as his body attempted to curl on itself, prohibited by the chains.

Every time Kin's knees weakened and praised the arrival of the ground, he'd be lifted back up for it to begin again. The shadows of his mind didn't offer enough comfort, and the taste of hot copper dominated his mouth.

In a moment of reprieve, Kin allowed the blood to pool on his tongue to remind himself he was still alive before he spat it on the stone at his feet. He offered no answers to Jarac or his tool, Killian, for he had none.

This is nothing compared to what he *will do to me for delaying my task. For Amarie.*

Muffled sounds came, but Kin couldn't understand the voices as his ears protested hearing anything but a distant ringing, droning like the bell of the Great Library of Capul, piercing through the fog at the beach.

A shaky breath vibrated through him, more grumbles. Wood dragging over stone. Sweet chimes of cold metal followed by a clicking.

Kin's arms fell loose at his sides but felt too heavy to lift.

Vision returned along with sound as they heaved him from the wall, his knees finally given rest as he plopped into a chair.

His neck burned as someone forced his head back again, and he focused on steel-blue eyes.

Jarac's mouth moved, but Kin couldn't make out the words. They moved again. "Tell me."

Kin shook his head again. "I don't know." His tongue tried to remember how to work, garbling his words. "I didn't know you existed, either."

A growl of rage echoed, and Kin's spine ached as Jarac tossed his head forward. A wave of what might have been adrenaline kicked in, a silent reaction to some outside source.

Killian faced the other way, looking over his shoulder at the staircase behind him as if waiting for something.

Jarac circled behind Kin, distracted by the clang of steel striking itself, and boots on stairs. "Kill him, Killian. He's of no use if he knows nothing."

Killian slipped his hand to his belt. Withdrawing a knife with a dull scrape of steel, he stepped towards Kin.

Too weak to stop the blade in Killian's grip from his throat, Kin grasped desperately at the man's wrist, but it did little. His right shoulder screamed in agony.

A sharp twang snapped from somewhere in the room, followed by a yell, and Killian's stance faltered. His blade clattered to the floor as he reached to the crossbow bolt embedded deep just above his knee. The wooden shaft protruded from his flesh, the sinister arrow head dripping blood down the inseam of his breeches.

Killian collapsed.

Jarac vanished from his vision in rapid movement. The scrape of a blade being withdrawn sounded behind Kin, his bad shoulder jerking backward. Jarac crouched behind him, pressing frigid steel against his twin's throat with an unexpectedly steady hand.

Kin blinked blearily at the staircase where the bolt had been fired from.

A bloodied figure stood with a parted stance. The most beautiful sight he'd ever seen.

Amarie stepped from the shadows in the dimly lit stairwell, a loaded crossbow raised to her shoulder. Her feet glided down the last few steps and she kept her back to the wall and her weapon aimed at Jarac.

Her shirt had seen much better days, speckled with patches of blood and white Lungaz ash. Smears of red streaked her neck. The shoulder opposite of where she held the weapon stained crimson.

Her chest heaved, but her aim held steady. "If you kill him, you'll only know the success for three seconds before my bolt goes through your eye."

Killian's head shot up, and he looked at her face with utter horror, which Kin wished he could better appreciate.

"But he'd still be dead." Jarac pushed the blade harder against Kin's throat, grazing his skin. "Which would be a shame with what you've surely been through to retrieve him."

"What I've been through is nothing compared to the hells in

store for you..." Amarie paused. "But I have something that might give you reason to reconsider dying for your cause." Her left hand moved to her pocket, withdrawing a familiar necklace.

Kin rocked forward at the sight of it. The attempt ended when the blade bit deeper into his flesh, forcing his head back against his twin again.

Jarac tensed, turning the blade over.

Amarie dropped the Berylian Key shard from her shaking palm, and as it swung on the chain around her fingers, the crystal pulsated with an unnatural sunset glow.

That's impossible.

But there was no mistaking the hum of the Art from the shard.

"Unless you prefer death." Her voice darkened, and she snapped the illuminated pendant up into her fist.

Silence came, but the blade in Jarac's hand loosened against Kin's neck, letting him breathe easier. "An interesting proposal. What assurance do I have of my safety, should I accept?"

He knows what it is. And it works here in Lungaz. How?

Killian gasped, turning towards Jarac. "You mustn't, my lord. It's too great a risk. We still don't know..."

"Shut up, Killian. If you say another word, the next bolt will be much more permanent."

Killian shifted uncomfortably, Jarac looking towards him.

Amarie looked back at Jarac. "You have my *word*." She tossed the necklace, and it landed near the exit of the room, the glow dissipating. "Take it, and your remaining men, and get out. You have the span of my patience to decide."

Time passed slowly, and when Amarie widened her stance, Jarac made a hurried response. "Done." He pulled the blade from Kin's neck.

Kin fell forward over his knees, grasping them for support.

Jarac's boots rasped across the stone, and he replaced his dagger on his belt as he stooped to pick up the Berylian Key shard. "Killian." Command emanated through his tone, and he glanced briefly over his shoulder to the Delphi family guard, warning in his eyes. Without another word, Jarac ascended the stairs, vanishing.

Growling under his breath, Killian stood despite the bolt through his leg. He left a trail of blood on the pale floor and grunted as he pulled his injured leg onto the first step. Pausing, he looked at Amarie with a darkness in his deep-set brown eyes.

Amarie turned her back to Kin, crossbow aimed at the doorway as she stepped backwards towards him. Even after the men disappeared, she held her stance, her body stiff.

Kin's gaze trailed to her limp left hand, where blood dripped from her fingers to the ashen ground.

Letting out a breath, she lost her rigid posture and dropped her crossbow before turning to Kin. "Dear gods." She touched his face, examining his wounds closer.

Her fingers sparked pain each place they traversed, and Kin winced as she inspected him.

He urged his functioning hand to move, trying to grasp her arm. "What are you doing here?" She wasn't a vision or dream, yet he almost believed she was. "You're here?"

"Yes, Kin, I'm here. I followed them. I came to get you."

Kin wished he had a response, but his brain couldn't decide what he should say.

She came for me.

The concept of someone putting themselves in such danger for him was unfathomable.

Amarie moved a hand to his injured shoulder, touching a spot which didn't hurt even though Kin believed it should. "Your shoulder is dislocated."

At the mention of his shoulder, he glanced towards it and foolishly shrugged. He cringed. "I think you're right."

"My uncle used to have this happen all the time. It's all right, but I need you to lie down."

Lying down sounds lovely.

She helped him slip from the chair to the ground.

The pressure of the hard stone against his back granted respite for the screaming muscles in his back. Closing his eyes, he sucked in a deep breath to urge the rest of his body to calm.

As Amarie's boots scuffed on the stone, she moved towards his right shoulder to straighten his arm and he held his breath.

A sharp exhale came from his lips at the pop and relief as she maneuvered his shoulder back into place, the pain dulling to something more bearable.

He gripped her hand as strongly as he could, wanting nothing more than to stay still. Somewhere in the back of his mind, he registered the sound of a drum, the rhythmic beats he'd heard before. He'd sat on something scaled, clouds ripping past his face when the drum had lulled him to unconsciousness.

Was I on a dragon?

"Amarie..." He tried to remember what exactly had happened. It was so strange to consider her there.

I should be dead.

Her warm hand closed around his.

"The shard?" The terror of it being gone reignited the numbness in Kin's mind. "What happened?" He'd seen it glow, seen energy flow in a place where the connection to the Art didn't exist.

She'd claimed she couldn't let the shard go before, when she'd taken it from him. But now she gave it to spare his life.

Amarie pulled a skin of water from her hip and opened the end. "Drink."

His lips opened gratefully for the cool liquid to stream down his throat. He tried to go slow, despite his body's demand for more.

"It's all right. He has the shard, but it doesn't matter." Her voice held not even the slightest bit of worry. She stroked his hair from his forehead in tender caresses.

"But... how did it glow like that?"

"That's not important right now. Can you stand? We should get out of here."

Pride prohibited Kin from doing anything but nod to her

question. It took a moment and all the strength he had left to make his body move. He accepted the hand she offered, bracing himself against her to find his feet beneath him.

Chapter 14

Amarie led Kin from the outpost, his steps weary. She steered around two motionless soldiers she'd fought at the top of the stairs. One had been the man to skewer her in Jaspa.

Viento responded to her whistle, and she latched the crossbow to her bags, along with the quiver of bolts. The horse stood patiently still, supporting Kin's weight as he clung to the saddle.

Amarie didn't care if Kin saw as she reached into the pouch where she kept her coin. It was more important for them to get out of Lungaz as quickly as possible.

Mounting Viento was yet another laborious process, but with a smaller shard gripped in her palm, she channeled enough strength to pull Kin up behind her. If she'd known the shards reacted to her while in Lungaz, she'd have used it on the way there, too.

Would have been useful at the inn, if I'd known.

The power pulsed through her and the stone, encouraging the energy into Viento for their exit. Gaining the power by such means took longer than usual, now required to travel through an extra channel, but it worked all the same.

Viento ran once again at unnatural speeds, leaving no room for conversation. She had no desire to stop while they were still within the barren lands.

Night fell, but she powered through.

Kin's grip didn't falter. Nor did he complain.

Her strength waned as the adrenaline diminished, her eyes blurring as they rode. Even her legs, well-adjusted to riding, quivered with the effort of maintaining Viento's speed.

The sight of trees, and shortly after, grass, couldn't come soon enough.

In her battle to free Kin from Lungaz, her shoulder wound had reopened. It'd stopped bleeding again during the ride, but the caked blood drying down her arm made her skin itch. Her body ached with the few minor wounds incurred during the combat, but most of the blood soaking her clothes wasn't her own.

She prepared her hiding aura as they neared the border of Lungaz, willing it to snap into place as the flood of her energy returned. As they entered Feyor's lush forests, her power and aura jolted back to life, but it couldn't satiate the rest her mind craved.

While riding through the shadows of the trees, dawn approached. Birds chittered to greet the coming day.

She pulled back on Viento's reins, bringing him to a halt near a small creek. The area had a thick canopy above, and Kin relaxed his hold on her.

He dismounted to the plush grass covering the forest floor, looking more stable. He hesitated at Viento's side, looking at Amarie. "Can I help?"

Amarie shook her head. "I just need a minute." She waved a hand at him, trying to catch her breath.

Kin furrowed his brow but turned towards the stream. Reaching the water, he knelt, scooping the clear liquid over his face and neck. His movements were stiff, but she hoped the water would refresh him.

Reluctant to follow just yet, Amarie's head spun with exhaustion. Grasping Viento's mane, she closed her eyes, willing her balance to return. She still clung to the shard in her palm despite it no longer serving any purpose, holding it so tightly it dug into her skin.

Her body unintentionally rocked to the side as her stamina finally gave out. She fell from the saddle to the ground, and Viento sidestepped with a nicker.

The shard bounced from her loosened grip and came to rest near her hand.

Amarie stared at the brightening sky with unfocused eyes, watching a cloud change shape as it moved.

Kin knelt at her side, far faster than he should have been able to reach her considering his injuries. The surrounding fabric altered as he came to her, and he lifted her head to his lap.

The scent of rotted leaves wrinkled her nose.

As the Art coursed through him, energy dissipated from something else nearby. His personal well of power should have been drained during his torture, just as his physical strength had. A disconnected source couldn't supplement a practitioner's energy.

But why does it feel like that's what's happening?

Trails of water dripped down Kin's clean face. His jaw and left brow swelled, colored with the beginnings of bruises. A thick gash ran down from his temple to the top of his left cheek, bleeding fresh from the cleaning. He grasped her fingers and pulled her hand to his chest. His torn shirt showed scrapes and bruising at his collarbone.

"You need rest." Kin's voice sounded distant in the haze of threatening dawn. "I'll be right here, and you…"

Unable to move, Amarie couldn't recover the shard from the grass beside her. His voice provided her with comfort, even though she couldn't make out the rest of his words. Her eyes slid closed, and her grip on his hand relaxed as unconsciousness took over.

A breeze brushed over her cheeks, and she blinked up at the rustling jeweled leaves above her. The sun shone brighter than it had it days, cycled to the afternoon. She turned her head to the west, squinting as she tried to focus on the birds flying in front of distant cotton clouds. Sucking in a deeper breath, she swallowed as her awareness returned to her.

Amarie's head rested on the bundle of Kin's cloak, recognizable by the scent of him. He'd tucked a blanket around her body. Her wounded shoulder felt strangely numb.

She twisted her head the other way to look for the shard, but couldn't find it. Panic flooded into her chest, but the feeling subsided as her eyes fell on Kin.

He knelt at the stream again and ran a cloth over his bare back, shivering as the cold liquid dribbled over his bruised skin.

Her stomach knotted at the vision of purple and blue, mixed with partially healed injuries he'd received during his imprisonment. A scabbed-over scrape traversed his lower back, along with hints of old scars.

He still wore his boots and form-fitting breeches, though they were battered and torn in places, showing superficial wounds he'd not yet tended to. His face was clean, but a purple lump marred his jaw, hidden only partially by his beard.

A wave of refreshment passed over Amarie, even after only a few hours' rest. She pushed the blanket back, sitting up, and looked around to see Viento drinking from the stream. He was still tacked, but Kin had removed the heavy bags.

She watched Kin another moment, feeling the relief of his safety all over again. "Kin."

He lifted his head, a smile coming to his lips. With a groan, he stood and dropped the cloth.

"Are you all right?" Her gaze trailed over his chest, which wasn't in much better shape than his back.

"I'll heal." Another cut marred his skin just below his collarbone, but he had pressed something into it. A thick green and brown paste. The same substance covered the gash on the side of his face.

He huffed as he crouched at her side, balancing on the balls of his feet. "How are you feeling?"

Amarie took a deep breath. "I didn't sleep much on the way to find you. I'm fine, though." Her eyes narrowed as she turned her attention to the injury on her shoulder. She only wore the sleeveless top, the strap of it pulled off her shoulder. The blood cleansed from her skin, she eyed the wound on her shoulder, covered in the same goop as Kin's cuts. She lifted a hand to investigate.

"Don't touch it." Kin took her hand. "I don't want it to open again when it's finally healing."

Amarie smirked and looked at him. "Always caring for my

injuries." Her gaze stayed on his, her breathing even as her mind contemplated the journey which came after the events at the inn. "I'm really glad you're safe."

Kin crossed his legs and moved her hand to his lap, squeezing it. He released her briefly to retrieve his cloak from the ground, and wrapped it loosely around his bare shoulders with a vague shiver. "I'm safe. But without you, I wouldn't be alive right now." He took her hand in his again, running his thumb over her skin.

"I had to come for you."

"No, you didn't. But I'll forever be grateful you chose to." Kin looked away as if he were deep in thought, and apprehension built within her. "I have a lot of questions, though." His smile grew grim.

Amarie sat back onto her feet but left her hand in his. "You're not the only one."

Where his connection to the Art came from was a more pressing matter than his apparent twin. Now that she'd been present as he used it, she knew it wasn't directly from his own energy source. The state of the surrounding air confirmed it. Her mind had recognized the feeling of the fabric being manipulated before she passed out. But there was no obvious explanation.

They sat with her knees touching his shins, both hands grasped between them. His hands were warm against the onset of the late-autumn chill and firm in their grip.

Would he tell me the truth if I asked for it?

He'd always been so evasive when she asked him anything, and the idea he might actually answer was intimidating.

Do I really want to know?

Her stomach twisted, but she kept her gaze where it was, fearing her eyes would give away her reservations. Another reassuring squeeze came to her hands as Kin's chin dipped down to catch her vision and bring it back to his.

"I know I haven't always been the best at giving straightforward answers, and I'm not sure I have many." Kin broke the silence. "But perhaps we can try now?" His lips curled handsomely in a smile.

Amarie hesitated at the biggest question lingering in her mind. As she watched his eyes, she admitted to herself she could never know him without hearing the answer. "Where does your ability in the Art come from?"

The ensuing silence wasn't unexpected but disappointing.

Kin heaved a sigh as he looked down to their hands. He held his breath for a moment, then slowly exhaled through his mouth. He chewed on his lip before he finally brought his gaze back to her with a pained expression. "You don't know what you're asking me to tell." He sounded ashamed. "It isn't my secret to share."

Her chest tightened out of discouragement that he'd rejected her first inquiry. She flexed her jaw and took a breath. "I'm asking you to tell me anything, Kin. Anything at all. Something..."

He held eye contact with her through her plea, though his eyes glazed over, and his shoulders slumped. His mouth opened as if to speak, but then promptly closed. He took his gaze from her, hands losing their grip on hers. Arms retracted, moving to settle against his own thighs.

Amarie's frustration grew, but a part of her wanted to comfort him. She could recognize the internal struggle and refused to let him pull away from her so easily.

She caressed the uninjured side of his face and urged his gaze to lift back to hers. "Look at me."

He stubbornly resisted her gesture at first, but his chin eventually rose, and their eyes met once more. His eyes bore into her, like a mirror reflecting pieces of her soul.

She leaned forward, shifting up to her knees as she closed the distance between their faces. Her lips brushed against his. Her heart pounded, but not with passion. She prayed he wouldn't move away.

His lips didn't immediately respond, but he didn't pull away. A slow breath passed between their lips as he inhaled and returned the pressure of the kiss on her upper lip.

Amarie let it linger for a moment, renewing it just once to kiss him with the same tenderness.

Sitting back on her heels, she searched his face, silently begging him to have faith in her. "You can trust me."

"I do trust you. But it's more complicated..." He shook his head, his voice trailing off. "I trust you with every fiber of my soul that still belongs to me."

Amarie could hear the words he said, but they didn't make sense. Her hand slipped from his face, falling to rest by her knees with her other. "What do you mean, still belongs to you?"

"I wasn't born with talent in the Art." Kin's hands twisted against each other in his lap, and he straightened his back with a wince. "I acquired it later in life. But even the power I have would never have allowed me to do what you did with the shard."

A sigh escaped her lips at his predictable deflection. She wanted to tell him she hadn't been born with access to the energies of the Art either, but she wasn't ready to share that information. Gaining talent in the Art later in life was rare.

Amarie tapped a finger on her dagger's hilt. "I didn't do anything to the shard."

"Then how?"

"You don't know what you're asking." Her voice was soft as she mirrored his earlier response.

She didn't know what to expect as a reaction, but it wasn't the half smirk curling up the edge of his lips. She couldn't help the touch of a smile creeping onto her face.

"We're quite the pair, aren't we?"

She supposed they were, but hoped there were still other things he might answer. "Why do you want the shard, anyway?"

He hesitated again, longer than she would have liked for such a vital piece of information. "Someone asked me to retrieve it for study."

Her eyebrow rose. "For study? Who wants to study it?"

"I don't know the details and I can't say who."

"Can you tell me if they have any shards already?"

"No..."

"How about if the person is respectable? Like a scholar or—"

"Amarie..." Kin chewed his lip and shook his head once. "I can't."

She wrapped her arms around her middle with an exhale. Her gaze drifted to the stream behind Kin.

What am I doing? This seems so pointless.

Absently, her eyes flickered to her horse, and she debated if her instinct to flee from Kin the first day they'd met had been accurate all along.

But there's one more thing I can try.

"I held a shard while we rode, but I dropped it. Do you know where it is?" Her eyes returned to his again, and she wondered if he would lie to her.

She watched him through yet another moment of hesitation before he leaned back and pushed his hand into his pocket. He brought a fist out towards her, opening it to reveal the small shard in his palm. It was more jagged than the one in the necklace, but roughly the same size.

He offered it to her. "Thought it was better if it didn't just sit out in the open, since apparently lots of people are after these."

Her mouth twitched with a slight smile, but she didn't take it. "Keep it. If you need it, then keep it."

Kin held his breath, his expression turning to confusion. He didn't pull his hand back from where he offered the shard to her. His next inhale came slow and long. Gradually, his fingers closed around the shard, and he tucked it back into his pocket.

He smiled warmer than before. "You have more, don't you?"

She scoffed, shaking her head. "Is that your way of saying thank you?" She kept the larger shards stitched within Viento's saddle, but he didn't need to know that. It didn't lessen the magnitude of letting him have one. She hoped this would help him trust her. This made two shards she'd given up for him.

I hope this habit doesn't continue.

"Thank you." He took her hand in his again.

Her mouth opened to speak, but she ended up biting her lower lip instead. "Are you a good person?"

Kin's grip tightened on hers, but he didn't speak.

Amarie looked at his hand, running her thumb over his knuckles. "You told me I made you want to change. Why?"

He toyed with her fingers as his smile faded. "I believe that opens up a much deeper conversation about what defines good versus evil."

Don't deflect again.

Kin cleared his throat. "But no, I don't consider myself wholly moral. The man I killed back at the inn in Jaspa wasn't my first."

"One fell at my hands too, along with two in the outpost. They aren't my first either, and won't be my last." Amarie paused, keeping her tone indifferent. "Will you hurt me?"

His gaze shot back to her. "Never. I'd never want to hurt you."

She didn't miss the words he chose. He seemed adamant in the 'want', but it was far from a promise.

But how much can a person guarantee another's safety?

It implied he could hurt her, perhaps even if he didn't want to. She could relate. She didn't want to hurt him either. Just like she hadn't wanted to hurt those she had. No part of her could chastise him for such an honest answer, because it would be the best she could offer him.

Kin's hand moved to her jaw, fingers soft against her skin as he urged her chin up so their eyes could meet. His irises were lighter, no longer tainted by the emotions they held before.

Amarie took another long breath, exhaling the plagued thoughts. His hand felt comforting on her face, and she moved her jaw into his touch with a smile. "If you don't ask me anything too specific, I might provide some wonderfully vague answers to the curiosities bouncing around in your head?" An offer she'd never made anyone before.

"I don't deserve answers from you. And honestly, my most pressing questions have nothing to do with you."

Her smile faded with a twinge of disappointment, but she wanted to believe he hadn't meant his words the way they felt. She seldom felt willing to open up to anyone. To tell even minor truths about her life. Usually, she was Samitha, or Lilia, but never Amarie.

She gave him the opportunity to learn something, anything about her, and his rejection stung. It made her recoil, regretting the offer. "Then I suppose I'll clean up." She went to stand, but Kin's grip tightened on her hand.

"Amarie." He spoke her name slowly, drawing her gaze back to him. "It's not that I don't want to know. I do. But I have to believe those answers will come in time." Running his thumb against her jaw, he held strong to her with his other hand, but it didn't feel forceful. "I want to take that time with you."

Another uncertain deep breath came from her mouth as she searched his eyes. She fought the overreaction quaking in her chest. The touch on her cheek banished the raging instinct to flee.

"I have to admit my distraction." Kin sighed. "There have been a lot of revelations of late. One being a man who looks like me, who I didn't know existed until yesterday."

She remembered the look on the face of the man he referred to, as she pointed her loaded crossbow at him. She'd thought Kin would have known exactly who he was.

How can he not know his brother?

In Lungaz, the Art couldn't be responsible for such similarities.

"I didn't kill him because I didn't want to assume you'd be all right with that." She smirked, trying to lighten her mood and rid herself of the bleak feeling in her stomach. "Perhaps I should have?"

He smiled half-heartedly. "I wouldn't have judged you for the decision, had you made it. But it's probably better he remains alive until I can find out who he is."

She nodded, glad her choice was apparently the right one, even if it lost her a shard. "Did you learn his name, at least?"

"Jarac."

Her eyes widened, recalling hearing the name while in the outpost, but hadn't expected to hear it regarding Kin's twin. "Jarac? Are you sure?"

His eyes narrowed. "Yes... Killian kept referring to him as Lord Jarac. I assume he's some Feyorian noble? I've never paid much attention to politics."

Amarie's infiltration of the outpost involved her sneaking between rooms, hiding at times to avoid unnecessary confrontation in her compromised state. Occasionally, she overheard conversations between the guards.

She'd kept to the shadows outside the outpost armory, eavesdropping on the guards. Many mentioned Kin, but they referred to him as the prisoner. Brought in on the back of a wyvern at the order of Lord Jarac, who arrived shortly before.

She discovered the shard necklace stashed in the armory after knocking the guards unconscious. Liberating it and a crossbow, she almost missed the crystal's reaction to her touch. There hadn't been time to dwell on it, but she'd use it to her advantage.

At the top of the stairs to the holding cells, a pair of familiar soldiers spoke in haste to each other. They knew she was coming, weapons ready.

Her boots made no sound as she crept towards them, listening.

"We must ensure his safety."

His companion soldier nodded. "Prince Jarac cannot come to harm."

At the time, it meant little to her. She didn't care who placed the order to take Kin, even if it was a prince.

Sitting on the forest floor, away from Lungaz, she stared at Kin for a long moment.

Is it possible Kin is a prince and doesn't know it?

If true, it made sense why his brother wished to kill him. With royal blood, Kin could challenge for the throne.

Her mind spun.

"Amarie?" Kin's voice rang through her thoughts, forcing her gaze to refocus on him.

She blinked and realized she needed to speak. "They called him a prince." Her voice softened at the revelation, and Kin straightened.

His hand dropped from her cheek, the other loosening its grip on her hand. "Prince?" His voice cracked, eyes wide. "Are you sure?"

"Definitely. The guards called him Prince Jarac."

"This has to be some kind of joke of the gods. I'm an only child, born and raised on an estate in Delkest. I've never been to Feyor in my life. My parents are winemakers, not royalty." He seemed barely aware of what he was doing as fingers twitched against hers. "This makes no sense. We need to go to Delkest, to my parents."

Amarie coughed.

We?

She hadn't thought so far into her plan to consider what might happen after escaping Lungaz. Whether they would remain together had been irrelevant to her purpose. Now he wanted to travel to his parents' home in Delkest, and he wanted to go together? Unless it was a slip of the tongue.

"Uh, what?"

Kin's grip returned. "Come with me, please? To Delkest. I..." He trailed off for a moment, his eyes going to their hands as he lifted hers and brought them to his chest. "Everything is more bearable when you're with me."

His words resonated through her, calming her insides of the chaos.

Not a slip of the tongue.

Amarie sighed. "All right. We'll go to Delkest. But is there anything else I need to know first?" Her own desire to remain close to him encouraged the thought.

Kin smiled and lifted her hand to his lips. He kissed her knuckles, drawing an involuntary inhale and wave of warmth to pass through her. "There is one thing."

She raised an eyebrow.

"My full name is actually Kinronsilis." He looked at her before another press of his lips. "In case you wanted to know."

"Pfft. Well, that changes everything."

 Chapter 15

Kin found it difficult to give in to sleep, despite how much his eyes protested being open. He battled the beasts raging within his mind.

As a child, Kin dreamt of having a brother, even pretended to have one for a time. Had there been a reason behind his parents' fervent disapproval of his imaginary sibling?

Every inch of his body ached. He'd treated the cuts, but the medicinal effects of the plants he used were fading.

Thoughts of Amarie came with a knot in the pit of his stomach. Fear that when he woke, she'd be gone again. His arms tightened around her, grateful she fell asleep with her head on his chest. Her rhythmic breathing assured him she slept.

He wished he could answer the questions she'd asked, but he kept the secrets for her own safety.

Amarie can't learn the depth of my shadows.

She gave him a shard, though. It pressed awkwardly in his pocket, bringing relief. It'd make everything simpler. He could complete his task, be given another, which would have nothing to do with the Berylian Key shards, and then continue his new double life.

He didn't control Kin's will and thoughts.

Kin didn't have to tell his master she possessed more shards.

He wanted to be with her and didn't care how unattainable it seemed.

It's worth the risk.

As morning crept in, her breath warmed his neck with each

peaceful fall of her chest. He wished she could eternally remain in his arms.

They departed their makeshift camp after a quick meal and another wash at the stream. Small, fleeting affection blossomed despite the dangerous tension accompanying staying within Feyor for too long.

The morning passed before they mounted Viento together.

During the journey south, Kin found what comfort he could in falling asleep with Amarie in his embrace and starting each day with her.

But since they knew the truth behind Jarac's identity, caution took priority.

Kin's warning from his master to never be seen in Feyor was now perfectly clear. He had known somehow, and it brought a whole new array of furious suspicions Kin couldn't express to Amarie.

Either Jarac or Kin's entire upbringing was a lie. That knowledge only encouraged his desire to see his childhood home.

He tried to remember the last time he'd looked on the vineyards.

Has it been five years already?

A new tension rose between himself and Amarie, one which hadn't existed before. An uncertainty about the future.

He forced his mind to stay focused on the danger of where they were. The potential for Jarac to suddenly appear and complicate matters.

Or *him*.

After Amarie gave Kin the shard, he tried to lock away his connection to the Art.

But cutting himself off from the source came with laborious moments of meditation and construction of barriers he'd never been good at. He couldn't sever the thirst for power, which hung over his head like an executioner's axe, ever threatening. Baiting him to devour the Art he'd relied on for so long and save himself from the coming terror.

He rubbed his temples, grimacing against the rising pain. A

tension gripped first at the tattoo on his forearm and snaked its way through his muscles to his throbbing head. His body quaked, but he fought to hide the shivers from Amarie.

"Are you all right?"

"Fine," Kin snapped, wincing at the volume of her voice. A whirling cyclone thrashed within his senses. Food had been difficult to keep down since he'd finally successfully erected the barrier between himself and the power. Only three days had passed since he'd used the Art, but it felt like weeks of starvation.

In her usual fashion as of late, Amarie ignored his irritability and responded patiently. "Can I rub your neck for you? Maybe it will help." Her soft tone sounded merciful.

Temptation to accept her offer fed the demand of his soul. Just a taste of power. He swallowed, rubbing at his stinging eyes. "Just a little."

With the touch of her skin, he let the wall crumble and absorbed the tiniest amount of energy from a nearby tree. Satiated, the hollowness quieted, and he relaxed against Amarie.

Disgust settled with the reestablishment of his connection to the Art. Even if he told himself he no longer wanted the power, he couldn't function without it. His connection to the Art seemed as necessary for his survival as water or air.

The moment they crossed the border between Feyor and Delkest, his mood lightened. Avoiding the border patrols proved less complicated than they feared. It'd been over two weeks of wilderness, and nothing sounded better than civilization and a bed.

Finding a place to camp for the night in a clearing densely surrounded by pine trees, Kin, more used to riding, dismounted first. His bruises were mostly healed, and he no longer winced when his body shifted to walk after riding. The cut on his face had closed, leaving a pink line which one day would fade to a white scar.

Something to always remember his brother by.

Amarie untacked Viento, humming a tune under her breath he'd heard her sing before. He enjoyed her voice, the way the melody carried over the wind. It brought him a sense of calm little else could.

They'd developed a routine while traveling together, which fell into place as she dug out the fire pit while he gathered wood for her ring of rocks.

A chill wind blew from the snow-capped mountains to the east, urging Kin to keep his cloak wrapped around his shoulders. Underneath, he wore only a thin, tan shirt. Amarie had appropriated it for him from a clothing line where some unfortunate woodsman left it to dry outside his isolated cabin.

The snow didn't drift to where they traveled, but a damp chill permeated the air.

He huddled eagerly by the fire.

Amarie sat wrapped in her deep-blue cloak, shoulders covered by a black fur pelt, waiting for the fire to grow into a blaze.

He'd watched from the corner of his eyes while she'd replaced her ruined layers with a black sleeveless tunic and a dark-blue shirt on top. The long sleeves hugged her toned arms, and he imagined undoing each button at the front. They hid beneath the vest she laced over it, another barrier for him to fantasize about playing with.

Despite a growing desire for her, the tension between them prevailed. Their affections rarely came to the surface amid strained conversations of half-truths and unspoken lies.

Kin watched Amarie while she added a log to the growing fire, and he settled down on the edge of his cloak. He reached into her saddle bags at his side to gather items to prepare their modest dinner. He'd taken on the responsibility of cooking, pleased to have a way to do something for her.

After eating, Amarie touched her chin. "You should shave that thing on your face."

Kin frowned as a hand went to his chin where his beard had grown coarse and thick. "I thought you liked it? You haven't complained before." He hadn't trimmed his hair either, and it nearly reached his shoulders.

She lightened his heart with a playful smirk. "I know..." She paused. "But now I rather miss your face." Her eyes glittered as she looked at him, biting her bottom lip.

Kin swallowed at the action. He was fairly certain she knew how effective the little mannerism was against his will. She'd used it many times to draw or gain things from him. While he believed himself to be in control of his own will against the one he served, Amarie proved to be more compelling in getting him to relinquish that control.

The sparkle in the depths of her azure eyes kept his attention and made it difficult to do anything but agree with her.

"I'll need a mirror."

The sun dipped below the horizon, but the fire warmed through his cloak.

Amarie stood and walked to her packs. "I'll do it." She stepped into the firelight in front of him. "Maybe cut off some of that hair, too."

Kin couldn't help but laugh at her apparent enthusiasm at fixing his unkempt appearance. He eyed her suspiciously before agreeing with a nod.

Despite the cold, he had no desire to be itchy for the rest of their journey. He abandoned his cloak at the edge of his bedroll and stripped off his shirt.

The cold air tickled his skin, the waves of heat from the fire encouraging him to sit on the ground close to it. The vibrant orange and yellow danced across his chest, no longer marred by the bruises incurred in Lungaz.

Betrayed by his own inclination, he eyed the onyx lines of the tattoo on his forearm. The thirteen geometric shapes marring his flesh throbbed with the power he'd tried to deny.

Steel glinted in the corner of his vision as Amarie walked behind him. If anyone else held the blade, he would have been nervous about it near his skin.

But I trust her.

Her hands were gentle as they twisted his head and jaw in the directions she needed to perform the task before her. The scent of her hair as she leaned forward brought a warmth to his blood and disguised the growing chill on his back as the rasping blade cut his hair in clean, practiced strokes.

"You must have done this before." He wished he knew more about her. Since he'd foolishly turned down her initial offer, he hadn't had the nerve to ask much.

"I have."

A subtle bitterness touched Kin's stomach. "Should I be jealous?" He tried not to imagine her cutting a half-naked Coltin's hair. The heir's face was often the one to haunt his insecurities.

She would've been so much better off with him.

Amarie lowered her lips to hover near his left ear, and goosebumps gathered over his forearms. "No," she whispered, and his tension melted.

She rounded to sit in front of him, running her fingers through his beard. Focus sharpened her gaze as she made slow draws of the blade across his skin, examining every inch of his face while doing it.

His chest fluttered to see her so close and careful in each movement. "You never cut Coltin's hair?"

Amarie laughed. "Gods, no. Ahria wasn't the touchy-feely type." She passed a damp cloth over his skin after she put down the blade, and the freshly exposed skin tingled.

His eyes locked with hers, amazed once again at how she'd come to be with him. The hope of finding this kind of happiness disappeared in the years following the life-altering decision he made at age seventeen. In the ten years since, he'd had plenty of time to accept the loneliness he deserved.

Amarie redirected his life. He'd told her she made him want to change, but so much already had.

His heart swelled at the thought, his hand taking hers holding the cloth. "Then, I'm the lucky one to know Amarie instead of Ahria. Though, I'm still fond of the name. Why did you use it?"

"Don't be daft, you know why."

"I do?"

She rolled her eyes, and he grinned.

"Maybe I want to hear you say it?"

"Say what? That even months later, all I could think about was a man I met in Capul? It was a terrible choice, using that name. Every time I heard it, all I thought of was you."

"And that's so bad?" Kin touched her wrist, turning it so he could kiss her palm.

Amarie smiled. "It is when I was trying *not* to think about you. What good would've come of that?"

"I can think of lots of good." His skin sparked as her fingers ran over his jaw. "You have to admit, it's a pretty name."

"It is. Perhaps I'll use it if I ever have a daughter."

Kin couldn't help the quirk of his brow. Kids had never crossed his mind when considering the name, but now he imagined a little girl with dark auburn hair and blue eyes.

"Who said you can lay claim to it?" A smile crept over his lips. "Maybe I planned to use it for my daughter, someday." Things as they were, a family was impossible to even consider. But he found what joy he could in the fantasy.

Amarie gave him an amused smirk. "I hadn't considered you'd want children. They're not particularly suited to our way of life. Besides, if I remember correctly, you came up with the name for me. Therefore, it's mine to use."

"I've imagined the possibility of children, if the gods bless me with them. But if you're going to be so stubborn about the name I so graciously gave you, I insist on some restrictions." Amarie rolled her eyes again, but he continued. "You may use Ahria in your escapades, *or* you may give it to your daughter... but only if she's mine too."

Amarie would be a wonderful mother to our children.

The thought made his body feel weak, and he coughed.

Wait... what?

Amarie gaped at him, wide-eyed, and then seemed to recover. "That's one big restriction." She rolled her lips together. "Maybe we should get a cat first."

Kin frowned. "I'm more of a dog person." He rubbed at the back of his neck, the cut hair itching his skin.

What's gotten into me? Kids...

Amarie laughed and tilted her head. "I'm finished. Is your face cold now?" She sat on her heels beside him, and he turned to face her.

He latched onto the change of subject and touched his jaw. "It is. Better, though? Do I still look like me?" He felt different somehow. His hand ran through his trimmed hair, cut far closer to his scalp than it had been in a long time. Everything felt right.

She smiled and shifted the cloth to her other hand, using it to brush away hairs from his shoulders and neck.

"Much better. Now I recognize the *Kinronsilis* I met in Capul." She rarely used his full name. It rolled nicely off her tongue, eliciting a response she likely didn't intend.

Or perhaps she does.

He lost himself in her eyes, distracted from the sounds of the forest and the crackle of the fire. Every instinct in his body drew him closer to her, wanting to taste her lips.

Amarie touched his chin with her thumb as he wrapped his arms around her, encouraging her onto his lap.

"Maybe I should have left you looking scraggly, now you're a little *too* handsome." She pinned her lower lip again, and a heat greater than the fire raged through him.

The rising inferno faltered with a ripple of shadow at the tree line behind her.

Dread overtook him, humming against the buried, ominous depths of his soul. A familiar tingle melded against his senses, turning the fever of affection in his veins to ice.

Kin's eyes focused on a tall form tucked among the trees. As his vision settled on the shadow, it sidestepped behind a monstrous pine. Even in the dark, he swore he saw the slither of a smile disappearing beneath a black hood. His skin crawled and the bottom of Kin's stomach dropped out, a tangible fear grabbing hold.

Another Shade.

He drew a steadying breath and returned his gaze to Amarie's, hoping she hadn't noticed.

Her eyes narrowed at him, and she glanced behind her. "What is it?"

Kin didn't have time to explain. If he even could. "Uh, I'll..." He pushed her shoulders gently, forcing her off his lap. He stood, plucking up his shirt and twisting the linen in his hands. His mind whirled to come up with a decent excuse. "I have to wash off." Kin watched her as she stood, and he hoped she'd listen. "Please, *stay here. I'll be right back.*"

She reached for him, but he stepped past her. "Kin."

"Everything's fine. Just stay by the fire." He walked into the darkness of the trees. They enveloped him with a regretful comfort as he pulled his shirt on.

Kin circled the wide tree the figure disappeared behind, but he was no longer there. The twist within his soul tugged at him as he let the senses he tried to ignore take hold and draw him deeper into the woods.

Moonlight refracted through the trees over the leaves crunching beneath his boots. A shiver passed down his spine as a chill breeze bit through his shirt, but he ignored it.

Venturing farther from their camp, Kin reached the shallow stream he'd used as an excuse, then steered over it and entered a grove of naked oak trees.

Stripped of their foliage by the encroaching winter, the branches cast eerie silhouettes on the ground at the bidding of the moon.

The knot in the pit of Kin's stomach hardened as the Art swelled in the darkness beside him. Decay assaulted his surroundings, and the corrosive scent of the dying ferns stung his nostrils.

"Kinronsilis." A familiar voice chortled his name, the hint of an Isalican accent elongating the vowels.

The shadows to Kin's side shifted within a beam of blue-white piercing through the barren branches. His eyes adjusted to cope with the dark, but the expanse of shadow made it difficult to focus on the spot. Narrowing his gaze at the base of an oak, he took a step back from the emerging form.

Sickening shadows curled around his lanky arms and legs as the Shade strode forward. The leaves crackled beneath the newcomer's boot as grey tendrils slithered away.

Kin stepped back, but not in fear, despite what the man's presence meant. "Ormon." The Shade's name tasted sour as he remembered it. Bark shed from the trees opposite Kin, responding to Ormon's drain of their energy. He leaned back against another oak, still solid and untouched by the Shade's power. Crossing his arms and ankles in feigned confidence, he examined Ormon.

How long has he been following us?

"I expected to find others who shared my task." Ormon's slim, pale hand pulled back his hood. His lean face boasted sharp features, with blond hair closely cropped at the sides. Long curled locks fell over his forehead. Thin lips sneered over yellowed teeth, arms crossed within his heavy woolen cloak.

The cloak prevented Kin from seeing if Ormon carried any weapons, but he didn't need physical weapons any more than Kin did.

Silence lingered, as if Ormon expected Kin to fill it.

Ormon frowned. "I didn't expect it to be you."

Kin's dread grew, but he hid it with a smirk. "Our master is no fool. He chooses those he knows will get the task done."

"While I may still be young in my service, I question the tactical benefit of achieving a shave and a haircut."

Kin laughed. It rolled too easily, like the wickedness he'd portrayed at the Delphi estate. "Then perhaps you aren't watching closely enough." The ice he trod on thinned. The presence of another Shade watching him was a significant concern.

A brief sick feeling overcame Kin as he questioned if their master learned about his attempts at defiance.

"Perhaps I am watching too closely. Though she is a pretty creature, that girl." Ormon's voice curled in stomach-churning greed. "Such a little thing, too, to have such power at her fingertips."

Kin's entire body screamed to react, but he forced a breath, careful to make it seem like all the others. He glanced at where he'd entered the grove, ensuring his eyes didn't give away his thoughts. "That's because you're still young and ignorant." He turned a taunting look on Ormon. "You should know better than most how little appearance matters when we're discussing power. It comes in many shapes."

Ormon let his arms fall to his sides with a shrug. "True." He walked forward, using the few inches he had on Kin in an attempt at intimidation.

Are all Isalicans this freakishly tall?

"But are we speaking of the girl, or the shard she carries?" Ormon's voice lowered.

Kin refused to satisfy him with a reaction, holding still. The reality of the situation struck him hard.

Ormon sought a Berylian Key shard, just as he was. Fear erupted at the realization the other Shade linked Amarie to a shard.

And this means our master is seeking more than one.

He could dissuade the man from his pursuit by giving him the very shard Amarie gifted to him if he hadn't foolishly left it within the pockets of his cloak at camp. He couldn't offer it without exposing Amarie and that she possessed more.

Kin steeled his expression. "I speak of the shard. The girl would offer little fight against me."

Even if the Shade conceded to Kin and went to chase another, it was possible the entire situation might make Amarie a target of their master. A revolting thought.

Ormon growled as if he found excitement in what Kin proposed, or at least how he interpreted it. "Now, what is it you speak of? The fight for the shard, or the fight to take her?"

Don't hesitate.

"Both," Kin hissed.

Ormon's teeth flashed in the darkness. "Resistance always makes it more enjoyable though, don't you think? Feeling a woman struggle and watching her will seep away?"

"I've always found greater pleasure in making her desire me, then watching her realization as I take her and then her life." Kin forced his voice to be steady, swallowing the bile that rose in his throat.

Ormon's eyebrow rose. "You mean to kill her when you're done?" His voice sharpened and held a hint of disgust, as if it were the worst offense. "Then perhaps the great Kinronsilis would share his conquest before doing away with her?"

Kin grinned and paused as if considering the idea, turning his vision away again to appear in thought. He humored the image of Ormon's bleeding body, crumpled on the ground before him.

With Ormon dead, Amarie would be safe.

However, her safety would be temporary if another could trace a shard to her. It would be better if they believed her dead by Kin's hands, using Ormon to spread the tale. Kin would give his master the shard, continuing the story of Amarie's death. Then, a new task would come, and he could focus on avoiding it to allow himself a life with Amarie.

"I've never been good at sharing my playthings. So, I suggest you find your own. You've entered this chase too late. Both prey and prize are mine." Kin pushed from the tree he leaned on, advancing towards Ormon.

"Oh, come now. Let one so young learn from one so long in service? We can both enjoy tonight."

"No." Kin stood his ground.

I need to get rid of him before I just kill him.

The anger rising in him allowed an instant of clarity to reach into the shadows at Ormon's back.

Kin plunged into the grim waters of the Art, drawing at the life deep within the hibernating oaks. The shadows slid along Ormon's body, wrapping like snakes around his limbs.

Ormon narrowed his eyes but didn't react.

Kin beckoned, urging action from the dark, dancing vines.

They jumped to Ormon's throat, the thrill of power echoing within him.

"You should remember professional courtesy." Kin clenched his hand into a fist. The tendrils on Ormon's neck tightened, and he gasped for breath before Kin's hand relaxed, and the shadows slid away. "Or I may forget mine."

Ormon took a step back, yielding to the more powerful Shade. With cynical eyes, he gave a swift nod. His jaw compressed, and his fingers twitched daringly near his side. "Fine." He gave a deep, mocking bow. "Always a pleasure, Kinronsilis."

The Shade disappeared, slipping into the shadows at his feet like a viper into water.

Kin's fingernails bit into his palm as he made a tight fist. Anger seethed, threatening to act on its own accord within his connection to the Art.

He let his mind drift to Amarie, imagining her smile, and it drenched his fury.

With a slow inhale, the rotten scent of death stronger than before, he turned to return to camp. His boots shuffled over the line separating the life of the forest from the Shade's destruction. He walked away, back towards the warmth of the fire and Amarie.

Amarie followed him. She had no desire to sit alone by the fire after Kin's blatant lie.

Creeping behind a wide oak, out of the moonlight and out of sight, Amarie halted when an unfamiliar voice spoke of enjoying a woman's resistance.

Kin stood with his back to her, leaning against a tree.

She waited for him to berate the stranger, but his voice came in a sinister response. "I've always found greater pleasure in making her desire me, then watching her realization as I take her and then her life."

Amarie swallowed, her heart quickening its pace.

He can't mean that.

"You mean to kill her when you're done? Then perhaps the great Kinronsilis would share his conquest before doing away with her?" The man's voice made her shudder.

Kin turned in her direction, and she jerked behind the tree, pressing her back against the bark. She closed her eyes, wishing for it to be a nightmare.

"I've never been good at sharing my playthings. So, I suggest you find your own. You've entered this chase too late. Both prey and prize are mine." Kin sounded angry, but it did nothing to quell her nausea.

I can't listen to this anymore.

Amarie darted into the shadows, returning to their camp. She eyed the crossbow by her saddlebags, controlling the urge to take it into the forest and hunt Kin's vile friend.

Her mind whirled, and she tried to calm her twisting stomach, but the words kept rattling around in her head.

After making bold statements about children... Does he plan to kill me?

She recounted each moment with him to decipher what was real.

The fire crackled under her glare, igniting cobalt flames within the orange.

Her fists tightened, matching azure sparks dancing around her knuckles.

Closing her eyes, she steadied her breathing. The colors of the fire through her eyelids shifted back to warm ambers.

Kin's footsteps crunched on the forest floor behind her and her gaze darted to her hands, ensuring the blue had vanished from them, too. At least he sounded like he was alone.

Feet dragging more than usual, he entered their camp. "Sorry about that. The hair on my neck was driving me crazy." His voice had a softness to it, so unlike what she heard in the oak grove.

Amarie refused to turn around. "Do you feel better now?" She held back the anger, trying to calm herself instead of immediately lashing out.

Maybe he'll tell me.

"Much." After a brief pause, Kin continued. "Though I have to admit, my face feels rather naked."

An attempt at humor.

The coil in her stomach tightened, and her distaste only grew.

She turned and glowered at him.

Kin's brow furrowed. "Everything all right?"

Her gaze moved from his eyes to his neck, where a multitude of tiny pieces of cut hair surely still irritated his skin, then back to meet his gaze. "It doesn't look like you did a very good job. Perhaps you became distracted with discussing your favorite ways to treat women?" Her arms crossed in front of her, muscles shaking with energy begging to be let loose.

Kin's eyes darkened, his expression difficult to read. His lips pursed, and he froze six feet away. "You followed me?" He sighed, lifting a hand to his head and pushing it through his hair. "Amarie... What did you see?"

"You... Talking to your friend. You can't walk away from me mid-conversation with a shit explanation and expect me not to follow you. You're supposed to be the one I can trust." She stood her ground, refusing her instinct to flee from him.

"I wish the trust you claim to feel would have encouraged you to stay like I told you to," Kin snapped.

Amarie lifted her chin. "Like you *told* me to? I'm not yours to command."

"I'm trying to protect you!"

"You're doing a fucking fantastic job." Amarie's hand shook as she ran it over her hair. "So which one am I? Your prize or your prey? What else have you lied to me about?"

Kin growled, pulling at his hair as he took a step back. "You're right, I lied. But only about going to clean up. I didn't mean one word of what I said in that conversation."

"You weren't even going to tell me, were you? Do you think me a fool? Those things you said... about women... about me!"

"Amarie, I said the things I had to say. I didn't mean any of it. I hoped to spare you."

She gaped at him. "Tell me you've never done that." Her mind felt so blurry, she could hardly comprehend him standing in front of her.

"Amarie." Kin's tone softened. "I've never taken a woman against her will. I never would. *Please* trust me in that."

She shook her head again before her gaze hardened. "Who was that man?"

A grossly familiar hesitation overtook Kin. He avoided making eye contact again. "Someone dangerous. He means you harm and I'm trying to stop that from happening."

More vague answers.

"And how do you know? How do you know he's dangerous?" She couldn't stop the questions from flying from her mouth. "Has he been following us? Me? None of this makes any bloody sense." She glared, watching him grow tenser with each question. Her tongue lashed the last question. "Is your goal to see me dead, Kin?"

"No. Never." Kin took a step forward, but stopped, meeting her eyes. "I want to protect you and keep you safe. Every word I uttered was intended to do just that. Ormon is not my friend, but I know his kind." His hands gripped into fists, eyes moving to the flames of the dying fire between them. "I don't know how long he's been following us, but he set his sights on you. I had to show him his presence wasn't welcome and use him as a tool to dissuade others who may follow."

Others.

The thought made her stomach lurch.

"Why does he know you?"

"His knowledge of me doesn't matter as much as his awareness of you. He knows you have a Berylian Key shard. It's what he wants."

"Just like you. Someone must really want to *study* it."

His gaze came back to hers with a shadowed look. "I've tried to shield you from the darkness I'm capable of." Kin dared another step forward. "But know, please, each word from my lips tonight made me want to—"

"At least you're equally disgusted with yourself." Amarie cut him off. "Some darkness you shouldn't be capable of. There should be a line in your head you will not cross. You're incapable of being honest with me."

"There *is* a line, and it's drawn between speaking and doing." Kin sighed, bringing his voice back down to a level just for them. "You don't know the monster that man is. If I hadn't responded the way I did, he never would have left. He'd still be watching you and thinking of doing those hideous things to you himself. And *that* is the truth."

"So he's the monster, not you? How can you associate with a man like that and not think of yourself as similar? I'd rather *he* thinks those things, hells, even tries those things. It would give me the opportunity to kill him myself. Better than hearing it from your mouth. The line isn't between saying and doing, it's not that simple. Only a fool waits idly by for a man to follow through on a threat."

"I wanted to kill him myself. Like the monster you so aptly describe me as. But if Ormon were dead, another would eventually find you, still looking for the shard he believed you to have. If he traced it to you, another will. But if Ormon believes I've already taken it and killed you, word will spread, and you'll be safe."

"Another what?" Amarie tilted her head, dropping her voice to a whisper.

Kin stared at her, tight-lipped and speechless.

She ground her teeth. "I don't need you pulling strings behind a curtain, dictating how my life unfolds. *My* life, not yours. I can take care of myself. Keep your half-truths. I don't want them."

A growl rumbled from Kin's chest. "Next time I'll just ask Ormon to patiently wait for me to consult you first how to best handle the threat." Sarcasm tainted his tone, and he opened his mouth to speak more, but Amarie cut him off.

"Don't you dare patronize me. You choose the company you keep. That's not what I said, and you know it. If I'm to choose between being—"

"I made a decision, and while I regret the things I said, I don't regret the intention behind them."

"Too much evil is justified with the excuse of good intentions."

Kin followed her words with silence and a locked jaw. Moving to the bedroll they usually shared, he snatched his cloak. "We both need time to calm down." He crossed to the edge of the clearing. "I'll sleep over here, if I may have your permission?" Without waiting for a response, he plopped down and leaned against a wide tree trunk. Pulling his cloak over himself like a blanket, he apparently planned to sleep fully clothed and in his boots.

"As if you give a shit what I think." Amarie crossed the camp and swung up onto a bareback Viento. Without another word, she nudged him off, away from their camp and into a fast canter.

Her body shook, limbs numb. The argument with Kin rocked her more than any disagreement in her life. Her mind warred between what she'd heard and his partial explanations.

Amarie rode up the stream, finding comfort in the beat of Viento's hooves and breath. Her thoughts cooled, but the knot in her stomach wouldn't budge. She couldn't help but feel Kin had been out of line without reason.

His words haunted the back of her mind.

A part of her felt he was trying to tell her the truth, and his vulgar words were to protect her. But he left out crucial details.

Who is he worried will come after me? Why was he worried about what I saw instead of what I heard?

Bringing Viento to a halt near the crest of a hill, Amarie looked over the tops of oak trees.

"Do you think he was really trying to protect me?" Amarie stroked her horse's neck, and he shook his mane. "I'm not used to this. What if I rely on him, and then..."

Viento turned from the view without her guidance, and she let him walk to a patch of grass.

"How can you eat at a time like this?" Amarie frowned, but a chuckle came to her chest as he munched on the green shoots.

Sighing, she shook her head.

It doesn't matter who he protects me from. What matters is that he's protecting me at all.

"And I bit his head off for it," she grumbled.

Once her horse lost interest in his snack, she guided him back around towards camp.

Dismounting, she patted Viento's neck and quietly made her way to their bedroll. She removed her boots, putting them to the side, and unlaced her vest. She glanced at Kin, though she could hardly see him by the dying embers of their fire.

He appeared to be asleep, still sitting at the base of the tree, his cloak camouflage among the shadows.

Sighing, she left the rest of her clothes on and laid down, pulling the single warm blanket over herself. Staring up at the sky glittering with stars, her mind took her down a familiar road.

It's simpler to be alone.

It would be the easier path, rather than enduring arguments like the one that night.

The thought left her heart hollow.

Amarie turned her head just enough to let her gaze fall on the man who meant so much to her, sleeping against the tree.

Tell me the truth one day, will you?

She missed the warmth of him as she drifted off to sleep, but found solace in the knowledge he was close.

Only a brief time passed before the bedroll next to her flexed under Kin's weight. He hovered over her as he sometimes did when they were affectionate, softening her heart.

Amarie rolled onto her back and opened her eyes.

A gaunt face, shadowed by the rim of a hood, leered down at her.

She gasped.

Ormon.

The pale light of the moon cast sharp definition on his skeletal face.

Before she could shout, his hand shot from the darkness and covered her mouth. Slithering vines of shadow ensnared her wrists and pulled them over her head.

Amarie winced as the deathly cold tendrils seared her skin. Craning her neck to stare at the manifestation of the Art, her eyes widened.

The shadow twisted and controlled her movement in a way it shouldn't have been able to. Not with the Art.

The stench of decay hit her nose, and she gagged. Her mind flooded with memories of tales told to her as a child, of villains who sucked the life out of everything around them.

By the gods. He's a Shade.

"Shhhh." Ormon leaned over her. His cloak fell, suffocating across her body. His free hand traced the bottom of her shirt and slid like ice on her skin.

She wanted to retch. Her power surged towards the surface. But that could only be a last resort.

Amarie struggled and, with more strength than she naturally had, she yanked her right hand free of the corrosive grasp. It darted to her thigh in the same instant she bit down on Ormon's hand as hard as she could.

The Shade reeled back from her bite with a curse before his other hand closed on the wrist reaching for the knife. He stilled the blade before she could sink it into his midsection.

She refused to drop it, struggling against his strength as he prevented the sharp point from meeting its target.

Crying out in frustration, Amarie kicked at his groin. Before she could land the blow, he shifted to pin her hips and legs between his knees.

"Get off me!" The energy within her begged to assault the scourge above her.

"Now, now." Ormon's voice curled with the shadows forcing Amarie's arm back, knife and all. They slammed her fist against the frosted forest floor, writhing against her skin, and the blade fell from her hand.

"I swear to the gods, I *will* kill you, you pathetic, impotent—" She couldn't finish her insult before the back of his hand collided with the side of her face. The web of pain expanded as his fingers dug into her jaw and wrenched her head back to him.

He tutted. "That's no way for a lady to behave." His fingers danced across her lowest rib, before the horrible sensation vanished.

Confusion clouded Ormon's eyes in the breath before his entire body folded against itself. An unseen force flung him across the campsite, freeing Amarie from his weight. He collided with the base of a pine tree, rattling the branches all the way up.

Amarie sat up in a rush, heaving a breath as she tried to take in the scene before her.

Shadow tendrils slipped away, shifting to form a protective barrier in front of her. Other black-purple shapes roiled across the forest floor after her attacker, swelling to embrace his chest and tear his cloak. He struggled to rip the material from his body to avoid being trapped.

Kin's broad form rose from the shade of where he'd slept. With silent booted feet, he crossed the pine-needle-strewn ground to where Ormon struggled. Kin's light-blue eyes shone, flicking towards Amarie with a look of concern.

She only returned his gaze, mouth agape in shock.

Kin's hand, clawed at his side, twitched with the flow of energy he manipulated. The scent of death doubled, and she lifted the back of her hand to her mouth.

He's one, too.

The realization tore through her like a lightning strike, and a rush of fear filled her chest.

Ormon ripped free of his cloak, and with it, the shadows holding him. His hand thrust to the falchion at his side with a roar of anger. His sunken eyes focused entirely on Kin. Relying on the length of his arms and his strength, Ormon lunged at his fellow Shade.

Amarie found the hilt of her dagger. She stood, bare feet planted among the frozen grass next to her bedroll. Her arm pulled back with an inhale to aim before her hand loosed the dagger towards Ormon's back. Her aim struck true beside his left shoulder blade.

Ormon's shoulder dropped with a scream of agony, his steps faltering.

Kin slid swiftly to one side, a foot catching his enemy's ankle on his injured side. With the forward momentum, Kin reached around to pull hard on Ormon's armed hand, rotating it with a crunch and forcing release of the falchion. The weapon thunked to the ground as Kin's full weight descended on Ormon's back.

Ormon's body collided with the rough bark of the pine, his neck snapping back, before falling to the floor with Kin on top of him.

Amarie stepped to her pack, retrieving the crossbow and loading a bolt. Her breath came in frosty clouds from her lips, her bare feet numb. The weapon lifted in her arms, she took aim at Ormon.

Kin's left hand gripped the handle of her dagger, twisted it, and then tore it free of Ormon's flesh. The handle spun within Kin's fingers before he pressed it against the base of the man's skull. It drew a thin line of blood as Ormon tried to scream, muffled against the forest floor.

Kin centered his weight on his knee, pressed against Ormon's shattered wrist, pinning it to the middle of his spine. Every muscle of Kin's body was taut, holding the larger man in place.

Ormon's body went still, his free hand lifting as if surrendering to his better.

Kin's anger rumbled deep in his chest as the man stilled. He pushed the blade against the back of Ormon's neck. "That was a mistake, Ormon."

Amarie approached, holding the crossbow steady and stopping a few yards away.

Kin's eyes moved from his opponent to Amarie.

A whirl of Ormon's power suddenly devoured the bush beside her. It withered before her eyes, branches curling into a dried husk as the energy coalesced into a rise of shadow beneath Kin's knee.

Ormon's body melted into the depths of black, vanishing impossibly into the flat darkness of shadow.

Her eyes widened, and she let the bolt fly. It sank into the frigid ground, passing through the shadow. She crouched to her pack to reload, tucking a third bolt under her arm.

Another tendril of shadow snapped at the hilt of the dagger, ripping it free of Kin's fingers as he struggled to regain his balance.

A roar reverberated from Kin as he leaned forward, tearing into the ground. Another surge of energy rustled through the wind. It felt different from the one Ormon conjured, more refined. The shadows danced on the forest floor like flames of a wicked fire, moving among the beams of moonlight in ways shadow was never meant to.

The darkness that was Ormon drifted away, fleeing towards the deeper parts of the pine forest before rattling to a sudden stop.

Power surged through Kin, balled within his fingertips. He stood, tensing his hand to control the energies as Amarie watched with her mouth agape.

This can't be true.

The writhing shadow bubbled into a rising boil which became Ormon's cloak and form, his shoulder bloodstained. His broken wrist nestled against his abdomen. Pale hands played in the depths of his cloak on the hilt of Amarie's dagger, debating its purpose.

"Come now." Ormon's voice rippled through the shadows as they flecked away like snow in a breeze. "What happened to professional courtesy?"

"You don't deserve to breathe," Kin snarled. "You have earned no courtesy."

An evil smile crept across Ormon's face. "Oh, Kin." He clicked his tongue. "I'd have thought you'd know better than to fail *him*." His gaze moved from Kin to Amarie, his eyes as dark as the shadow he'd been. His skeletal face beamed at Kin's silence. "Does she know? Does she know what you are, and what you've done? The time you—"

With aim as true as her intent, a bolt sank deep into Ormon's throat, protruding out the other side.

His voice gurgled to a halt, blood flowing into his windpipe and preventing the completion of his sentence.

Reloading the crossbow, her aim stayed on the wavering form of the man who'd climbed over her, touched her, disgusted, and revolted her. The man who would surely have done it to another, and most certainly had before.

Amarie's heart pounded in her ears like a drum.

His body collapsed to the ground, life draining from him.

The smell of blood weighed thick with the decay of the surrounding forest. Darkness around the body rippled with a gesture from Kin's outstretched hand, enveloping the corpse and lapping at the blood on the ground. He tugged at a stream of energy, engulfing the body in a pool of hungry shadow.

His arm shook as he lowered his hand, crouching to pluck her dagger from the ground.

Amarie stepped back, redirecting her aim at Kin and holding the crossbow steady.

He froze, eyes shining in the moonlight as he lifted his hands, dropping the blade back to the ground. "Whoa, Amarie. Still me."

Amarie's breath heaved, hands shaking. "You're a Shade."

Kin's eyes darkened, jaw twitching. "Yes." He swallowed, eyes darting to the crossbow then back to her. "But I won't hurt you. I never will."

Rolling her lips together, she kept her trigger finger to the side. Her face still burned where Ormon had struck her, mirroring the pain at her wrists. "That's how you escaped the chains. This whole time. You're a fucking Shade..."

Kin winced, but slowly approached, watching her. "Yes." He kept his eyes on hers. He didn't step out of the crossbow's path, instead just getting closer to it. "Did he hurt you?"

Amarie lowered the crossbow enough to look at him without the sights. "Nothing permanent," she whispered, searching his steel-blue eyes.

He still protected me, regardless of what he is.

After a moment, she relaxed her arm and let the weapon hang at her side. All the unspoken things between them, the memories of their fight only hours before, prevented her from going to him.

Kin stepped beside her, his soft hands closing over hers on the crossbow to take it from her. Shifting it away from her, he slipped his hand into hers, squeezing. "You sure?"

Amarie touched her face with her free hand. "It was just a hit." The burns on her wrist stole her attention, and she furrowed her brow. "And... whatever his shadows did to my skin."

Kin's thumb grazed the strip of tender flesh, and she flinched but didn't pull away as he lifted her hands. "I'll bandage them."

Her adrenaline faded, and she exhaled, collapsing forward into Kin's chest.

He wrapped his arms around her, drawing her into him as his lips pressed to her forehead. They lingered as he heaved a breath.

Shades are real. And Kin is one of them.

Her eyes slid closed, comfort washing over her, and she gripped his waist in response. She felt safe in his arms, despite every instinct telling her to fear the power he had.

"You didn't have to be the one to kill him." Kin leaned his head against hers. "I could have."

"I know. But that darkness was mine."

Kin loosened his grip and drew his head back to look into her eyes. His jaw flexed, and he nodded.

Her hands lingered on his sides as he stood before her.

He leaned his head forward against hers, closing his eyes. His breath flowed against her lips, relief in his gradual exhales. "I'm sorry. It's not an easy path. But, I'm grateful we found each other. Perhaps we can try to find another path, together."

Amarie's fingers found the back of his neck, and her hand moved to touch his hair. She hated arguing with him. "I felt the bedroll move, and I thought it was you."

"It should have been me. I should have been beside you. If I had been, he might not have even tried. I put you in danger."

"If he'd seen you, he would have known your previous words were lies. While I don't know what that would have meant, I can guess it wouldn't have been good. You still should have been next to me. Our fight should never have gone so far." She searched his face, looking for any sign of the previous anger between them.

He nodded again, his face grim. "I'm sorry."

"Me too." Her heart finally beat at a normal pace. "Thank you. For being here. For what you did."

His eyes opened, brows knitting together, and his hand slid around her waist. "Amarie." He said her name slowly, and she bit her bottom lip at his tone. "You don't need to thank me. I'll always do whatever is necessary to keep you safe."

I believe you.

"I'm sorry I aimed the crossbow at you." Amarie glanced down at the weapon and shuddered, leaning on Kin again.

"Considering what I am, I don't blame you." He pressed his lips into a kiss on top of her head.

Amarie cringed, glad he couldn't see her face. "Maybe. But I forgot *who* you are, and that's so much more important." She looked up at him. "Your Art doesn't define you."

Lifting her chin, Kin brought his mouth to hers, kissing her. It grew with each gradual movement of their lips, until she could hardly breathe and he pulled away. "I don't deserve you." He touched her jaw, his voice taking on a more serious tone. "We need to leave here, though, and should get as far away as possible."

Amarie nodded, understanding and not understanding at the same time.

It only took them a short time to pack their camp, call Viento, and get moving.

Carrying them both, Viento ran hard, with Amarie providing him extra strength. She wasn't sure how much Kin was aware of the energy transfer when it occurred between her and her horse, since he never mentioned it. But with the power she'd witnessed him use, there was little chance he hadn't noticed.

They continued towards Kin's parents' estate, riding through the remaining night.

When Amarie brought Viento to a stop, hints of early morning daylight peeked through the branches of the trees. The sky brightened with vibrant oranges and pinks, spreading across the rolling rain clouds encroaching from the west.

Frost clung to the shrubs in the small meadow, and curling fog billowed from Viento's flared nostrils as he caught his breath. His ribs heaved, body shifting anxiously at the dissipation of her power.

Slender birch trees lined the clearing. Their bark glowed with the colors of dawn.

Looking at Kin as he dismounted from Viento, she smiled.

I don't care about his shadows.

Amarie's boots touched the ground not long after his, and she pulled her cloak tighter to keep out the cool air still freezing their breath. Her eyes strayed from Viento grazing to find Kin watching her. Her heart jumped, his steel-blue eyes boring into her soul.

"I would've thought the prospect of hearing all about me and what I've done would have stilled your bolt, rather than encouraged it loose." Kin's tone came softer than she expected. The sky reflected in his eyes, and it only added to the spell he cast on her.

"Don't be fooled. I want to know everything about you... but I want to hear it from you. Your secrets are yours to tell, not your enemy's."

The meadow was so still and calm, she feared he'd hear her thoughts.

He smiled. "I definitely don't deserve you."

Amarie gravitated closer, slipping her hands over his chest, and bringing her arms to wrap around his neck.

The comfort of his embrace banished all the vulnerability Ormon might have caused. He'd shown her his power, which was more than she could offer him.

As she moved closer, his breath hitched against her lips, his chest pausing mid-breath.

She lifted her chin and brushed her lips against his jaw. "You underestimate your worth, Kinronsilis."

Chapter 17

Her lips, pressing against his bare chin, sent a shiver through Kin. The ember in his soul, which hadn't glimmered in weeks, woke at her touch.

"Either that, or you grossly overestimate it." It took everything within him not to pull her mouth to his. His fingers entangled at the base of her hair.

Thoughts of the night's events permeated his bliss, forcing him to consider if his master could sense the death of his Shade.

Ormon's body would re-emerge when the sun rose, banishing the shadows from the forest floor and, with it, the short-lived grave.

If he discovers my involvement, death would be merciful.

In hindsight, it was good Amarie was the one to kill him with the crossbow. It would lead to fewer questions than if Kin's use of the Art was detectable in Ormon's death.

While riding through the night, Kin had focused on the energies flowing from Amarie into her horse. He'd dismissed it as being her at first, because she needed the Berylian Key shard to channel it in Lungaz. Kin had assumed she tapped into the rumored power of the crystals without needing to assemble them. He might have continued to believe it, too, if she hadn't used the power to speed their departure from the oak grove. Without the presence of the shard, he recognized the flow of energy came from Amarie herself.

Her hiding aura is the most refined I've ever seen.

He could do it for himself when the occasion arose. But hers was constant. It never waned.

How much power can she possibly have to make it necessary to erect a permanent wall?

The slow shake of Amarie's head encouraged Kin's focus back to her. "Not a chance." Moving her face a little farther from his, she left the anticipation of a kiss hanging between them. "No one has ever had my back the way you do. I've been alone most of my life." Her voice sounded raw as her perfectly bow-shaped lips formed each word. "You became a partner the moment I met you. You defend me with ferocity and yet... you're kind to me. Gentle. I don't care what you've done in the past, because to me, you've been nothing but what I need." Her hand touched his face. "What I want."

The growing ember burst into an inferno within him, his entire being aching.

"With all my secrets, I fear I don't deserve to be yours. My gentleness with you isn't enough to make up for my sins. For being what I am." He caressed down the back of her neck, considering all Amarie had changed in him.

"I don't care what you are." Amarie's gaze flickered back and forth between his eyes.

"But you should."

Her eyebrows twitched. "It would be incredibly hypocritical of me."

Hypocritical? Her secrets couldn't be worse than mine.

Kin tilted his head. "You make it sound so simple to trust a Shade." He whispered the last word, his heart thudding in his ears and nearly drowning out the admission he'd never once spoken aloud.

Amarie leaned closer, breathless. "Isn't it?"

His mouth collided with hers, passionate. A kiss that had waited too long, lips parting simultaneously to plunge into each other's affection. Her sharp inhale only encouraged him, and he pulled her body tight against his. He became unaware of the cool air, heated by the desire growing between them.

Her nails dragged along his scalp. All the emotions he felt for her, every overwhelming ounce, threatened to take over his actions.

She accepted him, so blindly, in a way no one else ever had, despite all she'd seen.

Their tongues met, the taste of her having a dizzying effect. His mind and heart buzzed together. No doubt tainted his mind. He needed her. No limits existed for what he would do for her. A tangle of anxiousness and desire pressed against Kin's gut as his kisses grew more needy for her affection.

Her tongue ran along his lower lip while her hand slipped beneath his shirt.

Kin gasped and broke the kiss. A chill rush came between them with vapors of winter air. His mind needed to still for a moment, a breath to think. He touched her jaw, focusing on nothing but her.

A look of curiosity played on her face, her mouth slightly parted as she waited for him to speak.

Kin's soul whirled in discord, seeking to rediscover then finding the same thing every time.

This is what I've wanted all along.

"I love you."

Amarie's eyes widened, but he was too eager to show her his affections before she could respond. His fingers brought her chin up just enough for him to renew the kisses, banishing the frigid air again.

Her mouth responded affectionately, but her body tensed. She yanked away a moment later with a look of panic. With wide eyes, she gasped, letting go of him and backing up. "Gods. No."

In that same striking moment of cold, another draft surrounded Kinronsilis so suddenly it knocked all breath from his lungs. It wasn't a physical force, but the strength of it felt as if it should have been. The fabric of the Art around him swelled, setting every fiber of his soul alight.

He fell into an ocean of power, wrapped within its tides. Pulled by an irresistible current to where everything within him was awash in infinite strength. An energy composed it with more magnitude than he'd ever felt before. It coursed through him like strikes of lightning and thunder that left all his senses reeling.

Kin tried to remember how to breathe.

For a horrible, beautiful moment, there was no shore in sight. The warm sea banished the cold of the winter air he was only vaguely aware of, extinguishing the flame within him from Amarie's affections. He recognized the pressure of the pulse. But previously, it had been in the form of a jagged pendant hanging around his neck.

A sudden breath came with stark intensity. An all-enveloping sensation stirred against his own access to the Art, revealing to him the exact depth of Amarie's ability.

Her fathomless connection.

A daring swirl of crystal pink and purple mixed with the blue of her irises, distraught terror within.

He'd hoped to never see her fear directed at him.

Kin's stomach dropped, and he took a step back as his body instinctively recoiled from the massive source of power. All his thoughts whirled in a haze, clouded by the tidal wave of energy and the lingering passion clinging to his lips.

Amarie stepped back again, her expression refusing to fade. Her breath came fast.

She didn't mean for this to happen.

It all made sense now, except perhaps why she wanted the shards.

She doesn't need them.

Her feet abruptly moved, but not in the direction he would have chosen. His heart thudded harder as he watched her sprint to her horse and mount. Her actions were too swift for him to form words of protest, and before he knew it, the sound of hooves echoed in his ears.

Nymaera's breath. Her secret is so much more than mine.

Amarie's energy faded as Viento galloped towards the tree line.

The noise banished the remnants of the wave on his senses, dismissing the shock.

"Amarie." Her name came as a whisper as he tried to remember how to speak.

The winter air sent a shiver down his spine.

"Wait!" The shout came too late. She wouldn't hear.

Viento's black form disappeared into the densely packed birch wood.

Kin's chest grew heavy and his stomach rolled as he stared in the direction she'd vanished. The damnable legend he chased had dominated his life for the last year. He'd been sent to retrieve a shard and, instead, found the entire Berylian Key.

No rock held the infinite power, but a living, breathing person.

Amarie.

How is this even possible?

The pounding hooves faded, taking his happiness and the answers he needed with them.

His energy still buzzed from mingling with Amarie's, invigorated by her. The connection he sought for his Art came easily while surrounded by forest life, stealing it to feed his change. He faded down into the birch shadows cast by the rising sun.

Fueled by adrenaline, any doubt about manipulating his shape vanished.

His power shifted rapidly to gobble more, forcing feathers and beak to appear. This time, the change felt no more difficult than a step into the shadows.

Clawed black feet ripped at the grass. Wings beat against the morning air as the raven rose above the trees.

A decision loomed over Kin as he turned his wings into the wind. He needed to consider the two beings in his life who held his loyalty.

One by choice. The other by force.

He should turn towards his master, run to him with news of the Berylian Key. He should inform him of the frivolity of his search for the shards. Kin would receive a greater connection to the shadows and his master's well of power in exchange. And forgiveness if his master realized his involvement in Ormon's death.

Greater power. What he always thought he wanted, seeking it out from his master in exchange for a part of his soul. The corruption to the rest of it came through the completion of his required tasks. But gaining the power had been a means to an end. He wanted the love of a woman.

I don't deserve forgiveness.

He thought of all the things Amarie had said to him. The assurances of forgiveness for his past wrongdoings. Evaluating the twisty path he'd become lost within, Kin had started it all to be worthy of love.

Perhaps Amarie can help me find redemption.

His head twisted in the wind, in the direction she fled.

With Amarie rested the possibility of a different life. He yearned to follow her and tell her how much he needed her. Profess how he would protect her secret just as fiercely as he protected her from Ormon.

He'd betray everything he believed about himself for a chance with her. A chance for the family he'd given up hope on.

Bitter air sliced through the wings given to him by his master as he turned defiantly against the wind. They beat down beside his body, plunging him forward.

Kin caught up to Amarie quickly.

Viento would need a break soon, after riding through most of the night with both of them. She would never push her beloved horse too hard.

Just be patient.

He stayed behind her, not wanting her to know he followed, in case she misunderstood his pursuit.

She continued south as rain pattered against his feathers, gliding along the Dykul mountain range. She raced past the village which might have offered her respite and chose an open meadow roughly twenty yards across. It nestled against the side of a small lake with a babbling stream. Birch trees grew thicker in this part of the forest, prohibiting travel anywhere but on the worn hunting trails and paths.

As he looped a lazy circle above her, she dismounted and untacked Viento, the drizzling rain collecting on her cloak's hood.

Her subsequent movements were slow and unfocused. She faced

the lake before approaching the water's rocky edge onto a flat stone as wide as she was tall. Sitting with her legs bent in front of her, Amarie pulled her cloak tight against the freezing rain. Motionless, she stared at the still water.

Consecutive circles in the air brought Kin lower towards the meadow, wings brushing against the tips of the tree's branches as he landed in the soaked grass. His beaked head spun to look at Amarie's back, assuring she hadn't noticed his descent.

A breeze ruffled the fur over her shoulders, speckled with raindrops.

Kin drew power from the dense trees behind him. Taking as little as he could from the plant life, he surrounded himself with the embrace of shadow. The raven form dissipated easier than before, flaking into the mist as a foot fall brought him back.

Tugging on a lock of his hair, he ran a hand through to brush the water from his scalp as the rain stopped. The expansive energy no longer hovered in the air around her, and he strode closer.

He paused five feet away. "Amarie?" He pushed all of his concern and love for her into the syllables of her name, hoping she'd recognize it.

She instantaneously scrambled to find her footing as she rose, whirling to face him. Her wide eyes darted to her horse before looking back at him.

He lifted his hands. "Wait. Don't run. Please."

Amarie stared at him, her back to the lake. A serene background for her lovely form, which he appreciated along with her strength.

The realization of her power only enhanced the love he had for her. His original attraction came from his observation of her resilience. All that time she kept her power hidden and never used it.

How isolating keeping such a secret must feel...

Amarie found her voice a moment later. "You followed me..." Her words were softer than he expected and lacked hostility.

"What else should I have done? Nothing's changed, even if you think it has. This doesn't change the way I feel about you."

She moved one foot back, her toe coming to the edge of the stone overlooking the lake. "What about how you feel about the shards?"

Kin shook his head. "I don't care about the shards. I care about you. I'm on your side."

Fear tainted her eyes again. "You shouldn't have followed. I can't protect you from it. I meant it when I said I posed a threat to you. You shouldn't be here."

She's not afraid of me, but for me.

The truth of her concern left his heart aching. Sullenness in her eyes encouraged him to dare a step forward, to see if she would recoil. When she didn't, he took another and held out a hand to her.

"I'm good at doing things I shouldn't." He hoped the humor would draw a reaction from her. Anything. "You don't need to protect me. I'm not afraid of you. I know you wouldn't hurt me." He watched her gaze shift to his hand and linger there.

Her hand moved, but her intention faltered, and her motion paused as she looked at him again. "How can you not fear me? Knowing what I am..."

"I know *who* you are. We're not defined by our Art, right? I'd be a hypocrite otherwise."

The corner of her mouth twitched. "You're the only one who knows, Kin." Her eyes begged something of him. Her hand suspended partway to his.

The confirmation of his suspicion made his whole body thrum at the knowledge he held. He suddenly understood why she ran, the first time and this time, and what she might have been afraid of.

And with what I am...

"I'll remain the only one." He took another small step and lifted his hand closer to hers. "I'll do whatever is necessary to protect you. This doesn't change that, just as it doesn't change that I love you."

Her jaw flexed before her hand touched his.

He urged her closer, shoulders finally relaxing, and stepped into her.

Amarie moved to him. Her gaze never left his, but it softened, the fear within ebbing away. She released his hand when she was close enough to touch his face. After only a brief pause, she closed the distance between them with a hard kiss.

It released all the tension Kin hadn't realized was building within him. He responded to the feel of her lips as if the previous kiss had never ended. Nothing could make him regret his decision.

Kin drew her to him, his palm pressed against her lower back beneath her damp cloak. The feel of her tongue on his lips, and the heat of her breath stirred an immediate reaction from his body, yearning for her.

She fit perfectly within his arms as the kisses deepened, expressing the need they each had. The warmth of her expansive energy rose to encompass him once again. It banished the cold of their wet clothing, and the shock left him excited rather than afraid. He sensed the moment she released it, allowing him to join her within her hiding aura.

The willingness she showed encouraged him to let his own power mingle with hers. The dance ensuing between them felt primal. Each action felt powerful enough to move mountains. He became hyper-aware of each shift of her body and every delicate sound escaping her lips.

Her skin smelled sweet from the rain as he breathed her in through his nose. His hand slid along the top of her breeches, tugging at the hem of her shirt to seek her warmth beneath.

When she pushed his chest, he moved back, following her lead. His arm around her waist, he laid her back against the gentle incline of the grassy slope.

Amarie freed herself from her cloak, letting it provide a soft, warm barrier between her and the damp ground as he lowered his body to hers. She wrapped her legs around him, their hands seeking to do away with the layers blocking each other's touch.

The pulsing of her Art prohibited him from noticing the breeze as his bare chest received her caresses.

Kin tasted her, moving down her neck and playing along her

collarbone as his fingers deftly untied laces and unfastened buttons.

Amarie gasped when his tongue found the peak of her breast and he took her nipple between his teeth, tracing slow circles with his tongue. Her legs tightened around him as his hips flexed while he unbuttoned her breeches.

Taking the last pieces of clothing from her deliciously smooth body, he stroked her hips, his lips trailing down her abdomen and encouraging the arch of her back.

She tugged his belt, forcing him back up, and his mouth found hers in a heated exchange.

Amarie made quick work of his belt, loosening it just enough to push his breeches down. She used her feet to complete the task, leaving them both naked to each other in the soft light.

Pulling away just enough, Kin allowed himself a moment to take in the sight of her body. The morning sun glowed on her skin, and he traced his fingers along her hip.

Her violet eyes delved into him, cheeks flushed and lip pink beneath where she pinned it between her teeth.

The perfection made him slow and savor the feel of her. Leaning close, he freed her lower lip to nibble on it himself. Her soft inhale urged his hand lower.

She moved with his touch, legs entwined with his. His mouth traveled down her throat as his hand slid between her thighs.

The moan from her lips echoed in his ear, her hips rocking against his touch.

Kin listened to each change in the pitch of her voice as his fingers caressed, each gasp making his desire peak, colliding with his determination to take his time. He wasn't prepared for the jolt of pleasure when her hand closed around his hardness, enveloping his girth and stroking along his length. His groan vibrated against her neck.

Hot against him, her body arched as his hand rubbed the outside of her thigh. The play of her fingers returned to his torso and her lips bid his to return.

His hips tilted to meet hers, stilling to a pause as his sensitive tip dared trace her womanhood. Kisses grew deeper, his hands gripping her thighs.

He thrust into her, her tightness surrounding him, and gasped.

Amarie's brief cry vibrated against his lips, and her fingernails dug into his back, her other hand buried within his hair. Her hips rocked against him, urging a slow and steady withdrawal before he plunged into her again with fierce intent.

The slow rhythm grew, driven by the feel of her around him and the whimpers escaping her lips. He breathed heavily, forced to break the kiss, and a growl of desire rumbled in his chest.

Her heels squeezed into his thighs as she pulled him deeper. The moans trailing from her lips came quicker with each breath.

As Amarie tightened, it drove Kin harder. Pressing his forehead to hers, the heat of her breath touched his lips. His fingernails bit into her hips.

As they moved in tandem, her heart pounded against his chest, her whole body shaking. She held her breath and lifted her hips against him, the sensation of her around him growing taut.

She cried out, her voice shifting to a climactic pitch, tumbling him off the edge with her.

He groaned against her neck, his body quivering in ecstasy.

They rode the waves pulsating through them together.

Finding her lips again, pleasure's zenith wound down within him. The echo of her moans still rang in his ears as he kissed her.

She's everything.

Kin's eyes flickered to hers, temporarily entranced by the lush violets and pinks mixed with her natural blue. Adoration swelled in him as his hands moved back up the sides of her body, feeling her gentle curves.

Leaning in to kiss her bottom lip, his hand followed the line of her jaw, caressing as her breath finally slowed.

Amarie's lips parted, eyes searching his. "I love you, Kin. With everything I am."

Chapter 18

Two months later...
Winter, 2610 R.T.

Kin and Amarie finished the journey through the mountain pass before the snow overtook the roads, the icy breezes and storms on their heels.

Great white clusters of the encroaching season drifted down from the sky while they traversed a steep switchback road at the east side of the Dykul Mountains.

At its base, the meadows began. Though they were small compared to Olsa's great sea of grass and hills, the flatlands of Delkest held the densest collection of farming communities.

Snow turned to rain, and the chill in the air faded in the more temperate valley, where trees still clung to some of their leaves.

The Parnell estate was well known within the valley, with a reputation for their decadent wines.

Surprisingly, none of the residents in town recognized Kin, allowing him to play the part of a stranger. It made her wonder how long it had been since he visited.

As they rode together, Kin embraced her from behind. He leaned close, lips teasing near her exposed neck. She smelled the freshness of his clean hair, still damp from their morning bath together.

"My mother will think we're coming back from war." His playful tone almost masked his nerves as he nudged the hilt of her sword.

"At least you'll be clean shaven." Amarie shrugged. "Not looking like that wild man I broke out of prison."

"Let's leave that part of the story out for my mother's sake." Kin stiffened, drawing his face away as they exited a clump of trees around the main road.

The valley opened to expose the estate nestled among the hills. Its impressive stone-grey structure was larger than she expected, both east and west wings stretching off from the foyer at the center.

Dense rows of grapevines, hibernating in the winter cold, surrounded the structure. The vineyard met the front gate, wrought iron curved to imitate the vines beyond. It stood open, inviting guests down the gravel drive leading to the house.

Amarie's stomach knotted.

Kin had hinted he'd never brought a woman home before, which made Amarie wonder what her role would be in his story to his parents. She hoped he'd prepared her enough for what could happen. Would he tell his parents of their history together?

What will I learn of his?

The quality of Kin's clothes, which she'd thought a curiosity when they first met, now made sense seeing his family's wealth.

He'd have led a charmed life either way.

Whether it was the one he'd grown up in or the one he might have had as a prince.

She was grateful for that. For him.

Viento's hooves crunched on the drive.

Workers mulled about in the vineyards and near a structure buried into the side of a rising hill to the east. They rolled large oak casks deep into the open barn doors, storing the wine to age during the winter.

The front of the house was quiet, as if patiently awaiting their arrival.

Amarie turned to meet his gaze as his grip tightened on her waist. She placed her hand over Kin's. "Just a couple days. Then we can do and go wherever we want. The beach, maybe?" She kept her tone light, seeking the comfort of his confirmation as much as reassuring him.

She'd never had great luck staying in one place longer than a few days, so Kin's anxiousness to keep the visit short came as a relief.

He smiled, but it seemed forced. "Just a couple days." He took a deep inhale near her hair. "It's been a long time since I've been home."

As they approached the front door, a flicker of movement at the carriage-house entrance near the side of the mansion caught her eye.

A young boy, perhaps eight or nine, came forward in a well-trained manner to await his instruction. His eyes turned towards the doorway to the house.

Kin dismounted as the door to the lavish stone home opened. The wood caught on the frame and rattled before the door jerked open with a huff.

The girl who emerged was plain, but pretty, with her long blonde hair twisted back into a low bun on her neck. Wearing traditional-looking attire Amarie suspected to be of the estate's staff, the girl moved from the doorway, her hands folded in front of her.

Amarie stayed on Viento while she watched Kin approach the front stairs. She scanned the immediate area before returning her gaze to the girl who opened the door.

"Good afternoon." The girl smiled, in a nice enough way, though lacking genuine interest. "May I ask if you are expected, sir and madam?"

Kin unfastened the buckles of one of their saddlebags, removing it and placing it on the stone patio the girl stood on.

Annoyance rippled the girl's brow.

"I highly doubt it." Kin smiled as he continued to remove more of their bags from the saddle.

The girl shifted, clenching her hands tighter in front of her. "Then, perhaps I may have your name, sir, to announce your visit and inquire towards your welcome?" Her voice turned terse. She was much younger than Kin and even Amarie, perhaps only sixteen, yet her firm stance was respectable.

Viento picked up on the tension of his rider and sidestepped with a snort, prompting Amarie to pat him on the neck.

"Apologies." Kin sighed, turning towards the girl. "I—"

"Who is it, Niya?" A matronly sounding tone came through the doorway before the form it belonged to.

At the sight of the stout older woman, Kin straightened.

Lindora, Kin's mother, was strong in her appearance despite her apparent age. Her hair, fully grey, had been tied in a bun at the back of her head. Her glittering brown eyes went to Amarie first, before they continued to Kin.

Lindora's hands slapped over her mouth, but it didn't stop the high-pitched squeal of excitement which should have belonged to a far younger woman.

Niya spun towards her mistress, confused as Lindora skittered down the steps to the open arms of her son.

Far shorter than Kin, she pulled him down so she could kiss his face.

Kin offered small protesting sighs as he tried to stand straight again.

A knot grew in Amarie's throat at the reunion, and she busied herself dismounting Viento. Her black boots barely crunched on the gravel as she stood next to her horse.

"Missed you too, Ma." Kin smiled as he pulled himself away, putting firm hands on Lindora's shoulders to hold her still despite her apparent desire to leap for joy. He glanced at Amarie, but Lindora promptly turned his head back.

"Kinronsilis." She sighed happily, grabbing his arms. "Where have you been?"

Niya's eyes drifted to Amarie's, offering a warm smile perhaps meant to act as an apology for her rudeness, before she promptly averted her gaze. She stood aside, waiting for direction.

It took a few more pinches of Kin's cheek and arm as if Lindora needed confirmation she wasn't dreaming, but he offered no resistance to the prodding.

Gradually, his mother's eyes darted towards Amarie.

She could guess at the conclusions his mother was jumping to.

"Kin," Lindora cooed with a smile. "Are you going to introduce me?"

"Are you done fawning over me then?" He took a step back from his mother and turned to Amarie, inviting her to join them.

Amarie watched Kin, her gaze steady as she took a step forward and let go of the reins.

The stable boy, with a subtle gesture from Niya, hopped forward and snatched them. Viento protested, and it drew her attention back to him. A quick, Aueric word of reassurance calmed him enough to let the stable boy do his task.

Amarie walked over to where Kin stood, her eyes on his mother. She forced a smile.

"Ma, this is Amarie. Amarie, my mother, Lindora."

Lindora smiled brightly, her teeth peeking past her lips. Age lines appeared next to her mouth and eyes.

Before Amarie could extend her hand in greeting, Lindora pulled her into a hug. The lump in Amarie's throat returned, and a wince crossed her face during the embrace before she corrected her expression.

"So very nice to meet you," Lindora chirped cheerfully in Amarie's ear before she released her.

"And you as well."

"Welcome to our home. I hope you'll be staying for a while." She eyed Kin while she spoke.

He laughed and nodded. "A little while. But don't get too used to it, Ma. I have some things to ask you and Father about, but then Amarie and I will be leaving again."

Niya stepped forward. "May I take your things? I'll put yours in your old room, Master Kinronsilis, and shall I prepare a guest room for Miss Amarie?" She received an eager nod from Lindora.

"Please." Kin looked at Amarie and then his mother. "If the guest bedroom across the hall from mine is available, may she use that one, Ma?"

"Of course!" Lindora beamed, gesturing frantically to Niya. "You know firsthand that we rarely get visitors. My son included."

"I'm sorry. I know it's been a long time." A softness entered his gaze, the previous nerves no longer visible.

"So don't wait five years before you visit again." Lindora chided with a playful poke to his shoulder. "Please see to it, Niya. And Russel, take great care with their horse. Extra oats seem in order." She looked at the stable boy, who nodded.

Russel eyed Viento warily but then guided him towards the carriage house.

Amarie glanced over at her horse, who appeared to be behaving for the stable boy.

Niya walked ahead and carried their things up the stairs at the back of the foyer, following a second set from the landing towards the east wing of the house before disappearing into the hallway.

The main entrance foyer was large, surely intended for entertaining, with an unlit chandelier high at the center of the room. The open space smelled of fresh flowers, despite the time of the year.

Amarie wondered what memories this place held for Kin. She couldn't understand why he felt so eager to move on, especially after seeing the comfort such a place brought him.

I wish I could know that feeling.

Amarie walked next to Kin while he turned to speak to his mother, touching his arm in silent support. The physical contact was as much for her as it was for him.

"Where's Father?" Kin's baritone voice echoed through the hall.

"Oh, your father is in his study speaking with Talon." Lindora waved a hand as if to dismiss the very idea of her husband. She turned to look at her son, her eyes catching Amarie's touch. A surprised, but satisfied smile crept over her lips.

She's going to have questions about who I am...

Amarie wondered what conclusions Lindora came to on her own. She wished she had a definitive answer herself. Promises and desires to be together could only go so far without follow through.

What does it mean for the future?

"Talon? He's here?" Kin sounded surprised.

Instead of focusing on the questions of their relationship, Amarie considered the mention of someone unknown to her.

Kin had never mentioned Talon when they spoke of who would be at the estate.

"Yes, he arrived yesterday to stay the week. It's as if you timed your arrival perfectly so as not to miss your old friend."

Kin's muscles tensed against Amarie's touch.

Lindora motioned towards the west wing of the house. "They should be concluding their business shortly. Or did you want to interrupt?"

"No, no." Kin spoke quickly, shaking his head. "It's all right. Perhaps I can show Amarie around in the meantime?"

"A wonderful idea." Lindora turned towards Amarie again. "While the vineyards themselves are a little drab this time of year, I hope you'll make yourself very much at home here."

"Thank you." Amarie smiled. "And the estate is quite beautiful, no matter the season."

Lindora smiled wider. "You sure you still remember where everything is, Kin, dear?"

Kin shook his head with a laugh. "I'm sure I'll manage, Ma. You're right about me needing to visit more often, but I doubt much has changed. Father is too stubborn to let it."

"I suppose that's true." Lindora tiptoed forward to pull Kin down for another quick kiss on his cheek, which he obediently leaned over for. "No running off." She shook a finger at him.

"Nah." Kin stepped towards Amarie, taking her hand. "Go take care of all those things I know are whirling about in your head with our arrival. We'll still be here when you're done."

Lindora's eyes flickered to their subtle embrace before she spun to walk away. She climbed up the stairs to follow the way Niya had gone with their things.

Kin watched her go and heaved a sigh. He squeezed Amarie's hand, and she returned it reassuringly. "If my father is talking business with Talon, I might not get a chance to talk to them until after dinner. Talon is too good at tending to my father's whims when it comes to conversation. They tend to talk far too long about things I have no interest in."

Amarie rolled her lips together. "Who's Talon?"

Kin led her towards the open archways at the side of the foyer and out of the great room. They entered a hallway with a long rug which ran the length of it. It was at least quieter than where they'd been.

"I didn't think to mention him before. I'm surprised he's here. Talon is an old family friend." Kin glanced down the hall as if he was worried about being overheard. "He's known me almost my entire life, but we've drifted apart in the past couple years."

Amarie tilted her head with a furrowed brow, frowning at his vagueness. "I appreciate the details. I have a clear understanding of your relationship now."

Kin sighed and shook his head. "Let's just say my problem isn't necessarily with Talon but with the company he keeps."

Amarie gritted her teeth. "You think there'll be a problem?"

"I'm not sure. Talon is inherently sensitive to the Art in all its forms because of his heritage. He's auer."

Her shoulders relaxed. "An auer isn't a threat. I lived in Eralas for months, so I can't imagine your friend can sense deeper than all the auer I met during that time."

Kin's eyes widened. "You truly are a marvel," he whispered, his hand coming to her cheek.

She relaxed at his touch, some of the unsettled feelings dissipating. "Why is an auer here? I haven't seen many outside of Eralas."

"Talon is a rejanai."

A banished auer.

Amarie took a deep breath. "I'll watch my back, but I still don't suspect there'll be an issue."

Kin frowned. "Talon hides the extent of his power most of the time. He's the one who trained me when I had no clue how to control the Art when I first gained it. I'm hoping you two don't have to spend any time together."

"You don't trust him?"

"That's not it. I trust Talon wholly. He's more than earned it from me." Kin hesitated, his brow twitching as he contemplated his next words. He shook his head. "Nevermind. It's not important. He's here, but it doesn't change why *we* are." He took her hands and held them between them. "Are you all right, though? When you hugged my mother..."

Amarie looked at the floor. "I am. I will be. Just brings back memories, for me, of my family. My mother." Her voice matched his whisper.

His gaze shifted to catch hers, and his hand gave an extra squeeze. He touched her cheek, his thumb caressing her jaw. "You've never talked about her. Where is your mother?"

Amarie forced a smile. "She died when I was six."

Kin winced. "I'm sorry. How did it happen?"

Swallowing, she remembered looking through the trees as her home burned. "Some men came." Her eyes unfocused, trying to recall the details. "Mum shoved me out the back door, told me to run. They killed her. Set our home ablaze." Shaking her head, she looked at Kin. "It was a long time ago."

With a gentle step into her, Kin tilted his chin to kiss her forehead. He slowly withdrew, touching her cheek again as his pale eyes watched hers with concern. "What about your father?"

"I never knew him." She shook her head again, having no recollection of the man who should have been there.

Kin's grip tightened to encircle her waist. He embraced her, rubbing the back of her neck. "Please tell me you haven't been alone since losing your mother."

Her head came to rest on his collar, and she closed her eyes. "No. My uncle raised me after that. He suffered a similar fate as my mother, at the hands of Reapers, when I was fourteen. I've been on my own since then."

"Reapers." Kin's dark tone proved his familiarity with Helgath's goons sent to acquire Art users. "They didn't catch you? If Helgath knows about your power..."

"They don't. They never caught me, and my uncle died in the confrontation, so he was never interrogated." She furrowed her brow. "It was strange, though. When they came for me, Rennik told me to run. A Reaper had been waiting at the back door and grabbed me. This other man came out of nowhere and put a sword through the Reaper's chest. Terrified, I ran, but sometimes I wish I'd stopped to ask my rescuer who he was. He saved my life, and I never even saw his face."

Kin brushed her hair from her cheek, tucking it behind her ear.

Amarie laughed, clearing her throat. "Wow, I didn't mean to..."

"No. I'm glad you told me. I should've asked sooner." He kissed her forehead again. "I'm so sorry. I've been completely insensitive dealing with all my own family problems."

Amarie touched his chest, trying to find what comfort she could in the feel of him.

"Is Rennik the same uncle who taught you to fight?"

He remembers me saying that?

"Yes, he was..."

"I'm sorry that you lost them. It's not—"

"Stop, please. It's all right. It was a long time ago. Life isn't fair, and not all of us have families with grand estates." She smiled. "I know you came here with all sorts of questions, but... don't be too hard on them, no matter the truth. I can see how much your mother loves you, and regardless of how you came to be their son, you *are* their son."

He nodded his promise to her, his warm lips pressing against her temple. "Did you want to see the rest of the house?"

The tour ended on the back patio of the mansion, overlooking the gardens. The hibernating greenery curled up the large stone balconies, a series of short steps leading towards the hedges and manicured flower beds. Only the hardiest of flora clung to their leaves, the others having given up the struggle against the coming frost.

As Kin and Amarie stood in the withered gardens, she remained silent.

He stood perfectly still, hands resting on the banister as he stared out at the rolling hills of his childhood home.

Certain he'd forgotten her presence, she let her gaze wander over the winter-scorned landscape. She could only imagine how beautiful it was in summer. An odd feeling filled her, suggesting she would never bear witness to it in a different state than it currently was.

Perhaps he needs some time alone.

Despite an unwelcome wave of isolation, Amarie decided to give him the opportunity. She didn't want to interrupt his thoughts but didn't want to simply slip away either. "I think I'll go make sure Viento is settling in."

Glancing at her, Kin gave a subtle nod of understanding. "All right. Dinner should be ready soon and we can meet in the dining hall?"

Amarie nodded, a heaviness weighing on her chest as she descended the stairs in silence.

The fresh air welcomed her after the warmth of the house, and she made no effort to pull her cloak around her. A brisk breeze whipped through it and cooled her body. Her boots made little noise as they traversed the grass.

A persistent fog hung in the distance, dew still clinging to the grass in the shade.

Arriving at the stable, she surveyed the massive space with a large covered arena at its heart. Around the arena ran a walkway dusted with hay and feed, and outer stalls boasting attached paddocks for the horses to wander on their own accord.

The scent of horses and muck of stable hung with a familiar

comfort as she walked down the row of stalls in search of Viento. She turned a corner and spotted a big black head poking out, staring at her with pricked ears.

Chewing a mouthful of hay, Viento whinnied at her.

She stroked his midnight nose, encouraging the nickering sounds as he nuzzled into her chest. The talk of her family caused buried memories to venture towards the surface. "You're my family now."

Since she was seventeen, Viento had been her only constant companion. Remembering the day she found him, the winter chill dissipated into the summer memory.

Helgath's hot sun had beat down on her brow, reminding her of the tedium of traveling by foot as she approached the equestrian training facility. They bred warhorses, and while she had no illusions of purchasing one of their prized steeds with her scarce coin, she wanted to try her luck at bargaining for one of the less obedient mounts.

She kicked a stone across the flat terrain, and watched it skitter into a boulder. The ground radiated with as much heat as the sky, and she shook her shirt to fan air to her chest.

The shrill call of a horse brought her attention up, and her eyes focused on the breaking pen, where a man struggled to approach a young stallion with a saddle.

Frowning, she ducked behind the boulder to get a closer look.

Private breeders never saddle-broke their horses until they were at least three years old and fully matured. Helgathian forces tended to push those boundaries, wanting warhorses faster, but this horse couldn't be more than two years old, judging by his lanky frame.

The young soldier threw the saddle to the ground in his impatience, and picked up the lunging whip. Instead of flicking it behind the horse as it was made for, he struck the stallion's rump.

The horse reared and charged the man until he tumbled through the fence and into the dirt.

Amarie smiled, thinking the animal had won, but the man proved relentless.

He didn't abandon his task until the horse's rump bled, retreating to seek help or perhaps admit defeat. The soldier left the saddle in the dirt as he stomped towards the barn.

Her heart broke for the proud, black horse, still standing strong. While the horse was plenty big and sturdy enough to ride, he was too young and his mind wasn't ready.

Overcome with anger, Amarie left her hiding place and raced to the small paddock.

The horse pawed the ground, shirking away from the fallen saddle.

She held out her hands, cautiously entering the fenced area. Striding to the center, she walked in small circles as he cantered around the outside of the ring.

"Easy, boy." Keeping her voice low, she kept moving with the horse until his eyes relaxed and his ears swiveled forward. Turning her back to him, she halted and waited.

A few breaths later, he nudged her back with his nose, and she smiled. "Let's get you out of here."

Someone yelled from the barn, and she gasped, scanning for the paddock gate. Fumbling with the rope holding it in place, she freed it as several foot soldiers raced across the rocky landscape towards her.

Amarie spoke in hurried whispers to the horse the whole time. "I help you, you help me, all right?" She ran to the beast, who sidestepped, but didn't balk when she pulled herself onto his bare back.

He started running before she'd even settled, and they burst out of the paddock. The gate swung wide, colliding with the approaching soldiers, and throwing them to their backs.

Fleeing Helgathian persecution for horse theft, they made their way to Eralas. On the island, she took the time to name him and train him properly.

Amarie shook her head at the nostalgia, patting the neck of her protective horse.

The stable boy had thoroughly brushed and cared for him,

granting him ample hay, fresh water, and extra oats.

"I hope you behaved for him." Her mind eased, and she murmured to Viento in Aueric. She'd never broken the habit of the language she'd trained him in. "It'll be all right, boy. You'll see."

"I can't imagine any horse would be left wanting while stabled here. The Parnells are wonderful hosts." A melodic voice spoke from behind her.

She jumped but stopped herself from whirling around.

I have no enemies here.

The voice continued, a perfectly pitched masculine tenor, sweet, soft... and intrinsically auer. "I don't believe I've heard a human tongue say those words so smoothly before."

Amarie turned to look at the man approaching behind her, his feet quiet on the hay-strewn floor.

Viento snorted, and she smirked.

Talon stood as tall as Kin, and as he tilted his head, a lock of raven hair fell forward over his shoulder, framing his face. Vibrant green eyes bored into her, and she resisted the urge to shuffle her feet. As he stopped in the shadow of a beam, his Aueric pinpoint pupils swelled.

Amarie had grown accustomed to the unusual attractiveness of the auer during the time she spent in Eralas. Talon was no exception, with his flawless, deeply tanned complexion.

"Perhaps the reassurance is as much for myself as for him." Her eyes met his, refusing to balk at their gemstone hue.

Talon smiled, showing the pearly edge of his teeth. "The same applies. Unless you have been mistreated here?" He gracefully folded his hands behind his back, the front of his white silk tunic growing taut on his broad chest. "I could formally complain on your behalf, if I knew the name of the human who speaks Aueric so beautifully?"

His voice was so smooth, that she wondered why the auer people didn't just spread over all of Pantracia and simply ask kings and queens for their kingdoms.

It might just work.

"There's no need. I'm Amarie, and you must be Talon." She

offered her hand in greeting. Inwardly, she encouraged herself to be kind. The tension of his aura buzzed around her, shrouding the depth of his ability.

He moved a hand from behind his back, grasped hers, then bent his head into a bow and kissed the back of her hand. His lips were warm and feather soft before he rose again.

Amarie smirked. "You seem confident in your ability to assist, even when my worries are unknown to you."

Talon didn't immediately release her hand, taking his time in assessing her statement. "Should I not be? For I don't know a better home in which you and your steed could be so amiably treated. I have known the Parnell family for many years and have yet to see the limit of their hospitality." He stepped away, returning his hand behind his back. His plain, high-laced boots made no sound on the ground. "I'm flattered you already know my name. Though, you've caught me at a disadvantage as I know little about you."

"Perhaps there is little to know."

Why is Talon in the stable? If Kin's parents are both now unoccupied... is Kin speaking with them?

Amarie rolled her lips together. "Were you planning to go for a ride?"

"No. Perhaps I'm merely here to check on my horse and reassure her?"

She raised an eyebrow.

"Or perhaps my curiosity drove me here? Lady Lindora mentioned Kinronsilis has returned home for a visit. I assume you're the guest he arrived with?"

"That would be me. And what, if I may ask, were you curious about?"

"Forgive me." Talon didn't evade her gaze with the apology, as Kin so often did. "Kinronsilis hasn't been home in many years and never with someone at his side. You are my greatest curiosity. I'm interested in discovering the kind of company my old friend keeps."

"And what have you discovered? Aside from a woman who speaks to her horse." Amarie leaned on the stall door.

"Still unclear. My curiosity has only grown." Talon's smile faded and his tone gentled. "What is it that bothers you?"

"Perhaps my horse will enlighten you." Standing straight, she patted Viento's nose before walking past Talon towards the exit of the stable.

"Amarie."

She stopped and turned to him with a raised brow.

"Could I convince you to join me for a ride tomorrow? I'm sure Kinronsilis will be occupied if his mother has any say in the matter, and remaining within the walls of the main house can get rather... overwhelming. I constantly find myself in need of fresh air, and company would be most welcome."

Amarie smiled wider at his request. Asking the woman who spoke to her horse if she would go for a ride must have seemed like a good bet. She couldn't help but nod, even though Kin had expressed concerns over them spending time together.

I can handle myself around an auer. There's nothing for Kin to worry about.

"Of course. I'd be happy to join you. Perhaps I'll find you here around midday?"

Talon joined her as she walked from the stable towards the main house. "You most certainly will." He lowered his voice in a way she'd heard auer speak before. It was often meant to be alluring and seductive, but in her time in Eralas, she'd learned to see through the facade and recognize the subtleties of manipulation. Long lives made the auer masters of it.

While many may swoon over Talon's handsome face, he didn't hold a candle to Kin's rugged charm.

Chapter 19

Sitting on the worn couch in his father's study transported Kin back into his childhood. He kept his back awkwardly straight as his father paced about the room.

Hartlen's thick eyebrows knitted together beneath the dense, greying curls of ruddy-brown hair. "You're old enough to know, Kinronsilis."

Lindora closed a hand on her husband's wrist as he crossed near her chair, and they exchanged a poignant look.

"You don't deny it then?" Kin's stomach fluttered.

"No. Your father and I had been trying for so long to have a child, but..." His mother sniffed. "You were given to us."

Kin looked at the floor. "Ma. This doesn't change anything. I need to know the truth."

Lindora took a shuddering inhale, tears filling her eyes. "Can't we just keep pretending you're ours?"

"I *am* yours." Kin crossed to his mother, kneeling on the floor beside her. He drew the handkerchief from the pocket she always kept it in and dabbed at the tears.

"What happened, Kin?" Hartlen stood like a sentinel behind his wife. "Why are you asking now?"

Lindora reached for her son, touching his face.

Kin gave her knee a squeeze. "I believe I encountered my twin brother, which was a nasty surprise for us both." He looked at his father. "If you have any information about the family I was born into..."

Lindora and Hartlen exchanged an unreadable glance, a looming silence hovering before his father broke it. "We don't know anything. One rarely asks questions when given such a gift."

Lindora's breathing normalized, and Kin drew away, rubbing the back of his head. He crossed towards the large window at the back of the study, gazing out on the familiar sights of the valley. The frosty hills rolled into the lawn leading towards the horse pavilion.

"Who gave me to you, then?" Kin watched Talon pass through the open doorway into the stable. An odd feeling coalesced in his stomach as he realized who the auer likely sought.

"Alana."

The feeling evolved into a tumultuous cyclone.

"Alana?" Kin spun towards his parents. He couldn't hide the anger in his voice as he said her name, suddenly grateful he had this conversation without Amarie present.

The last thing I need is Amarie learning about Alana.

Hartlen cleared his throat. "Yes, I met her in Olsa originally, on a caravan trip. She was easy to talk to, and I divulged our plight to her. I was still young, and the power of the auer was a mystery. I'd hoped she could help."

Kin resisted the temptation to accuse his father of being taken in by Alana's enchanting appearance. "Alana is the one who brought me to you?" The sickening image of him as an infant in Alana's arms made his skin crawl.

"She insisted we not ask questions." Lindora fiddled with her handkerchief. "We weren't about to question a messenger from the gods, as we saw her. She brought us a child, and we couldn't appear ungrateful. We agreed she could visit anytime she liked. To check in."

The origin of the family's long-time friendship with the Di'Terian siblings became clear. Alana and Talon Di'Terian were a presence Kin had never thought to question growing up. As a child, Alana's fine Aueric features were enough to distract from any such curiosity. When puberty set in, she was a welcome sight he grew infatuated with.

And she did nothing to dissuade it.

Her brother, Talon, began visiting when Kin was eight, leading to the closest thing to a brother-like bond Kin ever knew.

Kin glowered and crossed his arms at the frustration of knowing what the next step was. "Then, I'll have to wait for answers until I can speak to Alana." He made no effort to disguise his disgust at the idea.

Hartlen frowned, and his mouth opened, but a touch on his arm from his wife halted it.

His mother understood his dislike for Alana more than his father, though neither parent knew the depth of her betrayal.

Movement drew Kin's eyes to the large window at the back of the study, where he saw Amarie and Talon, together, crossing the grass between the stable and the main house.

They were smiling.

A familiar roil of jealousy tangled in his stomach at the sight, but he didn't have time to process it before his mother delivered more grim news.

"Alana should arrive in the morning, actually, so there'll be no waiting. You'll be able to ask her yourself. Talon arrived today with the news. He's always so thoughtful and knows I appreciate the warning so I can see to preparing her room."

Alana's arrival was both fortuitous and horrendous timing. A fresh wave of anxiety overtook the feelings evoked by seeing Talon and Amarie together.

This is all becoming so complicated.

Kin considered telling Amarie a lie, that the horses of the estate were ill, and she needed to go back to Ingston with Viento to keep him healthy.

His father's gruff voice interrupted his scheming. "We will sit down with Alana to ask your questions together. We are still your parents, and we'll find the truth you seek as a family."

His father left no room for argument on the matter. It just meant he would have to endure a performance from Alana for his parents' benefit before he could confront her alone.

"Father... Ma." Kin evaluated the best way to speak his coming request as he turned towards them. "Please, don't tell Alana—"

Hartlen waved a hand, and Kin quieted. "How can we expect Alana to be honest if we ourselves are not? We keep no secrets." He locked his narrow jaw in a stern scowl, and Kin now understood why he never looked like his father.

Lindora's expression soured, then she apologetically looked at Kin, who balled his fists.

Uncomfortable silence followed.

"Well, dinner should be almost ready." Lindora crossed to her son, taking on a cheery tone. "Come, darling. Your father has a new vintage you need to try."

Kin and his mother descended to the dining hall for what would be an ostentatious dinner. Perhaps the drink and food would serve enough of a distraction for him to forget his frustration with his father.

Hartlen was never the empathetic or understanding type.

His mother ushered Kin to the table and pushed a glass of wine into his hand.

Amarie's laugh echoed behind him, mingled with that of the male auer he knew so well. A spark of surprise merged with a twinge of envy in Kin. Talon had somehow cheered Amarie up from the dower mood she left the garden in. Though, perhaps, Kin's attitude had influenced hers.

The talk about her family dying probably didn't help either.

Amarie's gaze found Kin and she absently bit her bottom lip, smiling in a way he hadn't seen for days.

He questioned if it was Talon's company, or the sight of him instigating the glitter in her eyes.

"There you are!" Lindora's happy voice trilled as she poured two more glasses of wine and shuffled over to offer them to Talon and Amarie as they approached the table.

Amarie took hers. "Thank you, Lady Parnell."

"Psht." Lindora waved her hand as she took a sip of her wine.

"Please, call me Lindora. I never much cared for the formalities."

Talon grinned. "She's tried to get me to drop the title many times, but I stubbornly refuse." He lifted Lindora's hand to his lips, giving it a light kiss. "You look lovely this evening."

Color touched Lindora's cheeks and she batted Talon's hand as she lifted hers away. Her eyes still showed a hint of red from her crying, and Kin wondered if the auer noticed.

"You should be saving those charms of yours for a nice *young* woman, Talon." Lindora turned to Kin's approach. "It's nice to have you boys in the house together again."

"Kin." Talon smiled, a hint of dry humor underlining the stoic greeting. "I thought I felt a chill in the air."

Kin couldn't repress the sideways grin as he lifted his wine. "Talon." He tilted his glass so it clinked against Talon's. "I didn't think you'd notice in the haze of all that hot air you bluster."

Talon beamed.

"You boys are always so rude to each other." Lindora huffed and smacked her son's shoulder with the back of her hand.

Amarie moved from Talon to stand next to Kin, and his hand wrapped around her waist to pull her close to his side. It took everything within him not to place a kiss on her hair, already able to smell its sweetness in the warmth of the dining hall.

Talon's attention flickered down Amarie to Kin's hand on her waist, a glimmer of amusement reflecting in his emerald eyes.

"It's the only way we know how to express ourselves to each other, Ma. You know that." Kin sipped his wine.

And he's the one who knows all my secrets.

Talon's displeasure of Kin's acquired Art preluded the steady deterioration of their friendship.

Kin once thought it jealousy, but Talon's accomplishments in the Art surpassed his own. Ultimately, the decay of their brotherhood could be blamed on Talon's elder sister.

Amarie looked up at Kin with a devilish smile. "Talon was telling me about your fourteenth birthday when your parents got you that grey mare." She rested her hand on his, lacing their fingers.

The realization of what she was talking about came in a single horrible memory. His smile turned to a frown as he remembered the creature he'd been gifted.

In his first attempt to ride the mare, Kin was unprepared for the obstinate bunny hop of protest from the animal, and the small bounce unseated him. He landed flat on his back in front of all the guests, and the laughter wasn't something a budding youth would forget. He neglected his gift until his parents eventually sold her.

Talon smirked, taking the wine to his lips for a slow sip. "I don't think he appreciates me telling you such things."

Kin sighed, hoping it would be the worst Talon would tell Amarie. Gods knew he had much worse he could share.

"Talon, don't speak of such things. Poor Kinronsilis never got on that horse again, or any horse for that matter." Lindora rubbed Kin's arm. "I would never have imagined you riding the beautiful Friesian that carried you both to our doorstep, if I hadn't seen it myself."

Grinding his jaw at his mother's failed attempt to change the subject, Kin took a sip of wine.

"It was even worse since *you* saw it happen." Lindora motioned to Talon, oblivious to her son's discomfort.

Talon's laugh rumbled in his chest. "Could you imagine what his reaction would have been if Alana had been there?"

Kin nearly spat out his wine and his arm tightened around Amarie.

Her head tilted towards him, eyebrows coming together as she failed to recognize the name.

Talon laughed again. Usually the sound would bring fond memories, but it stirred anxiety.

Why would he bring her up?

Silence fell between them as Kin narrowed his eyes, but Talon didn't acknowledge the look. He merely took another sip of his drink.

"I better go check on dinner." Lindora smiled uncomfortably and squeezed Kin's shoulder before bustling towards the kitchen.

Kin let go of Amarie to reach for the bottle on the table. He would require more wine to get through the meal.

Talon cleared his throat to end the silence before taking another gulp of his wine. "What brings you home, at last, Kinronsilis? It's been some time, has it not?"

At least he's making an attempt to change the subject.

"It's easy to lose track of time, which I'm sure you can appreciate. I didn't have much reason to return home these past several years."

"Time is something I often forget."

Auer were blessed with lives far longer than humans. Talon would often make fun of Kin and his anxiousness to accomplish things in his life. In some ways, Kin, at twenty-seven, was older than Talon, who was ninety-two.

"Have you seen Alana at all since I saw you last? I'm surprised you're not traveling together." Talon swirled his glass.

The tannin in the wine stuck to the back of Kin's throat, and he choked. He swallowed the sting before coughing.

So much for that. Bastard is determined to keep bringing her up.

Kin slipped away to top up his wine again.

Amarie ran a hand through her hair. Bringing her glass to her lips, she looked at Kin, her expression unimpressed. "I'm sorry." She forced formality to cover her annoyance. "Who, exactly, is Alana?" Her gaze moved from Kin to Talon, seeking an answer from either of them.

"My sister." Talon found words first. "I'm surprised Kin didn't tell you. She's the one who introduced me to him so many years ago. She's actually arriving tomorrow morning."

"I heard..." Kin tried to control the growl in his voice. "Unfortunately."

Amarie raised an eyebrow.

It was Talon's turn to frown, but there was a playfulness in it. "I didn't think Alana had fallen so very far from your good graces." He placed his empty glass on the edge of the dining table. "You used to follow her around like a love-sick puppy."

Amarie gulped her wine, and Kin's stomach twisted into knots as Talon casually laced his hands together in front of himself.

A deafening silence lingered.

Amarie stepped over to place her half-full glass on the table next to Talon's. "Excuse me." She avoided Kin's gaze and didn't wait for a reply before crossing to the doorway and exiting the room.

Kin glanced after her before glowering at Talon.

The auer's eyes lingered on Amarie's departing form.

Kin cleared his throat loudly and drew Talon's attention. "Are you really so callous?" He huffed in frustration, abandoning his wine glass on the dining table as well.

Talon's face was impossible to read, emotionless. "I didn't think you would be so careless as to not tell her about Alana. As if she wouldn't figure it out."

"You blatantly brought her up. Even after you could tell she didn't know about Alana. And love-sick puppy? Really—"

"I only spoke the truth. You probably still worship her." Talon gestured at Kin and lowered his voice. "You gave up your *soul* for her."

"Not anymore. And I refuse to let a mistake I made as a teenager continue to rule my life."

"As if you have a choice. Not with that infection."

"I'm not asking you." Kin stepped into Talon, and the auer didn't back down. They stood face to face, Kin's hand flexing in and out of a fist.

"But have you asked *her*?" Talon narrowed his eyes. "Does she know what you are? Who you serve?"

They stared, unmoving. Kin's mind whirled in anger. "You can be such an ass." He grumbled, shaking his head as he took a step back. "Stay away from Amarie." He turned to walk past his friend.

A strong hand clamped down on his bicep, pulling him back to face the jade eyes of the man he called his friend. "You think you can keep it from her?" Talon's voice deepened to a tone that could send a chill through any creature's body. "What game are you playing?"

Kin jerked his shoulder, tearing it from Talon's grip with another resentful look. "Don't you dare presume to know anything about me. We may have been good friends once, but time still passes for me. I've changed."

"I think you give time too much credit, Kinronsilis."

"Or perhaps I give you too much. Use that *charm* of yours to explain to my mother why Amarie and I will be taking dinner in our rooms tonight."

Kin prayed to the gods Amarie wasn't heading to the stable. He made his way into the foyer first and found Niya tending to a flower arrangement.

Her gaze lifted, and a practiced smile graced her face. "If you're looking for Miss Amarie, I only just directed her to her room."

"Thank you, Niya." Kin tried to control the relief in his eyes as he gazed towards the east wing stairs instead of the front door. He subdued a sigh as he started up the stairs.

The hallways of his childhood home were painfully familiar, smelling of polished wood and burning oil lamps on narrow tables against the walls. In the growing dark, the lamplight was necessary for Kin to see within the diagonal hallway that abutted the interior balcony above the foyer.

The rugs covering the wooden floor muted his footsteps as he made his way towards her room. He passed rooms he knew, heading towards the end of the hall where it opened into a small circular space with three doors. One belonged to him, and they had converted another into a study when he was old enough for schooling.

He moved to the guest room door and gently rapped on the wood with his knuckle. His hand closed on the cold iron doorknob but didn't twist. "Amarie?"

There was a lengthy pause before she replied.

"Come in."

Kin didn't withhold his relieved sigh this time.

The guest rooms of the Parnell estate were far less garish than the Delphi estate in Feyor, but Amarie's room still hosted a large four-poster bed with a fine-silk canopy. A bureau with large closed doors dominated the left wall, along with a vanity and mirror. Amarie's things had been placed near the latter.

Amarie had opened the window and cool evening air filled the room. She sat sideways on the wide ledge, her back against the frame and her face turned outwards to the view of the barren vineyard. Both her feet rested on the ledge in front of her, legs bent and her arms draped over her knees. She didn't turn to look at him, even as the door clicked shut.

Habit encouraged Kin to lock it. "I'm sorry." He stepped towards her, walking around two overstuffed, high-backed chairs. "I can't even imagine how uncomfortable that was for you."

It was odd to see her so perfectly placed in a window from his childhood. The familiarity of the two, never before presented together, sent strange cascades of emotion through him.

Amarie looked gorgeous in the twilight, the flicker of lanterns within the room highlighting the red tones within her long, dark hair. She turned to him, the anger he expected absent in her expression. The moonlight reflected in her deep blue eyes, adding to her haunted appearance.

"Uncomfortable." She repeated the word with a thoughtful air. "That's one way to put it, I suppose. I feel like I only have some pieces to this puzzle, with strangers handing me new ones. I'm afraid I don't know what to do with them." Her tone sounded distant, lost among her thoughts.

Kin's heart broke as he moved towards her. "I'm sorry for that, too." He caressed her hair and kissed the top of her head. He wanted to comfort her, make up for all the mistakes he made. "I owe you so many explanations. I just don't know where to start, or how to keep going once I have."

Surprisingly, a smirk rose to her lips as she tilted her head. "Perhaps you'd humor me and start by explaining who this woman I keep hearing about is, so I may accurately decide how jealous I should be." She took his hand.

The action brought a smile to his lips, regardless of his dislike for talking about the auer woman who'd damned him. "Alana." Her name tasted sour on his tongue, decayed. "Her involvement is growing more and more complicated by the moment."

Considering Alana's newly discovered involvement in his birth and relocation to the Parnell estate, Amarie would learn about her, eventually. Yet, he didn't fully understand her part in everything.

"I never really questioned Alana's presence when I was younger. I always assumed she was a friend of my parents who enjoyed the luxuries of staying here from time to time. I became rather…" He struggled to find the right word for it. "Infatuated with her. I'm sure you can imagine the allure of an Aueric woman to a teenage boy." He paused, pushing the images of her long, raven hair and large, jade-green eyes from his mind.

Amarie's gaze left him, her lips rolling together. "I can imagine. Quite easily, actually."

Kin paused, watching her until she met his gaze again. "Of course. While you were in Eralas?"

She nodded, waving her hand. "It's inconsequential. Continue."

He gritted his teeth and nodded. "Alana proved herself one of her people, despite being a rejanai. She manipulated my childish attraction and put me on a path I still regret. Nothing… *physical* ever happened between us, for which I'm now grateful."

No matter how much he once desired Alana, she ultimately always denied him. Even in the last moments before she made her true intentions clear.

When he finished, Amarie turned so her feet could touch the floor again. Standing, she sighed and shook her head. "Why didn't you tell me before?" Her free hand touched his chest.

As she moved into his arms, a wave of gratitude washed through him.

His hand pressed comfortably to her lower back, and the other tucked a loose strand of hair behind her ear. "Embarrassment. Regret. The path is one that made me what I am. I don't want to risk exposing you to the same danger Alana put me in."

Amarie considered his words for a few moments before lifting her chin and letting her lips graze his jaw. "So *not* jealous, then," she whispered, as if it were her singular concern in the matter.

A chuckle rumbled through his chest. Again, gratitude washed over him for her patience and ability to take his words for the truth without the poison of doubt.

"No." He tilted his head to allow her access to his skin, her lips making it tingle. "No jealousy necessary on your part. Though, I wonder if perhaps I should be?"

Amarie withdrew her face from his and looked at him with a confused expression. "Why in the names of all the gods would you need to be jealous?"

Kin groaned at the disappearance of her kisses. "Talon." He watched the curl of her lip pin under the edge of her teeth. "He's prettier than me. I have witnessed his ability to bewitch firsthand during our excursions to the taverns in Ingston."

Surprising him again, Amarie let out a brief laugh and released her lip. She wrapped her arms around his neck and brought her face close to his. Her lips traced delicately up his neck and hovered below his ear as a hand played with the base of his hairline.

"My love. I have spent..." She kissed his neck. "Many months and moments around Auric men." Her mouth moved against his skin again. "And I can positively say..." Another kiss buzzed against his soul. "None have ever come close to stirring within me the feelings you do."

This time, she bit him and elicited a low moan from his chest as his hands gripped her tighter, the familiar fire rising within him.

"No one, including Talon, could lure me away from you."

Her words coupled with her actions were too much for Kin to resist. His hands moved shamelessly to explore lower, slipping over the curves of her body.

"Is that so?" The baritone of his voice grew deeper. "Perhaps it was a fluke, and we should make sure I still have that effect?"

Amarie laughed and kissed his neck again before she moved her mouth closer to his. "Probably a good idea." Her eyes flashed with mischief as her lips teased his. "I'd hate to think you've lost your touch." She leaned into him enough for him to appreciate how her body felt against his.

"That would be a shame." Kin tangled his fingers in her hair and pulled her head roughly towards him to close the distance.

Their mouths met in a hard exchange.

His entire body desperately sought the affection capable of quelling the nervous energy which had dominated him since they arrived at the estate. The jealousy of seeing Amarie with Talon only heightened the desire for her.

Nothing will change. She's mine.

He craved the sound of her reaction to his touch.

Her response to him was immediate, her arms gripping tightly around him as his mouth claimed hers. A whimper came from her throat in the sudden surge of their passion.

He pulled her closer, his hands seeking bare skin at her waist.

Amarie's fingers ventured to the buttons of his tunic.

Kin found himself quickly bare from the waist up. The cool air from the open window touched his chest where her fingers drew fiery trails.

Her vest and shirt were tossed carelessly to the side. Heated kisses grew deeper and hungrier.

Wearing nothing on her upper body other than the cropped chemise covering her breasts, her exposed skin warmed his.

He found the closest wall he could to press her against to feel the entire length of her body. His fingers traced her arm as she freed him of his belt.

A sharp rap on the door echoed through the room.

Lips tore cruelly apart, hot breath passing anxiously between them as he waited to see if the person would go away.

The knock came again a moment later, along with Niya's voice. "Miss Amarie? I've brought your dinner."

Kin groaned his frustration directly into Amarie's ear. When he moved his head a little further from hers, he could see the fire in her eyes and her lips moving in a way that tempted him to ignore Niya.

Amarie pushed his chest, urging him to respond to the door as her pinned lip tormented him.

He moved his lips towards hers again for a kiss he kept as long as possible. "Don't go anywhere." He lifted a finger to her lips before he turned.

Chapter 20

Kin tore the door open with more aggression than the wood deserved, apparently having no qualms against letting the poor girl know what she interrupted.

Amarie stood to the side, out of sight of the door, and debated taking a step forward to see the reaction a shirtless Kin was about to receive.

The gasp and sputter for words from Niya was enough to give her a clear image.

Amarie's eyes lingered on the thin lines of the tattoo on Kin's forearm before returning to admire his torso. She wondered about the significance of the ink she hadn't asked him about.

Is it a Shade thing?

"Master Kinronsilis!" Niya stuttered. "I..."

"Thank you for the meal." Kin's voice came gently, and Amarie was certain only she could hear the subtle difference of it. It sounded deeper, tinged with the passion they'd been ripped from. "I'll take it from here, if you please."

Amarie unlaced her boots, pulling them off and tossing them to the side.

"Of... of course..." Niya whispered.

Silence hung in the air before Kin reached past the door, impatient. "Thank you, Niya." He pulled a jangling cart through the doorway with one hand.

"Good... good night." The girl shuffled down the hall.

Kin rolled the cart in past the entryway before he sealed the door, latching the lock. He hovered there for a moment, the strength in his biceps accentuated by the way he pushed on the door. He shook his head with a laugh before returning his gaze to Amarie.

She stood barefoot, leaning back against the wall with her hips hovering away from it. Chewing on her lip, she raised one eyebrow.

Kin's eyes bore an eagerness in them she'd seen before and craved again. His chest reflected the light of the lantern as he leaned over to untie the laces of his boots. While he did, his eyes remained on her. His chest rose faster when she unfastened her breeches.

Feet free, he crossed the floor to return to her. "Now..." His voice was gruff and hot against her. "Where were we?" Hands moved over the coolness of her skin and tickled beneath the edge of her chemise.

"Shall I remind you?" She slowly slid her hands up to unbutton the front of her chemise. Letting it fall, she watched his gaze wander down her body as the cascade of fabric left her torso bare.

Humming appreciatively, Kin pressed his hips against hers. "Oh, yes. I remember, now." Lifting her chin, he kissed her, cupping her breast.

Amarie gasped when he twisted her nipple between his finger and thumb.

His mouth teased hers before kissing down her neck, leaving her breathless. Pushing the top of her breeches, the material slouched to her knees before she kicked it off.

Running her hands through his hair, she closed her eyes, leaning her head back against the wall as she savored the feel of his mouth on her skin.

Damn, he's good at this.

His mouth trailed lower as he knelt before her, playing with the delicate fabric around her hips. Kissing her lower abdomen, he pulled her last article of clothing free of her body.

Amarie's feet lifted off the ground and she yelped in surprise as he held her to him, placing her down on the nearby vanity. "Bed too cliché for you?"

Kin gave her a sideways smile as he lowered himself again between her legs. Running his nails along the outside of her hips to her knees, he encouraged them apart. "This is a better height."

Her jaw clenched, body humming with anticipation with the increasing tempo of her heart. She found the inside of his thigh with her foot, teasing. "You're overdressed."

"And you can do something about that." His tongue danced along sensitive skin. "When I'm done."

Swallowing, Amarie breathed through her mouth and leaned against the vanity mirror, toes curling.

Morning came too quickly, the brilliant sun waking them well before Amarie wanted to rise from the comfort of the bed they shared all night.

She rolled over, groaning. Blinking her eyes open, she focused on a piece of parchment on the floor near the door. "We've received noise complaints." She pulled the blanket over her head.

Kin laughed, rising over her. He tugged on the blankets to reveal her face and leaned in to kiss her. "It's a big house. No one heard. But *I* wouldn't mind if they had, either."

Amarie smiled. "Me neither."

He grinned and kissed her again before rolling away to retrieve the note. He chuckled as he read it. "On the contrary, it appears someone believes we require sustenance."

She tilted her head, gaining a better vantage point to admire his naked backside. "Hmm?"

Kin glanced back at her as he unlatched the lock on the door. "Breakfast." He pronounced it slowly for her. "Or did you have other things in mind already?" He tentatively opened the door and hastily wheeled in a cart covered with pastries, fruits, and cheeses.

Poor Niya must have been afraid of interrupting again.

"You make it difficult to *not* have other things in mind."

Kin brought the cart to her side of the bed before crawling over the blankets to join her. "At least that's a problem we share." He traced the edge of her jaw and kissed the soft underside of it. "Sleep well, my love?"

Amarie closed her eyes. "Once we finally slept, yes. Can't we stay in bed all day?"

Except I promised Talon we'd go for a ride.

Kin caressed her shoulder. "As much as I wish we could, there are certain unavoidable conversations that need to happen today." His face grew grim. "Alana is arriving, and she has answers—"

Pressing her finger to his lips, she shook her head. "We're naked, in bed... Is that really what you want to talk about?"

"Is there something else you'd rather discuss?"

"What you did with your hands... while your mouth did that thing... that was really something."

Kin laughed. "I'm glad you enjoyed it."

Amarie pouted. "I don't want to face the day."

Reaching to the breakfast cart, Kin plucked up a piece of cheese and offered it to her. "We don't need to rush. There's still time."

Amarie took the cheese with her lips and nestled into his chest, burying her nose amid his scent and forcing him onto his back. "Good. This is all I want."

Kin's heart pounded in her ears as he wrapped his arms around her and encouraged her on top of him. Running his hand through her hair, he placed a gentle kiss on her lips. "And you're all I want."

Time passed slowly through the morning, broken between kisses and occasional nibbles of breakfast.

Eventually, after they dressed, Amarie turned to Kin as he rearranged pillows. She hesitated, loathe to discuss the day ahead. His meeting with Alana made her stomach curdle, but she refrained from admitting it aloud. It gave her slight solace to know the meeting would also include his parents.

"I agreed to go for a horseback ride with Talon today." She'd meant to mention it the night before, but became pleasantly distracted.

Kin's gaze shifted from the buttons of his tunic to her. "With Talon?" A distinct edge tainted his tone.

She met his gaze and nodded. "Yes. He asked me to accompany him." Crossing the room to Kin, she kissed his chin.

His jaw tensed and her affection seemed to do little to ease it.

"I promise, you have nothing to worry about, he has no effect on me. I love you." She kissed his chin again.

"It's not his effect I'm particularly worried about." Kin's arms surrounded her waist and pulled her close.

Amarie tilted her head, keeping her chin elevated. "Then what are you worried about, Master Kinronsilis?"

Kin's fingers traced her cheek, his eyes following. "Mostly his apparent lack of control in telling you stories about me." He smiled, but the tension in his jaw hadn't faded. "Promise me you'll remember that I'll always love you, no matter who or what we both are." He leaned close to press his lips to hers.

His words echoed eerily in her mind, and she delicately kissed his lower lip. "I won't forget. Besides, there'll be little room for conversation during a ride." Her mouth fully claimed his, which he ardently returned.

The kiss grew deeper and more passionate, threatening to develop into a primal need for physical intimacy, but the shrill chime of a bell marking midday interrupted.

Nothing Talon can say will change how I feel.

They parted ways at the foyer.

Kin returned up the stairs to go towards the west wing, while Amarie made her way to the stable.

As surprising as it was to see Talon attempting conversation with Viento, what shocked her the most was her big, black horse eating oats out of the palm of the stranger's hand.

Amarie paused and watched as the auer rubbed the stallion's dark forehead, speaking in the eloquent foreign tongue she only used with her horse.

A pure white Andalusian mare waited, tacked, off to the side.

"I'm sure he finds you just as attractive." Amarie approached them both.

A handsome smile graced Talon's lips as he turned towards her. "I believe he may feel more attracted to the oats than me."

Amarie laughed and nodded. "You're probably right." She unlatched Viento's stall door to slide it open. Instead of attaching a lead rope to his halter, she walked to his saddle resting on a post nearby. Ignoring Talon, the Friesian followed Amarie obediently and stopped behind her. She started with the saddle pad.

"I was hoping to have him tacked and ready when you arrived, but he resisted the idea. I'm sure you can imagine." Talon stepped beside Amarie as she lifted the saddle. "Did you have a late evening? I hoped I'd see you at breakfast."

A smirk adorned her lips as she remembered breakfast that morning. "It would've been wildly inappropriate for you to have seen me at breakfast."

A mirroring smirk touched his expression in her peripheral vision, but she gave him no further information.

"Viento isn't fond of other people." She cinched the saddle and removed the halter to replace it with a bridle and reins.

"Though he's quite fond of you. Perhaps he finds you more attractive than me after all. I can hardly blame him."

Her gaze flickered to him before she scoffed. "He *trusts* me. Do you have a route in mind for your ride today?"

"For *our* ride. I do." He turned, approaching the snowy form of his mare. He pulled himself onto the saddle, hardly straining despite not using the stirrup. Gracefully, he avoided the woven basket precariously secured to the back of his saddle, which she hadn't noticed before.

His dark leather boots fit into the loops at his horse's side. He wore no cloak, just a fine-crafted vest of green fabric only slightly darker than his eyes. The thin, black linen of the long-sleeve shirt beneath the vest, cuffs tied at his wrists, would hardly offer warmth.

His Aueric blood wouldn't notice the cold.

Amarie mounted with ease. She felt more at home in the saddle than anywhere else but missed the warmth of Kin's arms.

He's busy meeting with Alana.

She shook her head to rid herself of the lingering knot of worry. Something didn't sit right with her knowledge of Talon's sister, but it was more than jealousy. Kin left something out in his explanation, again, but she had a sense that Alana knew all his secrets.

But what more could there be?

Guiding Viento to the nearest exit, she let Talon lead the way.

Once out of the stable, Talon turned them east, following an old cart path towards the river at the back of the property. He glanced at Amarie before letting out a short, low whistle, guiding the Andalusian into a steady run. He didn't seem to hold back, trusting Amarie's ability to keep up.

They galloped along the curve of the river, hooves pounding against the thawing ground into a glade of trees. The flow of the water rushed towards the Nelmar Sea.

With the sun just beyond its zenith, most of winter's chill vanished. The warm rays beat on Amarie and Viento, flashing on the raven tufts of Talon's hair whipping against his neck.

Slowing the horses as the ground pitched downwards, a low roar rose in Amarie's ears.

Talon guided his mare down a well-worn switchback.

Riding single file, they dropped roughly thirty feet, passing by jagged grey stone protruding from the side of the hill.

The river cascaded into an elegant three-tiered fall, then curled north at the base before disappearing into the woods. Deciduous trees, barren of their leaves, mixed liberally with evergreen pines.

The curling river created a shallow outcropping of land surrounded by rolling water on three sides. The sun reflected within the low-hanging mist around the base of the falls and sparkled in a prismatic array of color.

Talon pulled back on his reins, bringing his mare to a halt before dismounting. "It's hard to talk while riding, but I was hoping for a conversation with you." He ran a hand through his long hair to detangle and flatten it before he untied the knots securing the basket. "I brought something for us to enjoy beside the falls. I hope I'm not being too presumptuous."

Amarie raised an eyebrow.

Presumptuous indeed.

"Was there something specific on your mind?" She swung down from Viento's back and patted his neck as he moved off to drink from the flowing water.

Talon set the basket on the ground before urging his mare to join Viento. With a gesture towards the outcropping of land, a tickle of energy buzzed through Amarie's mind. He manipulated the Art with the relaxed opening of his palm. He barely looked in the direction he willed the flows of energy before knobs of tree roots emerged from the ground. They budded up like flowers as the wood morphed. Roots formed two stools flanking a sapling with fanned-out branches acting as a table.

He lifted the basket, placing it on the branches as they finished growing into position.

While she couldn't deny being impressed by his casual use of the Art, she rolled her eyes at the showmanship.

Is he trying to impress me?

This felt more like a courtship than a casual ride.

"You know, most people just bring a blanket."

Talon smiled. "Usually women are a little more impressed." He sat with his back to the falls, releasing the flaps of the basket. "Perhaps I wanted to make sure my delicate auer backside didn't have to suffer the hard, cold ground. I thought it would be rude not to create a place for you to sit as well." He gestured to the stool across from him.

Amarie approached the wooden seating arrangement and joined him. "Most women are easily impressed."

A part of her found the lack of secrecy of his talent refreshing, even knowing there was likely more to his abilities than moving tree roots.

Kin was rarely so forthcoming.

With me, at least.

"I have a suspicion you're not like most women." Talon lifted a bottle of wine and two glasses from the basket first.

She raised an eyebrow.

He showed as little struggle in opening the bottle as he had in mounting his horse.

An unfamiliar tinge in the back of her mind wondered if Kin perhaps guessed Talon's intentions when he admitted his jealousy. Suspicion settled in her.

"May I?" He held the neck of the bottle near the glass closer to her.

"Please." She watched him as he poured and then accepted the glass. "I suppose not many women I've met speak to their horse." Studying the glass, she waited without raising it to her lips.

Talon poured himself a liberal glass of the drink before setting aside the bottle. "And in Aueric. I can't help but notice your familiarity with my people. Few take the time to learn such an archaic and difficult language."

He sipped the wine before circling it in his glass.

"I know enough to get by, but I'm quite familiar with your people." Tasting the wine, it reminded her of the previous night's events.

Talon smiled coyly. "Have you been to Eralas?" The name of the reclusive auers' island flowed fluidly over his lips, making it sound like a different place than when a human said it.

"I have. I spent many months there several years ago."

"You have visited my homeland far more recently than I, then." Sadness crept into his tone.

Her eyes narrowed as she tried to determine how much of his demeanor was genuine. Taking another sip, she paused in the conversation and watched him empty the rest of the contents from his wicker basket.

He unwrapped parchment packages, containing breads, cheeses, fine meats, and ripe, hearty winter fruits.

"Forgive me, but I can't imagine you going to all this trouble to ask about my travels." A raw coil of paranoia wrapped Amarie's gut.

Does he know what I am?

Surely, Kin hadn't said anything.

Maybe he's trying to keep me from the estate while Kin meets with Alana.

Talon's face remained as calm as it had been when they first met. "You're right. But it'd be rude of me to dive into such topics so brazenly. I'm not trying to be elusive, but rather the opposite." He pursed his lips. "My interest is sincere in sparing you from certain avoidable dangers."

"With all due respect, Talon, you know nothing about me. I'm well equipped to handle the current dangers in my life. Unless you believe there's something I'm unaware of?" She tilted her head, focused on the narrow circle of his pupils.

"You're quite right. I don't know very much about you. But, in this case, that's irrelevant. I don't believe you're aware of a danger you're quite close to." He paused, lifting his wine.

Amarie waited for him to continue.

"I was surprised Alana was unknown to you before last night. She played a pivotal role in Kin's life for many years, and in some ways, still does. I would've expected him to at least mention my sister to you."

Amarie bristled at the topic she least desired to discuss. "He was embarrassed. He explained she led him down a dark path he now regrets. I don't think it matters that she didn't come up sooner." Her shoulders tensed, and she hoped the direction of conversation would alter. If this was to be Talon berating Kin, she wouldn't sit still and listen to it.

"Dark path." Talon scoffed. "Hardly adequate to encompass the totality of Kin's sins. Alana can't be wholly blamed for his choices. It'd be a slight to the memory of the innocent lives he's destroyed."

The accusation lit a wildfire within her, fanned by a writhing in her gut. Her immediate instinct was to leave Talon to drink his wine alone. She'd said it before. She didn't want to hear Kin's secrets from the mouth of another. But Amarie wasn't aware of innocent lives lost, and it gnawed at her resolve, keeping her seated.

Shades can still be good, can't they? But Ormon...

"Kin wouldn't kill innocent people." She shook her head, taking a hasty drink. Guilt surged within her for letting Talon speak further.

"Death, for some, would've been more merciful." Talon's tone lowered, and he eyed her. "I don't want to upset you, but I feel you need to know. The power Kin accesses isn't easily kept. Nor is his will entirely his own. Many have died at his hands either directly or indirectly." He settled his glass down again, the crimson within sloshing back and forth.

Amarie's throat clenched, unable to respond to the allegations Talon leveraged against Kin.

He said he trusted me with every fiber of his soul that still belonged to him. How much of it doesn't?

Talon toyed with the stem of his glass. "You must have suspected something already... but I wonder if you know Kinronsilis far less than you believe. Has he truly told you nothing about the one he serves?"

Serves?

"No, he isn't like that. He was searching for something for his employer. A Berylian Key shard, to be studied. It's how we met, but no one has told him what to do since I've known him."

A single-breathed laugh burst from Talon as he shook his head. "Study. A perversion of the word. That creature studies nothing. He only seeks to control through fear, corruption, and power. Kinronsilis *serves*. He doesn't have the luxury of choice in what tasks he does or does not complete for the one who cursed him with access to the Art."

A shiver ran up Amarie's spine, and she gripped her wine glass tightly before putting it down to avoid shattering it.

"My *sister*." Talon's use of the familial title was twisted on his tongue, showing his own disgust. "She's the one who manipulated

Kin into pledging himself. It was too late by the time I realized her intentions."

Talon appeared sincere, yet what he said made Amarie feel nauseous. She'd given Kin a shard, and he knew the reason she collected them. To keep her secret safe.

If what Talon says is true...

Kin couldn't be acting. She refused to consider he'd been less than genuine in his love for her. Her mind struggled with whether she could trust Talon.

He used the word creature to describe the person Kin worked for.

The creature he serves.

Her blood ran cold.

Kin can explain.

"Kin told me you're his friend." Her voice softened. "Which led me to believe I could trust you. But what you're telling me makes me to wonder if Kin is aware of what kind of friend he's keeping." Her heart pounded, unable to cope with how many of Talon's assertions made sense to her.

She didn't know the truth about Shades.

No one did.

"I *am* Kin's friend. I'm telling you these things to protect him as much as you. I wish to stop Kin from putting himself in a self-damning position, assuming what I sense between the two of you is correct. He's told me about the punishment he'll suffer should he deviate from his service. In horrid detail. If Kinronsilis falters, he'll face worse than death."

He would, for me.

Talon didn't know all of the story, however. He didn't know who, and what, she was.

But Kin did.

"Is that all?" She half-heartedly lifted her gaze to meet the auer's once more. "Is that everything you wanted me to know?"

His hand moved to touch hers on top of the table, fingers grasping with surprising strength as if trying to comfort her. "I urge you to remember the role my sister plays in Kin's life. I'm certain you're aware of the skill we auer practice in manipulation, which I swear by the gods I don't use on you now. Kin's a quick student and was focused solely on Alana for many years. While it's possible he's sincere, if there's anything Kin knows about you of value, I insist caution. He's no fool and will make use of any information he can."

Each tiny hair on the back of her neck stood straight. It took a moment for her to compose her expression.

Kin won't do that. He isn't like Talon's sister.

She couldn't tell from Talon's steady gaze if he saw her panic or not.

He broke away first and rewrapped the food. "I'm sorry. I thought it was important for you to know. I wish I was wrong. But I couldn't sit aside and allow Kin to drag you into his shadows."

She rose from her seat on shaky knees, looking at Viento. "I think it would be best if I spoke with Kin myself."

Talon stood with her, offering a quick nod. With a flick of his wrist, he dumped the rest of his wine and placed the glasses into the basket before clasping it shut. "I understand."

He snapped his fingers, a ripple of energy radiating from the staccato. The branches of their table and stools shriveled and shrank back into themselves, melting away like ice in a raging heat.

Amarie watched with a furrowed brow.

Auer never use the destructive Art.

Typically, the auer practiced exclusively what they considered life-giving Art.

Maybe this is why he's a rejanai.

The main focus of her thoughts kept her from lingering on such innocuous matters. She needed to see Kin immediately.

Would he deny the things Talon told her?

A sickening twist in her stomach suggested he couldn't.

Chapter 21

With the door to the study ajar, low conversational tones drifted through the crack.

Kin hesitated, one hand hovering above the knob.

"I apologize for the short notice of my arrival, Lady Lindora." Alana's tone grated like razors against Kin's ears. "I had an urgent need for the Delkest countryside and your company. I couldn't wait longer."

Her show has already started, the lying bitch.

"No need to apologize, Alana."

Kin could imagine his father lifting a mug of coffee beneath the thick, silver mustache.

"Your arrival is fortuitous, actually." Lindora used a more serious tone than usual. "Kinronsilis arrived last night."

"Oh?" Alana's feigned surprise made Kin roll his eyes. "How unexpected. I didn't think I would be so fortunate as to see him, too."

The sweetness of her tone brought a sour taste to Kin's tongue. He steeled himself to enter the study.

"Did he arrive alone?"

Before either of his parents could answer, he shoved the door open with excessive force.

The room might have been misconstrued as a lounge if not for the bookshelves and slatted compartments filled with ledgers from the winemaking business. The parchment was arranged in careful piles and rows on a formidable desk positioned towards the enormous windows on the back wall.

His parents sat in overstuffed chairs with a tea table before them, their backs to the door. Between their heads was the view of Alana perched exactly in the middle of the couch, the only remaining seating in the study.

A wide smile spread across her ruby lips, hovering above the porcelain teacup nestled in her hand. One leg delicately crossed over the other created a cascading waterfall of the thin, violet satin of her dress. Narrow straps on her tanned shoulders held the Aueric-style attire in place. Her bare arms would be unaffected by the winter chill lingering in the house.

She lowered the tea to her lap. "Kin."

Lindora and Hartlen turned towards their son.

"It's such a lovely surprise to see you. I hadn't—"

"I need the truth, Alana," Kin interrupted, frowning. He stepped forward, ignoring the scowl from his father.

Alana pursed her lips, still maintaining the smile, and tilted her head. Her black hair didn't move, pulled back at the sides and pinned in place.

Hartlen huffed in the silence. "I apologize, my dear. Kin may be a little hasty. He recently had an unsettling encounter. We wish to consult you about it."

"Of course." Alana's brow knitted in concern. The cup clinked onto its saucer. "I hope I have the answers you all seek. Especially you, Kin." Her hand idly brushed aside a loose section of her hair, her exposed arm unmarked by their master.

"Won't you come sit?" Her delicate hand, nails painted a shade of green to match her eyes, patted the couch beside her.

"I'll stand," Kin growled.

Hartlen gave him a disapproving look, but Lindora rested a hand on Kin's elbow. Her touch felt a great distance away.

Alana shrugged and offered Hartlen an understanding smile.

He opened his mouth to chide his son, but she raised a hand.

Her demeanor might have seemed concerned to his parents, but Kin only saw a serpent positioned to strike

"Why don't you tell me about your encounter? I'll speak what I know. You have my word." Alana pressed three fingers to her forehead with a curt bow of her chin towards her chest.

She always tries using her heritage to her advantage...

She hardly believed in the Aueric gesture.

Lowering her hand into her lap, she folded her fingers together.

"Kin?" Lindora's prompt reverberated in the silence.

"Who are my birth parents?" Kin had no intention to play her game of niceties. "Where did you take me from?"

Alana frowned and lowered her gaze as if embarrassed.

She better not try to deny this.

Kin's skin heated in his fury at her continued act.

"The answers to your questions are far from simple. I hope you are ready to know the truth." Alana's eyes flitted to Lindora. "I didn't take you. I saved you. If I hadn't, you would've died."

Kin's mother leaned forward, a hand on her knee as she placed her tea down. "We must know the truth, Alana. Regardless of how distasteful."

"The truth." Alana lowered her gaze. "Yes, I suppose it's time. But I need to know what happened, exactly."

Kin sucked in a breath, hesitating before he accepted the necessity of explaining. "I met my twin. Jarac. In Lungaz, where he imprisoned and questioned me."

Lindora gave a frightful gasp, squeezing Kin's hand. "Lungaz?"

Kin patted her hand. "I'm fine." He turned back to Alana, who gave him a knowing sigh.

"Jarac is the elder of you. Born to King Hendrick Lazorus and his wife, Queen Izadelle of Feyor."

"*What?*" Hartlen bellowed.

Hearing Alana say the names sent a chill down Kin's spine.

"You said he'd been abandoned," Hartlen pressed. "But by a royal family?"

"He was." Alana lifted her hands in defense. "The chief advisor to the throne perceived Kin as a threat. He recommended death, insisting that twins, let alone identical ones, aren't good for any kingdom. When the time came for the elder to rule, the jilted younger would surely protest. It would throw Feyor into chaos. Bitter disputes leading to avoidable civil wars.

"King Hendrick grew convinced his country, and his family, would be torn apart if both Jarac and the unnamed second-born lived. To protect the throne and the country, you needed to be disposed of.

"Fortunately, I was summoned by the rather distraught midwife tasked with the deed of dispatching you." Alana's eyes sparkled as if struggling to hold back tears. "I was serving as a secondary advisor of the Art to the throne. Upon discovering the king's sinister decision, I forwent my service and absconded with you. I assured the midwife I would complete the duty for her. Clearly..." She gestured towards him with a wry smile. "I did not."

"And you brought him to us." Hartlen coughed, covering any emotion he might have harbored. "Remembering what I'd told you during our meeting in Olsa."

"Of course." Alana nodded and dabbed at the corner of her eye with her fingertips.

Kin's stomach twisted, acid rising in his throat.

"I felt a responsibility to check in on him, considering the importance that his existence remains a secret." Alana smoothed the creases in her dress. "I must insist his origin remain undiscovered."

"Absolutely." Lindora turned to Kin as her hand closed hard on his forearm. "You mustn't go anywhere near that country again. It's too dangerous."

Kin gripped his mother's hand and squeezed, reminding himself not to scream at Alana in present company. His parents didn't know what she had done to him. They didn't know about his service or his power. They didn't understand that because of Alana, Kin had lost a part of his soul.

Alana knew, from the very moment she took me into her arms, the shadow she would lead me to.

"It's all right, Ma." Kin released her hand and took a deep breath.

"But I need some air. Excuse me." He hid the scowl on his face as he turned and hurried out of the room. The anger swelling inside him sparked a need to reach out and destroy something.

Anything.

The Art pulsed, responding to his emotion like a dog on the end of a leash. It radiated through his chest regardless of how he tried to quell it.

The gardens were the first place he thought might bring him reprieve, and he hurried into them before he lost all control. They used to offer him comfort, but did little now.

Kin seethed at Alana's continued involvement in his life, barely noticing the cold outside. His knuckles popped as he paced between the rose bushes, trying to connect all the pieces of the jigsaw.

His master surely knew of Kin's birthright.

Has his intention always been for me to claim it? Was the entire situation in which I came to him carefully designed?

Soft shoes scratched on the stepping stones of the garden, accompanied by the lazy swish of a long skirt.

As Alana ambled beneath the hanging arbor at the base of the stairs, she offered Kin a smile. She looked not a day older than twenty.

While the attraction to her feminine features and dulcet scent was long gone, he felt disgusted for ever having the emotions at all.

He glowered at her for interrupting his solitude.

"Your parents are very gracious." Alana's smooth voice rolled from her lips. "They only just told me you arrived here with a girl at your side."

The tangled mass in Kin's stomach twisted. Of course she'd learned of Amarie. He wouldn't have been surprised if she'd known before her arrival.

I need to keep a better watch for her vile little spies.

"I don't see it as any of your business," Kin growled.

"But it is my business. Any distraction from your task concerns me. *He* isn't pleased—"

Kin spun to face her. "You can assure the master I am still focused on my task and will deliver the shard shortly. I only chose a delay to seek answers to the lies both of you have spun. The company I keep is none—"

"Careful, Kin." Alana's sweet voice turned to sharp steel and cut off his words.

A flicker of energy passed between them, a tainted cloud of her will forcefully binding his own.

How much of his silence now and in previous encounters was compelled by her power? Had he simply not noticed?

The brackish sensation unnerved his soul.

"You know how the master deals with insubordination. I urge you to show restraint and remember his gifts to you." Alana's eyes darkened, the narrow auer pupils swelling in the dimming afternoon light. Her voice held power, demanding the same respect the master did. She was, after all, his loyal right hand in many ways.

Once, in this very garden, Alana made Kin see himself as undeserving of the love he sought from her.

She was beyond him.

An Aueric woman with years of practice within the Art could never choose him, a winemaker's son with no potential to speak of.

She wove a web of promises and forgeries to make Kin believe in a way to cheat the fates and the gods. To merit Alana's love.

"This was always your intention, wasn't it?" Kin took a step towards her, determined to appear stronger than he felt. The surge of his energy pushed against hers, willing it away from his body and forging a barrier between them. "You always intended to manipulate me into his hands. Was it his idea to keep me alive, rather than yours? I'm sure a viper like you would care little for a human child. You'd never have made that decision if you weren't commanded to."

Alana's lips moved to reply, but Kin didn't allow the breath.

"I can guess his intentions. And I refuse to be his pawn."

A wicked smile curled Alana's lips, her pearly teeth flashing like a predator's in the night. A laugh jangled from her throat and sent a shudder down Kin's spine.

"It's adorable how you believe you have a choice, Kinronsilis." She closed the distance between them.

The power he'd assembled crumbled, and he hurriedly turned away.

Alana pushed against his chest. Her nails bit through the fabric of his tunic. He felt the sting as she forced him to turn, his feet shifting to face her. Her hand crawled up his neck, caressing his skin in an icy blast, the very opposite of the feeling Amarie evoked within him.

The pit of his stomach wanted to flip but remained oddly silent.

No living being could deny Alana's beauty. She'd been the center of his affection for many years. It was impossible to ignore the effect her graceful movements would have had on him once. They echoed hollowly now, his mind going to Amarie as Alana's hand cupped his jaw.

He tried to pull away, to reject her touch, but his body refused.

Alana had rarely been so forwardly physical. Each time carefully orchestrated to maximize her manipulative power over him.

"The girl is a distraction." Alana purred, her eyes meeting his. Taller than Amarie, her face came close to the same level as his. "I know everything about her. Her thievish tendencies... There's still a poor boy in Jaspa looking for her. And I'm sure there are others whom her habits have upset." She scraped her nails over his stubbled jaw. "You can't believe she'll remain with you when she learns the truth. It's better if you do away with her first, and I wish to help you. There are ways less damaging than others." Her voice sounded uncharacteristically sensual.

A ripple of heat passed through Kin, his body shaking with anger. *Amarie wouldn't leave. I know her.*

He loved her and didn't care what it meant to Alana, or even his master. He wouldn't allow them to continue to define his future.

Kin considered reaching for his power to force Alana away, but her will readied, poised to respond. Without even trying, he already knew he'd lose.

Movement flickered in the corner of his eye. Two forms

approached. The instinct to turn came, washed through him, and departed with no response from his muscles.

A pulse of energy surged against his very being, tightening his limbs and making it impossible to move. It disoriented him, crippling his ability to reach for the arcs of power running within him. His body was fully aware of every sensation, but unable to obey his own commands.

"Kinronsilis." Alana's finger traced his chin, scratching like sand on a rock. Her clawed fingers curled back to the hair at the base of Kin's skull, tilting his unwilling head towards her. Her thin lips curved in a sinister smile, her eyes flecked with satisfaction. "I'm merely acting in your self-interest. It's far easier this way."

A disgusting shock passed through Kin as Alana pulled his mouth to hers.

His lips responded, no matter how much his brain screamed against the concept.

Alana tasted sickly sweet, her lips coarse against his.

His muscles fought to pull away, but did the opposite, his arms wrapping around Alana's thin waist.

The acid of her energy choked him, drowning all hope for him to regain control of his own will.

Chapter 22

Amarie opened her mouth to call out to Kin as she approached the back gate of the garden, but stopped in her tracks as her eyes beheld the last thing she expected.

Alana looked fragile in Kin's arms as he pulled her into him.

Unable to fully see the face of the man she loved, she couldn't mistake the connection between his and Alana's lips.

The woman Kin swore to be his enemy had her hand tangled within his hair, her eyes closed as their mouths parted and the kiss renewed, curdling the contents of Amarie's stomach.

Resisting the urge to retch, she couldn't look away.

Something closed on her shoulder. Talon's hand.

A fierce swell rose within her, as her feet dared her to approach Kin and the woman she hadn't met.

The grip on her shoulder tightened, forcing her to halt.

Kin wouldn't do this. He wouldn't.

Her first instinct was to tear him from the grasp of the auer woman he claimed he so adamantly detested.

Amarie swallowed hard, gazing at the ground. She lifted her head again in the hopes the scene before her had changed. She hoped Kin would pull away, free himself from her clutches, but her eyes settled on the motion of his lips responding to hers.

She steeled herself against tears. "Kin?" Her voice shook, and her hands balled into fists.

The kiss between them broke, and Alana peered over Kin's shoulder and met Amarie's eyes. She placed a hand on him, and he turned to face Amarie, his arms wrapping around the auer's waist from behind.

"You must be Amarie." Alana's sweet tone made Amarie want to vomit. "Kin told me all about you..." She reached behind her and entwined her fingers in his hair, pulling his lips to her neck.

Amarie clenched her jaw, blinking as she backed into Talon. She shook her head, staring at Kin's eyes. "Why?"

"Have you really fallen so far, Kin?" Talon stepped beside her. "This is crass, Alana, even for you."

Kin didn't look up from where he nuzzled Alana's neck, and she only smiled. "I see no purpose in feeding the girl's false beliefs. Kin is mine. Always has been."

Amarie turned from them, running out of the gardens. Her heart beat wildly as she struggled to breathe and maintain her aura.

Keep hold.

Talon foot steps thudded behind her, his hands squeezing her upper arms. Steering her to see only his chest, he kept her back to the gardens.

She tried to focus on his rich, green vest, and the rise and fall of his breath to match hers. The minimal amount of clarity it brought her was enough for her to think about what came next.

Rapidly losing control of her emotions, the urgency to get away grew. She already made the mistake of letting Kin know her secret. She wouldn't allow anyone else to.

Except maybe Alana already does.

"I need to get out of here. I can't go back in that house." Her mind whirled as she strove to maintain any semblance of composure. She watched Talon's lips move in a response but couldn't make out his words.

Talon gripped her upper arms and lowered his face to be level with hers, speaking louder. "I'll get your things and meet you back at the stable."

All she could do was nod as the auer strode back into the garden to get to the house.

Amarie didn't look back before rushing to Viento, who waited nearby, and threw herself into the saddle.

What did Talon say?

Thoughts became difficult as she struggled to remain in control.

Meet him in the stable.

She spun Viento and took up the reins of Talon's mare to return her to her paddock. She took what comfort she could from the steady beat of Viento's hooves on the hard ground.

Arriving back at the stable, Amarie sloppily dismounted and pulled her supplies from the storage closet next to Viento's stall. She latched them onto her saddle, fingers moving deftly in their practiced routine, despite a tremble.

If she allowed her negative emotions to take hold, anyone in the vicinity would see. It had occurred several times in her life, the first time terrifying her. Now, it served as a reminder to calm down.

I'm failing.

The energy of the Berylian Key within her demanded to manifest visually around her, seeping through the cracks of her control.

When she touched her things, cold fire licked at her fingers, but failed to singe what she touched. She shook her hand to do away with the visualized emotion and hooked the crossbow and quiver to the ties of her saddle.

Viento pawed the ground.

Tears threatened her eyes again. Her aura buzzed as she combatted its desire to be set free. Every time she gained ground, her mind brought back the image of Kin.

His lips pressed against those that weren't hers, his hands on Alana's waist.

Faster than she expected, Talon arrived with her two bags and her short sword. He carried another pack she didn't recognize.

He didn't speak as he tied her things to the other side of her saddle. His gaze flickered to her fingertips.

They finished their tasks simultaneously, azure sparks rippling across her hands.

Amarie wasted no time in lifting herself onto her horse. Her heart ached, pain ripping through her and finally wetting her cheeks. Fear accompanied it, with what Alana might know.

Without a word, she wheeled Viento around.

"Amarie."

She paused.

Talon's hand came down on her knee. "You shouldn't be alone. You need a friend right now. Please allow me to come with you?"

His request brought a multitude of concerns to the forefront of her mind, starting with the knowledge he'd see more of the visual manifestations of her power if he accompanied her. Of course, he'd seen a glimmer of it already and, if she waited, the entire estate might be witness to the side effects of her agony.

With a quick decision, she nodded her agreement, not trusting her voice to maintain a steady tone.

Talon tied the third bag to his mare's saddle. He mounted and nudged his horse to come beside Amarie and Viento. His caring expression was odd from an auer. It brought a vague sense of reassurance as he gestured for her to lead.

He'll have to keep up.

Emerging from the stable, Amarie paused briefly to look at the estate one last time.

No sign of Kin.

She kicked Viento into a canter, their speed quickly escalating to a full gallop, racing down the gravel entrance and spraying rocks behind them.

A second set of hooves thundered to the side.

Her nails bit fiercely into her palms around the reins as she fought to hold on a little longer.

Once they crossed through the gate of the estate and hooves hit grass instead of rock, the lick of flames again surrounded her hands.

Her control waned, and she had to choose between maintaining the hiding aura or fighting the ignition of the Berylian Key's demands.

The flames would be safer, and more difficult to understand than the wave of energy Talon would definitely pick up on if her aura collapsed.

She closed her eyes, letting Viento run south as hot tears escaped, cooling quickly in the winter air.

Cobalt flames erupted as she accepted her grief and the heatless inferno spread over her reins. The fathomless energy flowed through her and into her horse.

His hooves left a wide trail of fire dancing in the frozen grass. It dissipated fifty yards behind her where the land remained unscathed.

Damn you, Kin.

The story continues in...

BLOOD
OF THE KEY

www.Pantracia.com

Even a stone can bleed.

On the run again with an unexpected acquaintance, Amarie suspects her new ally could be working with Kin behind her back. After a dangerous encounter, her trust in her companion grows, and he sheds light on Kin's master and what wickedness may come for her.

After a vile reminder of his vow, Kin must decide whether to remain loyal to the man who gave him power or to tell Amarie the truth. But following his heart could grant him a fate worse than death.

As they journey through the wilderness, much more is at stake than Kin and Amarie's future together. New enemies and allies shake reality, shoving everyone towards the precipice of disaster...

Blood of the Key is Part 2 of *The Berylian Key*, and Book 2 in the *Pantracia Chronicles*.

Manufactured by Amazon.ca
Bolton, ON